Peter Sailly Palmer

History of Lake Champlain

Peter Sailly Palmer

History of Lake Champlain

ISBN/EAN: 9783741180811

Manufactured in Europe, USA, Canada, Australia, Japa

Cover: Foto ©Andreas Hilbeck / pixelio.de

Manufactured and distributed by brebook publishing software
(www.brebook.com)

Peter Sailly Palmer

History of Lake Champlain

HISTORY

OF

LAKE CHAMPLAIN,

FROM ITS

FIRST EXPLORATION BY THE FRENCH

IN 1609,

TO THE

CLOSE OF THE YEAR 1814.

BY

PETER S. PALMER

ALBANY, N. Y.
J. MUNSELL, 78 STATE STREET.
1866.

LAKE CHAMPLAIN.

INTRODUCTION.

General Description of the Lake and of the most important Points along its Borders — Ancient and modern Names of Places — Distances — Old Forts — Scenery — Original Indian Name.

LAKE CHAMPLAIN extends from 43° 30′ to 45° north latitude, and lies between Vermont and New York — the boundary line of those states running through its centre. The lake is ninety miles long, in a right line from north to south, with a length of coast, on either side, of about one hundred and twenty-five miles: its southern extremity, or head, being at Whitehall, and its northern near the boundary line between the United States and Canada. The lake varies in width from one-fourth of a mile to thirteen miles, and covers an area of about five hundred square miles. It receives the waters of Lake George, at Ticonderoga, and discharges itself into the St. Lawrence, through the river Richelieu. There is no perceivable current in the body of the lake, and its waters, at ordinary stages, pass into the Richelieu with a velocity of only one-third of a mile per hour.

The lake has two arms; one on the west side, near its southern extremity, called South Bay, the other on the east side, near its northern extremity, called Missisco Bay. This last mentioned bay stretches into Canada and covers about thirty-five square miles. The area of country drained into the lake is variously estimated from seven thousand to nine

1

thousand square miles. It probably approaches nearest to the larger estimate. Numerous rivers and creeks discharge themselves into the lake, among the principal of which are, on the New York side, Wood Creek,[1] the outlet of Lake George, the Bouquet, Great and Little Ausable, the Salmon, the Saranac, and the Big and Little Chazy rivers. On the Vermont side are the Poultney River, Otter Creek, and the Winooski, Lamoille and Missisco rivers. The lake is subject to a rise and fall of from six to eight feet during the year; the waters attaining their greatest height about the twentieth of May, after which they fall gradually, until about the twentieth of September, when they usually reach the lower level of the remainder of the season.

Lake Champlain commences at the junction of Wood Creek with East Bay, in the town of Whitehall. The Indian name of this place was *Kah-cho-quah-na*, the place where dip fish. Philip Skene, an English major under half pay, located there in 1763, and established a settlement at the mouth of Wood Creek, which was called Skenesborough. This, for many years, was the most important settlement upon Lake Champlain. In 1778 it numbered seventy-three families, all of whom, with but two exceptions, were Skene's tenants. The name of the town was changed to Whitehall in 1788.

About two miles north of the village of Whitehall is South Bay, an arm of the lake seven miles long and one mile wide, extending to the south-west and separating the town of Whitehall from the town of Dresden. It was on the shores of this bay that the Baron de Dieskau landed, in 1775, with an army of fifteen hundred French and Indians, when marching against the English encampment at the head of Lake George.

---

[1]Called by the Dutch *Hout Kil*, and by the French *Rivière Chicot*.

Twenty-four miles below Whitehall is old Fort Ticonderoga on the west, Mount Independence on the east side of the lake. Here the waters of Lake George discharge themselves into Lake Champlain through an outlet called, by the Indians, *Cheonderoga*. The French erected a fortress here in 1756, which they called Fort Carillon, and which was a place of great strength. Mount Defiance lies on the south side of the mouth of the outlet of Lake George, opposite Ticonderoga. The summit of this mountain is seven hundred and fifty feet above the lake, and within cannon shot of the old fortress.

Twelve miles north of Ticonderoga is Crown Point, called by the French *Pointe à la Chevelure*. Here the French built a fort in 1731, which they called Fort St. Frederic. The fort was destroyed by them on their retreat to Canada in 1759, and the same year General Amherst commenced a much larger work, the ruins of which are still to be seen.

Opposite Crown Point is a landing place called Chimney Point, which was settled by the French about the time they commenced building Fort St. Frederic, and was destroyed by them in 1759. So complete was the destruction of the settlement that when the English arrived, a few days after the retreat of the French, they saw nothing but the blackened chimneys of the consumed houses, standing as grim sentinels amid the surrounding ruin. These chimneys were permitted to stand for years, and gave to that locality the name of Chimney Point; a name it yet retains.

For more than fifty years, the waters between Crown Point and Whitehall have been included within the limits of Lake Champlain, but in the older histories and maps of the country the passage between these places is frequently called *Wood Creek* and *South Bay*. Kalm[1] speaks of that part

---

[1] Kalm's *Travels*, 1749.

of the lake south of Crown Point as "the river which comes out of the Lake St. Sacrement to Lake Champlain," and again as "Wood Creek which flows to Fort St. Frederic." Doctor Thacher, who was stationed at Ticonderoga in 1777, refers to South Bay as extending from that place to Skenesborough, "a distance of thirty miles." These changes in the name applied at different periods to the narrow part of the lake should be carefully noted. I have referred to them at this time to guard the reader against the confusion which they have frequently produced, and to explain an occasional apparent discrepancy between this work and the narratives here collected.

Two miles north of Crown Point, and on the same side of the lake, is Port Henry, and about eleven miles further north is Northwest Bay, called *Baie du Rocher Fendus* in Sauthier's map of 1779. The village of Westport stands at the foot of this bay. On the opposite side of the lake, about ten miles north of Crown Point, is a small bay in which Arnold grounded and burned his galley and five gondolas, after the engagement with the English of the 13th October, 1776. Otter Creek, called by the French *La Rivière aux Loutres*, empties into the lake about seven miles north of this spot. The creek is navigable for lake vessels as far up as the falls at Vergennes, a distance of eight miles. In this creek, Macdonough fitted out the fleet with which he gained the victory of the 11th of September, 1814. In the course of the last war, a small breast-work was thrown up on the north side of the creek at its mouth, where Lieutenant Cassin of the navy, and Captain Thornton of the artillery, with two hundred men, repulsed a large British force, sent out from Canada to destroy the American fleet fitting out at Vergennes. A few miles north, and on the opposite side of the lake, is Split Rock, called by the French *Rocher Fendu*. This rock has always been considered a great natural curiosity. It projects one hundred and fifty feet into the lake, and is elevated about thirty feet above the level of the water. The part detached contains half an acre, and is separated from the main rock by a channel about fifteen feet wide. The prominences and cavities of the opposing sides are said to correspond; and hence the popular opinion that this rock was separated from the main land by an earthquake,[1] but Professor Emmons, who examined it particularly, supposes the separation to have been occasioned by the wearing away or decomposition of an intermediate mass of rock containing a large quantity of pyritous iron.

The lake between Split Rock and Thompson's Point, formerly called *Pointe Regiochne*, is not quite one mile wide. A light-house has been erected upon the main land, a few rods south of the rock. From this point the lake increases in width as it extends towards the north. Between Essex and Charlotte, four miles north, it is three miles wide. Opposite Burlington it is nine and three-quarters miles, and from shore to shore, opposite Plattsburgh, about thirteen miles wide.

Between Essex and Charlotte is Sloop Island, so called because an English vessel of war, during the revolution, fired upon it, mistaking in a fog the stump of a pine tree standing near its centre for the mast of a sloop. A short dis-

---

[1] In the winter of 1663 there was a severe earthquake in Canada. "Lakes appeared where none ever existed before; mountains were overthrown; rivers sought other beds or totally disappeared. The earth and the mountains entirely split and rent in innumerable places, creating chasms and precipices, whose depths have never been ascertained."—*Jesuits' Relation*, 1663.

"On the fifth of February we had an earthquake which continued during half a quarter of an hour, sufficiently strong to extort from us a good act of contrition. It was repeated from time to time during nine days and was perceptible until the last of the month, but always diminishing."—*Baron d' Avaugour to the French Minister*, 4th August, 1663.

tance below Essex, on the New York side, is the mouth of the Bouquet River. At the falls, two miles up this river, Burgoyne encamped and gave a war feast to a party of about four hundred Indians, previous to his attack on Ticonderoga in 1777. Fourteen miles north-east from Essex and on the opposite side of the lake, is the village of Burlington. About midway between these two places are four small islands called the Four Brothers. They are called *Isle de Quatre-vents* on Charlevoix's map of 1744, and the Four Winds Islands on Sauthier's map. Two and one half miles south of Burlington is Potier's Point, called *Erkly's* by Sauthier. It forms the west side of the mouth of Shelburne Bay. Three miles south-west of Burlington is Juniper Island, on which stands a light-house erected in 1826.

North-west from Juniper Island, and near the west shore of the lake is Schuyler Island, called by the French *Isle aux Chapons*. Under this island Arnold collected his fleet on the morning of the 12th of October, after his retreat from Valcour Island. A little to the south of this island is Douglass Bay, called *Corlear* by the French and Indians. It is supposed that the humane and noble Corlear was drowned in this bay in 1666.

A mile to the north of Schuyler Island is a bold promontory called Pointe Trembleau. At the foot of a small bay formed by this point, stands the village of Port Kent, and about two miles to the north are the mouths of the Great and Little au Sable rivers, which empty into the lake near a sandy point, called Pointe au Sable. Six miles further north, and half a mile from the main shore lies the island of Valcour, or Valeur as it is sometimes called. This island is celebrated on account of a severe naval engagement fought near it between the Americans and English on the 11th day of October, 1776. One mile north of Valcour is St. Michel's, or Crab Island, and about three miles further north is the mouth of the Saranac river, called *Salasanac* on Sauthier's map. The village of Plattsburgh lies on both sides of this river at its mouth. Three miles east from Plattsburgh is Cumberland Head, on which a light-house has been erected. Cumberland Head was called by the French *Cap Scononton* or *Scononton.* It extends about three miles into the lake in a southerly direction, and forms Cumberland Bay. This bay was the scene of Macdonough's naval victory of the 11th of September, 1814. To the east of Cumberland Head is a large island called Grand Isle. The Lamoille River empties into the lake on the Vermont side near the south end of this island. Eight miles south of the Lamoille is the mouth of the Winooski. North of Grand Isle, and separated from it by a narrow channel, is another large island called North Hero. This is the *Isle Longue* of the French.

Twelve miles north of Cumberland Head, and lying between North Hero and the western side of the lake is Isle la Motte. This island was named from Sieur la Mothe, a French officer who built a fort on the north end of the island in 1665, which he called Fort St. Anne. It was afterwards called Fort la Mothe. Kalm says this was a wooden fort or redoubt, standing on the west side of the island near the water's edge. It had disappeared when he passed through the lake in 1749, but he was shown the spot where it stood, which he describes as " quite overgrown with trees." Opposite the north end of this island, on the New York side, is the mouth of the Little Chazy River, and a short distance further north is the mouth of the Big Chazy. These rivers are called *Chasy* on a map of a survey of the lake made in 1732, and were originally named from Lieut. de Chasy, a French officer of distinction who, in 1665, was killed by a party of Mohawk Indians, while hunting in their vicinity. King's Bay lies north of the mouth of the Big Chazy. The

north side of this bay is formed by Point Au Fer, which
separates it from Rouse's Point Bay.

Point Au Fer was formerly separated from the main shore
by a channel or deep morass connecting Rouse's Point Bay
with King's Bay. Kalm says the first houses he saw, after
leaving Fort St. Frederic, were on the western side of the lake
about ten French miles above St. Johns, in which the French
had lived before the last war, but which were then (1748)
abandoned. These houses probably stood either on Point
Au Fer or near the mouth of the Big Chazy River. Prior
to the revolution a brick house was built on this point, which
was known as the *White House*. It was fortified with an
intrenchment and cannon by General Sullivan, at the time
of the invasion of Canada, and was then considered a very
advantageous position to command the navigation of the north
end of the lake. Burgoyne, when he entered the United
States, threw a body of troops into this place, and it was
retained by the British as a military post until after the
peace.[1]

Opposite the northern part of Isle La Motte, on the Vermont side of the lake, is Alburgh Tongue, called by the
French *Pointe Algonquin*. The entrance to Missisco Bay is
on the east side of this point. About eight miles north of
Isle La Motte, also on the Vermont side, is Windmill Point.
The French built a windmill there about the time of the
erection of Fort St. Frederic at Crown Point, and had collected a small settlement near the mill; but the English
having burnt the houses several times, on their incursions
into Canada, the settlement was at length abandoned. In 1749
nothing but the mill, which was built of stone, remained.[1]

Opposite Windmill Point is the village of Rouse's Point,
and one mile north is the terminus of the Ogdensburgh

---

[1]Kalm's *Travels.*

(Northern) Rail Road. A connection is there formed between the Ogdensburgh and the Vermont and Canada Rail Roads by a bridge and floating draw. The boundary line between the United States and Canada, as fixed by the Ashburton Treaty of 1842, is about one mile below this bridge. This line is located 4,200 feet north of the true parallel of the 45° of latitude, and was so established in order to secure to the United States the site of an old fort commenced by that government soon after the close of the war of 1812.

The parallel of 45° was originally located correctly by the French, but in 1766 Governor Moore and Brigadier General Carleton visited Lake Champlain and fixed the boundary between Canada and the province of New York about two and a half miles below Windmill Point, which Governor Moore says was further to the northward than they expected to find it from the observations said to have been made by the French some years before.[1] Moore's line was recognized as the true one until about the year 1818 when, on taking new observations, it was found to be too far to the north. As soon as the error was discovered, the United States suspended work on the fort, and the unfinished walls were long known as Fort Blunder. Since the treaty of 1842 a new and larger fort has been commenced on the site of the old one, called Fort Montgomery. It is not yet completed.

Fort Montgomery stands at the foot of the lake. There the river Richelieu commences and conveys the waters of the lake to the St. Lawrence. This river, for several years after the first settlement of Canada, was called the River of the Iroquois. Charlevoix says it was afterwards called the Richelieu on account of a fort of that name which had been built at its mouth in 1641. This outlet of Lake Champlain is also called the Sorel or Chambly River.

---

[1] Gov. Moore to the Board of Plantations, 1766.

2

Three and a half miles below the boundary line is Bloody Island, said to be so called from the murder of two lumbermen who were killed there by a party of soldiers sent to protect them from the Indians. Three-fourths of a mile below is Ash Island or *Isle aux Têtes*. One mile below Ash Island is Hospital Island, and six miles still lower down the river is *Isle aux Noix*, where the French established a military post on their retreat from Crown Point in 1659. Thirteen miles below Isle aux Noix is the village of St. Johns. That place was selected for a military post by Montcalm in 1758. It was occupied by the French prior to 1749.

About thirteen miles below St. Johns is the village and fort of Chambly. A fort was built there by the French in 1664, which they called Fort St. Louis. It was at first built of wood, but had, prior to 1721, been replaced by a strong work of stone, flanked with four bastions, and capable of containing a large garrison. Fort Richelieu, at the mouth of the river, was afterwards demolished, and a new fort built there by Mons. de Sorel, to which his name was given.

Lake Champlain lies on the western side of a valley formed by the Adirondacks of New York and the Green Mountains of Vermont. This valley is from one to thirty miles in width, and about one hundred and eighty miles in length north and south. Its greatest depression has been found to be between Westport, Burlington and Port Kent. Between Burlington and Port Kent the water of the lake is two hundred and eighty-two feet in depth. Professor Emmons found the depth, four miles north of Westport, to be three hundred feet, and he was told that soundings of six hundred feet had been made in other places in that part of the lake. The surface of the lake is ninety-three feet above tide, and if Professor Emmons was not misinformed, its bottom at this last point is at least five hundred feet below the level of the ocean. It is the popular opinion that the waters of the lake are gradually subsiding, but I judge this to be a mistake for the reason that the soundings made seventy-five years ago do not differ materially from those of the present day. The water in the bays and along the shores is not so deep as it was formerly, on account of the washing of the banks and the deposit of earth, saw-dust and rubbish brought down by the creeks and rivers, but the surface is probably as high above tide as it was when the lake was first visited by Champlain in 1609. It is evident, however, from an examination of the adjacent shores and rocks, that the lake at one time filled a much larger portion of the valley than it does at present. Geologists suppose this entire valley to have been twice occupied by the ocean — but these speculations are of little interest to the general reader, who, usually, is satisfied to take things as they have existed for the last five thousand years.

This lake has ever been celebrated for the beauty of its scenery and the bold and imposing configuration of the surrounding country. Upon the eastern side the valley is wide and fertile until we pass Mount Independence going south, when the hills approach the lake, and in some places rise abruptly from its shores. On the New York side the mountains in many places extend to the water's edge, as in the case of the Black Mountains south of Ticonderoga; the Kayaderosseras range which terminates with Bulwagga Mountain near Crown Point; the northern end of the West Moriah range at Split Rock, and of the Adirondack Mountains at Trembleau Point, near Port Kent. These several ranges run from the lake in a south-westerly direction, increasing in altitude as they recede, and presenting a scene at once bold and beautiful,—hill after hill rising gradually above each other, until the highest peaks attain an elevation of over five thousand feet. From the west the snow-crowned rocks of Mount Marcy, old White Face, and half a dozen

other giants among the hills look down in solemn grandeur
on the lake; while, on the east, the eye passes over green
fields to trace along the horizon the clear blue outline of
Jay's Peak, Old Mansfield's Chin and Nose, and Camel's
Hump, the poetic *Lion Couchant* of the French.[1]

The original Indian name of Lake Champlain has been a
subject of much speculation and research. By some it is
supposed to have been called *Peta-wa-bouque*, meaning
alternate land and water, in allusion to its numerous islands
and projecting points of land. Among the other names
ascribed to the lake are *Caniaderi-guarunte*, the door or
mouth of the country; *Petow-par-gow*, the great water, and
Ska-ne-togh-ro-wah-na, the largest lake. The early French
writers do not refer to its Indian name, but speak of the
lake as the passage that leads to the country of the Iroquois.
Among the papers published in O'Callaghan's *Documentary
History of New York* in relation to the old French grants
on Lake Champlain, is a letter from Governor Tryon to
Lord Dartmouth, in which he states that this lake is called
on Blain & Ogilby's and other ancient maps the *Mer des
Iroquois*, the Richelieu River, *Rivière des Iroquois*, and
the tract on the east side of the lake *Iroscosia*. From
this it has been conjectured that the lake was called *Yroquois*
by the Indians. But this is explained by Charlevoix, who
says that the name was given to the river and lake by the
French, because the Mohawk Iroquois were in the habit of
passing through those waters in their incursions into the

---

[1] The following are the elevations, above tide, of some of the
peaks seen from Lake Champlain.

On the New York side, Mt. Marcy 5,467 feet; Dix's Peak, 5,200;
Nipple Top, 4,900; Whiteface, 4,900; Raven Hill, 2,100; Bald
Peak, 2,065.

On the Vermont side, The Chin, 4,348; The Nose, 4,044; Camel's Hump, 4,083; Jay's Peak, 4,018; Killington Peak, 3,924.

French settlements on the St. Lawrence. Champlain affixed his own name to the lake during his exploration of its shores in July, 1609. At a later day it was sometimes called Lake Corlear, in honor of a Dutchman who in 1666 saved a party of French and Canada Indians from being destroyed by a war party of the Mohawks, and who, in the year after, was accidentally drowned in it while on his way to Canada.

In the following chapters I propose to collect many facts connected with the history of Lake Champlain. No part of the United States is more interesting from its historic incidents. Every bay and island of the lake and nearly every foot of its shore has been the scene of some warlike movement—the midnight foray of the predatory savage, the bloody scout of frontier settlers, the rendezvous of armed bands, or the conflict of contending armies. These stirring incidents extend in tradition far beyond the first discovery of the lake, and are brought down by scattered and unconnected history, in an almost uninterrupted series of strifes and contentions, to the close of the war of 1812.

CHAPTER I.

But little progress was made by the French in their American discoveries until the spring of 1534, when Jacques Cartier sailed from France with two small vessels, and in the month of May reached Bonavista in Newfoundland. Cartier coasted around the north shore of the island, and along the Gulf of the St. Lawrence, returning to France in September. The following year he left France with three ships, and entering the mouth of the St. Lawrence, ascended that river as far as the St. Croix (St. Charles), near the Indian village Stadacona (Quebec), where he passed the winter. While his party were preparing their winter quarters, Cartier, with thirty-five armed men, proceeded up the river as far as Hochelaga (Montreal), where he arrived on the second day of October.

"Hochelaga," says Warburton,[1] "stood in the midst of great fields of Indian corn; it was of a circular form, containing about fifty large huts, each fifty paces long and from fourteen to fifteen wide, all built in the shape of tunnels, formed of wood, and covered with birch bark; the dwellings were divided into several rooms, surrounding an open court in the centre, where the fires burned. Three rows of palisades encircled the town, with only one entrance; above the gate, and over the whole length of the outer ring of defence, there was a gallery, approached by flights of steps,

---

[1] *Conquest of Canada*, vol. I.

and plentifully provided with stones and other missiles to resist attack. This was a place of considerable importance,
even in those remote days, as the capital of a great extent of
country, and as having eight or ten villages subject to its
sway. The inhabitants spoke the language of the great
Huron nation, and were more advanced in civilization
than any of their neighbors; unlike other tribes, they cultivated the ground and remained stationary." This was
Hochelaga in 1534. Seventy years later it had sunk into
a decayed and unimportant place.

On the 11th of October, Cartier rejoined his party at St.
Croix, and the following spring returned to France. Early
in the spring of 1541 he again sailed for America, and entering the St. Lawrence, passed up that stream as high as the
rapids of Lachine. The next spring he returned to Europe
and soon afterwards died. No effort was made by the French
to colonize Canada, after the return of Cartier and his associates, until the year 1603, when an armament was fitted
out, under the command of Pontgrave, to make further discoveries in the St. Lawrence. Among the officers who accompanied this expedition was Samuel de Champlain, a
captain in the French Navy and a native of Saintonge.
Pontgrave and Champlain explored the St. Lawrence as far
as the Lachine rapids, which was the highest point reached
by Cartier sixty-eight years before. In 1604 Champlain
accompanied De Monts to Canada, and again returned to
France in the fall of that year.

In 1608, De Monts, who was at the head of a trading
company, equipped two ships at Honfleur, and sent them
out under the command of Champlain and Pontgrave, for
the purpose of establishing the fur trade at Tadoussac.
Champlain reached Tadoussac on the 3d day of June.
After a brief stay there he ascended the St. Lawrence and
on the 3d of July, arrived at the ancient village of Stadacona,

which he selected as the site of the future capital of Canada.[1]

When the French first visited Canada the Indians residing north of the river St. Lawrence were engaged in war with the Five Nations of Indians. who occupied the territory south of the St. Lawrence. The Five Nations were a powerful confederacy. consisting of the Mohawks. the Oneidas, the Onondagas. the Cayugas and the Senecas. They called themselves *Aganuschioni*. or United People.[2] By the Delawares they were called Mingoes : by the French. Iroquois, and by the Dutch the Maquas. Lafitau gives them the name of the *Agonnonsiorni*. as does Charlevoix. who says, "Leur nom propre est Agonnonsionni. qui veut dire. faiseurs de cabannes : parcequ'ils les batissent beaucoup plus solides. que la plupart des autres sauvages."[3] In 1712. the Tuscaroras. who had been driven from the south by the English. were admitted into the confederacy. which was afterwards known as the Six Nations.

Prior to the settlement of Canada by the French, the Iroquois occupied all the country south of the river St. Lawrence, and resided in numbers around Montreal and in the valley of Lake Champlain. but they had been

---

[1] An ancient Castilian tradition existed that the Spaniards visited these coasts before the French. and having perceived no appearance of mines or riches. they exclaimed frequently. "Aca nada." *Acu ia nothing:* the natives caught up the sound, and when other Europeans arrived. repeated it to them. The strangers concluded that these words were a designation. and from that time this magnificent country bore the name of CANADA. *Warburton.* vol. I. Charlevoix gives another derivation : "D'autres dérivent ce nom du mot Iroquois *kannats.* qui se prononce Cannada. et signifie un amas de cabanes."—*Hist. de la Nouv. France,* tom. I.

[2] Governor Clinton's *Discourse* before the New York Historical Society.

[3] Charlevoix, tom. I.

driven off towards Lake Ontario by the Adirondacks, who lived near the Three Rivers. The success of the Adirondacks was of short duration, for soon afterwards they, in their turn, were driven from their ancient seats to a safer position below Quebec.[1] In 1605 the Iroquois resided upon the banks of the Mohawk and in several villages to the west of that river. They claimed the whole country lying on both sides of Lake Champlain, as far north as the St. Lawrence. The northern bank of the St. Lawrence was held by the Algonquins, the ancient and inveterate enemies of the Iroquois. The Hurons, a numerous nation residing west of Lake Ontario, were in alliance with the Algonquins and joined them in their wars against the Iroquois.

The Iroquois were powerful, politic, warlike and courageous. They have been termed by Europeans the Romans of the West.[2] Charlevoix says the name Iroquois was formed from the Indian *Hiro*, which means *I have said*, with which these Indians always finished their speeches, and *de koue*, a word often used by them, and which, when pronounced with a drawl was a cry of grief, and when spoken short and quick, one of exultation.[3] They lived in villages around which they had extensive cultivated fields. These villages were enclosed with strong quadruple palisades of large timber, about thirty feet high, interlocked with each other, with an interval of not more than half a foot between them. On the inner side of the palisades were galleries in the form of parapets defended with double pieces of timber.[4] The Algonquins were a warlike nation, and the most polished of the northern tribes. They were a migratory people, disdaining the cultivation of the soil and depend-

[1] Gordon.
[2] Warburton, vol. I.
[3] Charlevoix, tom I.
[4] Champlain's *Voyages de la Nouv. France.*

ing altogether on the produce of the chase. The Hurons had some slight knowledge of husbandry, but were more effeminate and luxurious than the other tribes, and inferior in savage virtue and independence.[1] They lived in villages, of which the nation possessed twenty, but which were inferior in construction and strength to those of the Iroquois.

When Champlain landed at Quebec he found the Algonquins and Hurons engaged in active war with the Mohawks, one of the oldest and most powerful branches of the Five Nations. Learning from some Indians who visited his encampment in the winter, that they intended an inroad into the country of their enemy in the course of the approaching summer, he determined to accompany them, and by that means, not only explore a river and large lake through which the war party would pass, but by his powerful assistance strengthen the friendship which then existed between the French and the neighboring Indians. For this purpose, on the 18th of April, 1609, he left Quebec on board a pinnace accompanied by a small party of followers, and ascending the St. Lawrence as far as the mouth of the Richelieu, passed up that stream to the foot of the rapids near Chambly. Here a war party of sixty Algonquins and Hurons joined him, and commenced preparations for the incursion.

It would seem that it was Champlain's intention to take his whole party with him; but the men, intimidated by the small number of the Indians, or from some other cause, refused to proceed any further, and after the strongest appeals on the part of Champlain, but two would accompany him. With these alone he determined to join the Indians on their long and perilous expedition. All their arrangements being completed, Champlain and his two companions, on the 2d of July, embarked with the Indians in twenty-four canoes and

---

[1] Warburton, vol. I.

that day proceeded up the river to a point about nine miles
above the island of St Theresa, where they encamped for
the night. The next day they continued on as far as the
lake, which they entered on the following morning, and
coasted along its west shore until they came within two or
three days journey of the place where they expected to meet
the enemy. After this they traveled only by night, each
morning retiring into a barricaded camp to pass the day.
The party advanced with the utmost caution, keeping their
canoes close together, and making no noise which might be
heard by the enemy should they happen to be near. During
the whole journey they used no fire and lived upon dried
Indian meal soaked in water.

In his account of this expedition, Champlain particularly
refers to the superstition of the Indians, and the importance
they attach to dreams.[1] Whenever he awoke they would
eagerly inquire whether he had dreamed of or seen their
enemies. One day, while the party lay concealed near
Crown Point, Champlain fell asleep and thought he saw the
Iroquois drowning in the lake within sight of the encampment. On awaking he related the dream to the Indians,
which, he says, "gained such credit among them that they
no longer doubted but they should meet with success." That
same night about ten o'clock, while proceeding cautiously
along, they met a war party of the Iroquois, who were passing down the lake in canoes.

As soon as the two parties discovered each other the Iro-

---

[1] The Indian trusts to his dreams, and invariably holds them
sacred. Before he engages in any important undertaking, particularly in war, diplomacy, or the chase, the dreams of the principal
chiefs are carefully watched and examined; by their interpreta-
tion his conduct is guided. In this manner the fate of a whole
nation has often been decided by the chance vision of a single
man.—*Conquest of Canada*, I, 192.

quois hastened to the shore, and having first secured their canoes, began to cut down trees and form a barricade. The others pushed out towards the centre of the lake, and proceeded to fasten their canoes together, and then secured them with poles in a position within arrow-shot of the barricade. Two canoes were then sent towards the shore to inquire whether the Iroquois wished to fight, who answered they did, but proposed, as it was then dark, that the battle be deferred until morning. To this the Algonquins and Hurons agreed, and both parties passed the night in singing and taunting their rivals with cowardice and imbecility. Champlain and his two companions were equipped in light armor, and each carried an arquebus. They were placed in different canoes and kept themselves concealed from sight, least the Iroquois might be alarmed at their appearance and decline the combat.

On the following morning an engagement took place which is thus recorded by Champlain.[1] "The moment we landed they (the Algonquins and Hurons) began to run about two hundred paces towards their enemies who stood firm, and had not yet perceived my companions, who went into the bush with some savages. Our Indians commenced calling me in a loud voice, and opening their ranks placed me at their head about twenty paces in advance, in which order we marched until I was in thirty paces of the enemy. The moment they saw me they halted, gazing at me and I at them. When I saw them preparing to shoot at us, I raised my arquebus, and aiming directly at one of the three chiefs, two of them fell to the ground by this shot, and one of their companions received a wound of which he afterwards died. I had put four balls in my arquebus. Our party, on witnessing a shot so favorable for them, set up such tremendous

---

[1] *Voyages de la Nouv. France.*

shouts that thunder could not have been heard; and yet there was no lack of arrows on one side and the other. The Iroquois were greatly astonished at seeing two men killed so instantaneously, notwithstanding they were provided with arrow-proof armor woven of cotton thread and wood; this frightened them very much. Whilst I was reloading, one of my companions in the bush fired a shot, which so astonished them anew, seeing their chiefs slain, that they lost courage, took to flight, and abandoned the field and their fort, hiding themselves in the depth of the forests, whither pursuing them I killed some others. Our savages also killed several of them and took ten or twelve prisoners. The rest carried off the wounded. Fifteen or sixteen of our party were wounded by arrows; they were promptly cured."

This battle was fought on the 30th of July, near what Champlain describes as "the point of a cape which juts into the lake on the west side." Some writers have located the battle-ground on Lake George. Doctor Fitch[1] thinks it was upon one of the points of land in the town of Dresden or Putnam, south of Ticonderoga; but, from an examination of Champlain's map of New France,[2] it is evident that the engagement took place somewhere between Crown Point and Lake George, probably in the town of Ticonderoga.

As soon as the victorious party had gathered the weapons and other spoils left behind by the Iroquois, they embarked on their return to Canada. Proceeding about eight leagues down the lake, they landed after night fall, when the Indians put one of their prisoners to death with the most horrible and protracted tortures. The rest of their captives were taken to Canada. At the rapids of the Richelieu the party separated, and the Indians returned to

---

[1] *Historical Survey of Washington County.*

[2] A copy of this map will be found in vol. 3, of O'Callaghan's *Documentary History of New York.*

their homes, well satisfied, says Champlain, with the result
of the expedition, and uttering strong professions of gratitude and friendship for the French.[1]

The above is, in substance, Champlain's narrative of the
first visit of civilized man within the limits of the state of
New York. Two months later Henry Hudson entered New
York Bay and ascended the North River as far as the present
village of Waterford.[2] Thus were the northern and southern sections of the state almost simultaneously explored by
the European.

After the departure of the Indians Champlain returned
to Quebec. He continued governor of Canada until 1629,
when he surrendered the government to the English and returned home. In 1632 Canada was restored to France, and
the next year Champlain was reappointed governor of the
colony; which situation he continued to hold until his death,
at Quebec, in 1635.

Champlain was brave, high-minded, active and generous,
and eminent for his Christian zeal and purity. "The salva-
tion of one soul," he often said, "is of more value than the
conquest of an enemy." During his life he fostered Chris-
tianity and civilization, and succeeded in planting them among
the snows of Canada. The only great mistake of his administration was an injudicious interference in the quarrels be-

---

[1] Charlevoix and most English writers say that Champlain, on
this expedition, ascended a rapid and passed into another lake
afterward called Lake St. Sacrement. Champlain, in his account,
says the Indians told him of a waterfall and of a lake beyond,
three or four leagues long, and adds that he saw the waterfall, but
says nothing of the lake. Had he explored the lake he would
not have represented it as only three or four leagues long.

[2] Hudson first entered New York Bay in September 1609. He
sailed up the river as far as Albany, and embarking in small boats
continued on to Waterford, where he arrived on the 22d of that
month.

tween the Indians. By this means he directed the hostility of the warlike Iroquois against the French, and created an implacable hatred on the part of that powerful nation which time could not heal, nor the blood of a thousand victims soften.

Mons. de Montmagny succeeded Champlain as governor of New France. In 1641 he erected a fort at the mouth of the Richelieu, as a protection against the repeated inroads of the Indians by the way of Lake Champlain. M. de Montmagny was succeeded by M. D'Ailleboust, in the course of whose administration, of three years,[1] the Iroquois made several incursions into the territory of the Hurons and drove them from the fertile banks of the Ottawa. These victories of the Iroquois rendered them more audacious than ever. Breaking a solemn treaty of peace made with M. de Montmagny several years before, they again appeared among the French settlements despising forts and barricades and insulting the humble husbandman with impunity. In their attacks no force was too strong for them to overcome; no hiding place too secret for them to discover. So great, at length, became the audacity of these savages that they suddenly fell upon a body of Algonquins under the very guns of the fortress of Quebec, and massacred them without mercy.

A dark and unpropitious gloom hung over the affairs of the colony until the arrival of the Marquis de Tracy, as viceroy, in 1664. M. de Tracy brought with him the Carignan-Salieres, a veteran regiment which had greatly distinguished itself in the wars against the Turks. Immediately on the arrival of these troops they were sent, accompanied by the allied Indians, against the Iroquois, and soon cleared the

---

[1] The Governors of New France held office for three years only; in consequence of a decree that no one man should hold the government of a colony for more than that length of time. — *Warburton.*

country of those troublesome enemies. Having established peace throughout the colony, M. de Tracy prepared to adopt measures to make the security permanent. The hostile Indians had been accustomed to approach the French settlements by the way of Lake Champlain and the Richelieu River, and to effectually block up this avenue three captains of the Carignan regiment, M. de Sorel, de Chambly, and de Salieres, were ordered to erect forts on that river.

M. de Sorel built a fort at the mouth of the river, on the site of old fort Richelieu erected by de Montmagny in 1641. M. de Chambly constructed one at the foot of the rapids, in the present village of Chambly, which he called Fort St. Louis, and M. de Salieres built another nine miles above, which he named St. Theresa, because it was finished on that Saint's day. The next year M. de la Mothe, another captain in the Carignan regiment, was sent to Lake Champlain to construct a fort on an island near the lower end of the lake, which was intended to serve as a place of rendezvous, "from which continual attacks could be made on the enemy."[1] This fort was called St. Anne.

As soon as tidings of the erection of these forts reached the Iroquois, three of those tribes sent deputies to Quebec with proposals of peace. M. de Tracy gave them a friendly audience, and sent them back with valuable presents.

About the same time he determined to invade the country of the Mohawks, who with the Oneidas remained stubborn and inflexible, and to inflict summary punishment upon them for their former insolence and treachery. With this view M. de Courcelles was ordered to fit out a military expedition, with the utmost despatch. On the 9th of Jan., 1666, he started with three hundred men of the regiment of Carignan-Salieres, and two hundred volunteers, *habitans*, for Fort St.

---

[1] *Relations, &c. en la Nouv. France,* 1664-5.

Theresa, which had been designated as the place of rendezvous. The weather was so severe that before they had advanced three days' journey many of the men would have perished, had they not been carried along by their companions. On the 24th, Sieurs de la Fouille, Maximin and Lobiac, captains of the Carignan regiment, joined the army with sixty men and some *habitans*, but before they reached St. Theresa so many men had become disabled that it was necessary to withdraw four companies from the forts on the Richelieu to supply the vacancies in the ranks.

On the 30th of January de Courcelles marched out of Fort St. Theresa at the head of five hundred men, and passing the lake on the ice, crossed the country towards the Mohawk villages. The snow was nearly four feet deep, and the men were obliged to use snow-shoes to pass over it. As horses could make no progress through the deep snow, a large number of slight sledges were prepared which were loaded with provisions and dragged along by the men, or by large dogs brought on for that purpose. Each man, including all the officers, carried upon his back from twenty-five to thirty pounds of biscuit or other supplies.[1] The intention of the French had been to march directly against the Mohawk villages, but having lost their way, through the ignorance of their guides, they turned too far to the south, and on the 9th of February arrived within two miles of Schenectady, where they encamped. Here they were met by a small party of Mohawks, who, pretending to retreat were carelessly pursued by sixty of the French fusileers, who were thus drawn into an ambuscade of about two hundred Indian warriors securely posted behind the trees of the forest. At the first volley of the Indians eleven of the French, including a lieutenant,

[1] Relations de ce qui s'est passé en la Nouv: France en années 1665-6.

4

were killed and several wounded. The fusileers discharged their pieces and immediately fell back upon the main body of the army, while the Indians retired with a loss of three killed and six wounded, taking with them the scalps of four Frenchmen which they exhibited in the streets of Schenectady. It is said the whole company of fusileers would have been massacred, but for the intercession of Corlear, a Dutchman greatly beloved by the Mohawks, who humanely interceded in their behalf.[1]

Information of the approach of the French having been sent to Fort Albany by the authorities of Schenectady, three of the principal citizens were sent to M. de Courcelles to inquire what were his intentions in invading the country belonging to the English. De Courcelles replied that he had no desire to molest the English in their possessions, but came solely to seek out and punish the Mohawks, who were the unrelenting enemies of the French. He also represented to them the state of his army, worn out with fatigue and hunger, and requested that they would sell him provisions and consent that he might send his wounded to Albany. The English readily assented to this, and the next day seven wounded Frenchmen were sent to Albany. The inhabitants also carried large quantities of beans, bread and other provisions to the French camp, for which they were liberally paid.

De Courcelles having rested his men until the 12th, suddenly broke up his camp and hastily retraced his steps to Lake Champlain, and from thence to Canada. The Mohawks, who were at their first village, learning the retreat of the French, immediately started in pursuit, and followed them as far as the lake, where they took three prisoners and

----

[1] Gordon says the whole of De Courcelles' party would have been destroyed but for the intercession of Corlear.

found the bodies of five men who had perished of cold and hunger.[1]

The expedition of M. de Courcelles, although it had failed to reach the Mowhak villages, through the mistake of the guides, caused much anxiety to the Indians; nor were their fears diminished by the information communicated by the prisoners that M. de Tracy intended to send a much larger force into their country the next summer. To avert the threatening storm they determined to make immediate overtures of peace. Accordingly, in June, 1666, ten ambassadors from the Mohawks, accompanied by a delegation of Oneidas, repaired to Quebec, asking protection for their people and a renewal of the old treaties of peace. M. de Tracy at first refused to receive their wampum belts, but perceiving that this caused them great anxiety, he finally accepted their proposals. But while the negotiations were in progress at Quebec, and just as the French viceroy began to congratulate himself upon the future security of his colony, a tragedy took place on Lake Champlain, which for the time defeated his plans, and destroyed all his confidence in the professions of the Indian deputies.

Fort St. Anne was at this time garrisoned by several companies of the Carignan regiment, one of which was commanded by Sieur de Chasy, a nephew of the viceroy. Apprised of the friendly professions of the Mohawks and their desire for peace, the ambassadors of that nation having passed the fort on their way to Quebec, the officers relaxed their usual vigilance and amused themselves with fishing and hunting in the neighborhood. While a small party of French officers and soldiers were thus engaged, they were suddenly attacked by a band of Mohawk Indians, who killed

---

[1] *Doc. Hist. New York*, I, pp. 64 et seq.

two Carignan captains, de Travesy and de Chasy, and took several volunteers prisoners. Information of this treacherous act was immediately sent to Quebec, and one of the Indian deputies had the vain audacity to boast, at M. de Tracy's table, that he had slain the officers with his own hand. The Indian was seized and strangled on the spot; and M. de Tracy, breaking off all negotiations, sent M. de Sorel, at the head of three hundred men, against the Mohawk villages, with orders to overrun the whole country, and to put every inhabitant to the sword. M. de Sorel had by forced marches crossed Lake Champlain, and was pushing rapidly towards the Indian villages, when he was met by a new deputation from the Mohawks, bringing back the Frenchmen taken prisoners near Fort St. Anne, and offering every satisfaction for the murders committed there.

Still desirous to secure peace, and in the belief that the demonstration already made had over-awed the Indians, M. de Sorel retraced his steps to Quebec, where negotiations were again resumed with such success that, on the 12th of July a treaty was signed by which the Indians agreed to restore the Canadian, Algonquin and Huron prisoners in their hands, and to become the fast friends and allies of the French. On the other part, the viceroy promised to extend his protection over their nation, "to send some black gowns (Jesuit missionaries) among them " and " to open a trade and commerce by the *Lac du Sainte Sacrement.*" [1]

---

[1] *Relations,* en années 1665-6.

CHAPTER II.

M. de Tracy collects a large Army at Isle La Motte—He marches against and destroys the Mohawk Villages—Condition of Canada—De Callieres' Project for the Invasion of New York—Burning of Schenectady—Captain John Schuyler's Attack on Fort Laprairie—Major Philip Schuyler's Expedition to Canada—De Frontenac marches against the Mohawks.

War is the delight of the savage. It furnishes an excitement necessary to his happiness. Without it he pines and wastes in insufferable quiet; a restless, miserable being. To gratify his passion for war he hesitates not to violate the most sacred treaties, or break the ties of long-continued friendship. "We must either," says Sir William Johnson,[1] "permit these people to cut each other's throats, or risk their fury on our traders and defenceless frontiers."

M. de Tracy soon found that he could only secure permanent peace and quiet to the colony, by an expedition into the Mohawk country of such force as to make that implacable nation feel the destructive power of the French arms. With such an army he now prepared to march against the Indian villages on the Mohawk River. Never had Fort St. Anne presented so lively a scene as was beheld there in September, 1666. Within the fort and close under its defences were collected six hundred veterans of the Carignan-Salieres, while on the main shore opposite lay encamped an equal number of volunteers, *habitans* of the colony. One hundred Huron and Algonquin warriors, bedaubed with paint and bedecked with feathers, stalked majestically among the crowd, and rendered the night boisterous with their war songs and dances. The labor of preparing this expedition,

---

[1] Letter to Earl of Hillsborough.

the largest which had yet been collected on Lake Champlain, was confined to M. Talon, intendànt of New France.

On the 1st of October M. de Courcelles started from the fort at the head of four hundred men. On the 3d the main body of the army moved off under the immediate command of M. de Tracy, who, despite his advanced years, was determined to lead the expedition in person. Four days afterwards Sieurs de Chambly and Berthier followed with the rear guard. The progress of the army after it reached the upper end of the lake was slow and laborious, as the men dragged with them two small pieces of cannon and three hundred bateaux or bark canoes, which had been provided for crossing the lakes and rivers on the route. It was de Tracy's intention to surprise the Indians before they should learn of his advance; but, notwithstanding the great caution of the troops, the Mohawks received timely information of their approach, and abandoning the villages, secreted themselves in the surrounding forests, or ascended the mountains, and from a distance fired random shots at the soldiers. The French found the cabins of this nation larger and better built than any they had seen elsewhere. The villages were surrounded by a triple palisade twenty feet in height, newly repaired and strengthened and flanked by four bastions. Large quantities of Indian corn, beans and other provisions were stored away in magazines sunk in the ground; and numerous bark-tanks, filled with water, stood within the enclosure to supply the inhabitants, and to aid in extinguishing fires when necessary. Everything indicated that the Indians intended to make a strong defence, had they not been intimidated by the strength and numbers of the invaders. But as it was, not a warrior or able-bodied man was to be seen; they had fled, leaving behind only the women and a few old and decrepit men too feeble to escape. These M. de Tracy retained as prisoners. In this manner he passed through the whole country until he reached the most remote Mohawk village, which he burned. After celebrating mass and returning thanks to God for the success of the enterprise, the French retraced their steps towards Canada, on their way burning the other villages and destroying all the provisions they could not carry off.[1]

While the army was passing near Schenectady on its return, M. de Courcelles called upon Corlear, who it will be remembered had rendered the French such signal service the preceding winter, and invited him to visit Canada. On Lake Champlain the fleet of boats encountered a heavy storm, which capsized two canoes with eight persons on board, all of whom were unfortunately drowned. Among the persons thus lost were Corlear and Lieut. Sieur de Luges, an officer of great merit and distinction.[1]

The expedition of M. de Tracy effectually subdued the Mohawks, and for the next twenty-years secured the settlements on the St. Lawrence from the inroads of that nation. But Canada was not destined long to enjoy the blessings of profound peace. Ten years had scarcely elapsed before she found herself again engaged in a destructive war with the Western Iroquois, which continued, with short intervals of truce and with varied success, until the treaty of Utrecht in 1713. For several years after the commencement of this

---

[1] *Relations, &c., en la Nouv: France,* en années 1665-6.

[2] The accounts of these expeditions through Lake Champlain do not clearly indicate the route followed by the French, but it was probably along the western border of the lake as far south as the outlet of Lake George, then up the outlet and through that lake to its head, from whence it crossed the country to the waters of the Hudson River. In the treaty between the French and Iroquois, referred to at the close of the preceding chapter, it was expressly provided that trade and commerce be opened to the Iroquois, with New France, by the lake du Saint Sacrement.

war the English colonists were on friendly terms with those
of Canada, and repeatedly refused to aid the Western Iroquois in their controversy with the French. They were
equally careful to do nothing to prevent it. "The five Nations are a bulwark between us and the French," said Governor Dongan.[1] That bulwark was strongest in war. In
times of peace it might crumble into atoms.

The accession of William and Mary to the throne of England in 1689, was followed by a war between the English
and French, which continued until the peace of Ryswick in
1697. The news of the quarrel between the mother countries
soon reached America, and found the colonists of both nations
not only willing, but anxious to participate in the struggle.
The Chevalier de Callieres, who was governor of Montreal
and commander-in-chief of the troops and militia in Canada,
visited France in the year 1689, and submitted to the king
a project for the reduction of the province of New York,
the reëstablishment of French ascendency over the Five
Nations, and the consequent control of the lucrative fur
trade of America.

De Callieres' plan was to lead an army of two thousand
men up the Richelieu River and Lake Champlain as far as
the carrying place between Wood Creek and the Hudson
River, where he would build a small log fort, and garrison it
with two hundred men to guard the bateaux during his
absence. With the rest of his army he would march directly against Fort Orange (Albany) which he would seize, and
then, embarking in the boats and canoes found there, would
push on for New York. This town he represented as containing two hundred houses, and protected by a small fort
which could offer but a slight resistance to his attack. To
prevent succor reaching the town from Boston or England,

---

[1] Dongan's Report to the Committee of Trade: 1687.

he required that two ships of war should be sent to cruise in the mouth of the river until his arrival. De Callieres predicted the greatest benefits to France from the success of his project. "It will," he declared, "firmly establish the Christian religion as well among the Iroquois as among the other savages to whom we shall be able to speak as masters, when they are encircled on the side of Canada as well as of New York. It will secure and facilitate the cod-fishery, which is carried on along our coasts of Lacadie and on the Great Bank. It will give his majesty one of the finest harbors in America which can be entered during almost all seasons of the year, in less than one month of very easy navigation." Accept the favorable opportunity which presents itself of becoming masters of New York, adds de Callieres in conclusion, and the trade of our colony will flourish ; reject it and English intrigues with the Iroquois and other savages will destroy Canada in a little while.[1]

The French king received de Callieres with favor, and in June of the same year sent instructions to Count de Frontenac, then viceroy of Canada, to organize an expedition to carry out the proposed plan, and directed that de Callieres should be appointed governor of the conquered province. The king also ordered Sieur Begon to send out two ships of war under command of Sieur de la Caffiniere, who was instructed to place himself under the direction of de Frontenac. Should the proposed expedition fail, de Caffiniere was ordered "to make war against the English, and to range along the coasts of New England and New York, to capture as many prizes as possible, and to remain there until he have no more provisions than are necessary for his return to France."[2]

While the French were engaged in prosecuting the war

---

[1] De Callieres to the Marquis of Seignelay, January, 1689.
[2] Instructions to Count de Frontenac, June 7th, 1689.

with the Indians at the west, they seem to have been regardless of the exposed state of the frontier towards Lake Champlain. The old forts of St. Anne and St. Theresa, which had
proved so great a protection twenty years before, were
suffered to decay. Montreal was not fortified; a triple
palisade, in poor repair, being its main defence. Indeed the
only work in that quarter of any strength was the fort at
Chambly, which had been rebuilt of stone and was surrounded
by a small but flourishing settlement. On the 12th of
November, 1687, a formidable party of the Iroquois suddenly
attacked this fort. The garrison made a successful resistance,
but the settlement around was ravaged and several of the
inhabitants taken prisoners. A few days later the whole
country between the St. Lawrence and the Richelieu swarmed
with a savage host, who demanded immediate audience
with the governor, M. de Denonville, and haughtily dictated
peace to the weak and terrified inhabitants. "Look," cried
the proud chief, pointing towards a band of twelve hundred
warriors at his back, "we are like the leaves of the forest in
number, and stronger than the mighty oak. Your people
are few and weak. We have no occasion to lift our whole
hand, for our little finger is sufficient to destroy you."
Denonville bowed before a storm he could not resist, and concluded a treaty upon the terms proposed by the savages.

Of short duration was this boon of peace to the French,
the acceptance of which alike proclaimed their own humilia-
tion and the power of their savage foe. On the 26th of July,
1688, twelve hundred Indian warriors landed on the island
of Montreal, and having overpowered a force of one hundred
and fifty Canadians and fifty Indians imprudently sent against
them, devastated the whole settlement, killing nearly a
thousand of the inhabitants and carrying two hundred of
them into captivity.[1] The St. Lawrence frontier was now at

---

[1] Gordon — Warburton, vol. I.

the mercy of the fierce and relentless Iroquois. The power of the French was paralyzed; trade languished, agriculture was interrupted, and the very existence of the colony threatened.

Such was the gloomy condition of affairs when the instructions of the king for an invasion of New York, reached the Count de Frontenac. The troops in Canada consisted of thirty-five companies of regulars, each of which, when full, numbered fifty men. But at least four hundred and fifty were required to fill the ranks, so that the actual number did not exceed thirteen hundred.[1]   Of the *habitans* three thousand were able to bear arms.[2]   Although de Frontenac could not send out an expedition of the magnitude and strength proposed in his instructions, he nevertheless determined to organize three small detachments to march against the English.   One was to rendezvous at Montreal, and was to proceed against Albany ; another was to assemble at Three Rivers, from whence a descent was to be made upon the settlements near the Connecticut; and the third was to start from Quebec to attack the settlements on the seaboard, east of Boston.

The party which left Three Rivers surprised and destroyed the English settlement of Salmon Falls, and on their retreat, falling in with M. de Mamerval, who had marched from Quebec, they joined him in an attack on the fortified village of Kaskebe upon the sea coast, which they captured after a severe struggle.[3]

The third and most important detachment numbered two hundred and ten men, including ninety-six Huron and Algonquin Indians.   This detachment was placed under the com-

---

[1] De Callieres to the Marquis of Seignelay.

[2] This was the estimated number in 1687.   It had probably decreased during the two succeeding years.—See Gov. Dongan's Report to Board of Trade.

[3] Warburton, vol. I.

mand of two Canadian officers, Sieur la Moyne de St. Helene
and Lieutenant d'Aillebout de Mantet, having under them
d'Iberville and de Montesson. Attached to the expedition
as volunteers were Sieurs de Bonrepos and de la Brosse, two
Calvinist officers, and Sieurs de Blainville and de Montigny.
The party left Montreal about the middle of the month of
January, 1690, and crossing to the Richelieu ascended that
river and Lake Champlain on the ice. At the close of the
sixth day's march a consultation was held to determine the
route to be taken, and to regulate the plan of attack. The
Indians asked where the officers proposed to lead them. To
this de St. Helene replied that he had received no orders to
march against any particular place, but generally to act as
he should think best, and that he wished to attack and surprise Fort Orange, which he represented as the capital of
New York and a place of considerable importance. The
Indians, remembering the defeats of the French during the
preceding year, and holding their prowess in light esteem,
opposed this plan as rash and impracticable. "Attack an
armed fort indeed," cried a swarthy warrior sarcastically.
"Since when have the French become so desperate?" "We
wish to regain our honor," replied de Mantet, "or perish in
so glorious an enterprise." The Indians, however, remained
unconvinced, and the party moved on without coming to a
decision.

Eight days after this the party reached the point where the
two routes to Albany and Schenectady diverged. The Indians took the road leading towards Schenectady, and the
French followed without objection. Nine days afterwards they
arrived, about four in the evening, within two miles of that
place. Here the savages were addressed by one of their
chiefs, who urged them to lose all recollection of their fatigue, and to prepare to take ample revenge for the injuries
they had received from the Iroquois at the instigation of the

English. Having halted here to refresh themselves and prepare their arms, the party moved on, and about 11 o'clock came within sight of the village. The night was intensely cold and the citizens had retired early to bed—even those who usually guarded the gates of the palisade had withdrawn, leaving the entrances open and undefended. In profound silence the Canadian officers marched into the village and distributed their forces among the scattered houses. As soon as each man was properly posted, the savages raised the war cry, and the whole force rushed upon the unconscious inhabitants. De Mantet, at the head of one party, assaulted a small fort which he captured and burned; putting to death all who defended it. De St. Helene rushed against the barricaded doors of the private houses, beating them down with muskets and slaughtering every one who opposed his progress. In the confusion, M. de Montigny was wounded by the thrust of a spear. The massacre lasted for two hours, and during that time sixty of the inhabitants, including women and children, were butchered in cold blood. Having pillaged and burned every house in the village but two, the French and Indians, early the next morning, started on their return to Canada, taking with them twenty-seven prisoners and carrying off fifty horses, besides a quantity of other property.[1]

The news of this murderous assault reached Albany about five o'clock the next morning, and created the greatest consternation among its inhabitants. Alarm guns were fired from the fort, messages were sent to Esopus for assistance, and Laurence, a Mohawk chief then in Albany, hurried to the Mohawk castles to bring down the warriors of that nation. In three days a party of fifty young men from Albany and

---

[1] M. de Monseignat's account. In this account it is stated that "some twenty Mohawks were spared, in order to show them that it was the English and not they against whom the grudge was entertained."

one hundred and fifty Indians were collected at Schenectady, and started in pursuit of the retreating marauders. At Crown Point the young men gave out, but Laurence and his Indians continued on as far as Canada, and succeeded in overtaking a party of Canadians, who had dropped to the rear of the main body, of whom they killed six and took twelve prisoners.

The accounts given by these prisoners were of the most startling nature. Count de Frontenac, they said, was busily engaged preparing for an invasion of New York. He had already built one hundred and twenty bateaux and one hundred birch canoes, and he intended to pass up Lake Champlain in the spring at the head of fifteen hundred regular troops and one thousand allied Indians. Letters were now addressed by Lieutenant Governor Leisler to the governors of the different provinces, calling earnestly for aid to protect the exposed frontier beyond Albany. The Five Nations were also assembled in council, and agreed to furnish eighteen hundred warriors to fight the French.

Nor were the authorities of Albany idle. On the 26th of March they ordered Captain Jacob to proceed to Crown Point with seventeen English and twenty Indians, and there watch the movements of the enemy. Four days later Captain Abram Schuyler was sent with nine men and a party of Mohawks under Laurence, to take post at Otter Creek, for a similar purpose. Captain Schuyler, while posted at Otter Creek, led a scouting party of eight Indians as far as Chambly, where he encountered a small party of the French, of whom he killed two and took one prisoner. [1]

About the 10th of April, one of the parties on Lake Champlain sent in word that they had discovered the track of twelve French and Indians, proceeding in the direction of Albany. Warning of danger was immediately sent through-

---

[1] *Documentary History of New York.*

out the country, and the inhabitants were advised to retreat into the neighboring towns for safety. Two families, residing near Schenectady, neglected the advice, and were attacked during the night, eleven of their number being killed or captured. [1]

Apprehending that this success might excite the French to further outrage, the New York colonists hastened their preparations for the invasion of Canada. On the 1st of May an agreement was concluded between the provinces of Massachusetts, Connecticut and New York, by which each was to furnish its quota of troops for the expedition. [2] At the urgent request of New England the command of the expedition was conferred upon John Winthrop.

A naval expedition was also fitted out by the colonists and sent against Quebec, under command of Sir William Phipps.

The army under Major General Winthrop, numbering eight hundred men, left Albany about the 1st of August, and proceeded on its march as far as Wood Creek. There Winthrop waited a few days for the promised reinforcement of Indians, but these not arriving, nor furnishing a supply of canoes to cross the lake, as they had promised to do, he called a council of war, who decided it inexpedient to proceed further. The expedition was therefore abandoned, and the troops returned to Albany, where they were disbanded.

Attached to Winthrop's army was Captain John Schuyler of Albany, a man of great bravery and energy of character, and of considerable experience in border warfare. Schuyler, who was dissatisfied with the decision of the council of war,

---

[1] *Documentary History of New York.*

[2] New York was to furnish four hundred men; Massachusetts, one hundred and sixty; Connecticut, one hundred and thirty five, and Plymouth, sixty. Maryland promised one hundred men.

which he considered weak and cowardly, declared the campaign should not be abandoned so easily. Beating up for volunteers he soon gathered around him a little band of twenty-nine followers, each as bold and daring as himself. To these he added one hundred and twenty Indians who had arrived at the camp under command of Juriaen, called *the Ferocious*, and having loaded a number of canoes with provisions, proceeded, on the 13th of August, as far as Canaghsionie (probably Whitehall) where he encamped for the night. The next day he again embarked with his party and on the 21st of the month reached a point "one mile below the sand bank of Chambly."[1] In the course of the journey one of the Indians died. "He died of sickness," adds the brave captain, evidently surprised that so quiet a death should be reserved for a Mohawk.

On the 22d the little party having first secreted their canoes and provisions, started by land for Laprairie, which lay on the south shore of the St. Lawrence River about fifteen miles distant. While Schuyler was slowly approaching Laprairie, the inhabitants of that place were having a gala day in honor of their governor, the brave old Frontenac, who having learned from his scouts that Winthrop's army had retired, was marching with eight hundred men to Quebec, to repel the threatened attack of Sir William Phipps in that quarter. Little did the quiet husbandmen imagine, as they sat near their doors at evening, chatting over the stirring incidents of the day, repeating to listening ears the wonders they had seen, and rejoicing perhaps at a security

---

[1] Schuyler in his journal of this expedition gives the Indian names of several localities on Lake Champlain. On the 16th the party, he tells us, reached *Kanondoro*, and traveling all night, arrived the next morning at *Oghraro*. The next night they traveled as far as *Ogharonde*, where "they determined, by the majorities, to fall upon Fort Laprairie."

which the departure of the troops seemed to confirm, that a band of fierce and determined warriors lay secreted under the very trees which bordered the little settlement, ready with the morrow's sun to bring destruction and death about their rude but happy homes.

Early on the morning of the 23d, Schuyler sent forward his spies, who soon returned with information that the inhabitants were leaving the fort to go into the fields to cut corn. It was Schuyler's intention to wait quietly until they reached the fields, and then place his party between them and the fort, so as to intercept their retreat; but through the eagerness of some young savages, the war cry was prematurely raised, and both the English and Indians rushed to the attack without waiting for orders. The French, taking alarm, hastily retired to the fort, but not until six of their number were killed and nineteen taken prisoners. As soon as the prisoners were secured, the assailants fell upon the cattle feeding around the fort, and killed one hundred and fifty head of oxen and cows. They also set fire to all the houses and barns outside the fort, which were speedily consumed. The English wished to attack the fort itself, but did not do so, as the Indians refused to aid them. The forts at Montreal and Chambly now answering the alarm guns fired at Laprairie, Schuyler hastened his departure, lest his retreat might be cut off. Before leaving, his Indians burned the body of one of their number, who had been killed during the affray.

The party retreated about seven miles, when they halted for dinner. The same evening they reached the river and embarked in their canoes. The next day they went as far as the ruins of old Fort St. Anne, and on the 15th stopped on the long sand point near Port Kent, where they killed two elk. The next day's journey took them to a place which

6

Schuyler calls The Little Stone Fort,[1] from which a canoe was sent forward with the news. On the 27th the party reached the mouth of Wood Creek, and on the 31st arrived with their prisoners at Albany.[2]

During the winter of 1690-1, the New York colonists were too much occupied with their internal disputes to give much attention to military affairs. In the spring however their difficulties ceased, and active measures were at once adopted to carry on the war with Canada. The frontier posts of Albany, Schenectady and Half-Moon were repaired, the militia reorganized and a conference held with the Five Nations, with whom the French emissaries had begun to tamper. The Indians not only promised to abandon all negotiations with the French, but pledged themselves to make war upon that people so long as they should live. An expedition was now planned against Canada ; the English colonists wisely concluding that the only way to secure the coöperation of the savages was to give them active employment.

On the 22d of June, 1691, Major Philip Schuyler left Albany at the head of one hundred and fifty English and three hundred Indians, and crossing Lake Champlain by the route taken by his brother, Capt. John Schuyler, appeared unexpectedly before Fort Laprairie, which he carried by surprise, killing several of its defenders. De Callieres, then governor of Montreal, hastily collected eight hundred troops and crossed the river, when the English retired to the woods, where they met and destroyed a small detachment sent forward to cut off their retreat. A short time afterwards M. de Vallerennes coming up with a large force, a

---

[1] This was probably a slight work thrown up by Capt. de'Waim at Crown Point the March previous, or one erected at Ticonderoga by Capt. Sanders Glen while he was waiting there for the advance of Winthrop's army.

[2] Journal of Capt. John Schuyler.

severe and desperate battle was fought between the two parties. Schuyler posted his men behind trees, and for an hour and a half withstood the fire, and repelled the charges of the Canadian troops. In this engagement the loss of the English was trifling, while not less than two hundred of the French were killed or wounded. Schuyler, fearing to be overpowered by superior numbers, now hastily withdrew and returned to Albany.

The favorable result of this expedition gave a new impetus to the warlike temper of the Iroquois, and strengthened their friendship for the English. These Indians for the next two years so harrassed the French that de Frontenac determined again to invade their territory. For this purpose he collected a force of six or seven hundred French and Indians, and about the middle of January, 1693, set out from Montreal, for the Mohawk valley. The march upon the frozen surface of the lake and through the deep snows of the forest was attended with great hardships, yet such was the energy of the invaders that early in February they passed Schenectady unobserved, and falling suddenly upon the first Mohawk village, killed many of the inhabitants and took more than three hundred prisoners. As soon as the intelligence of this incursion reached Albany, Major Schuyler collected a party of about three hundred men, principally Indians, and started in pursuit of the assailants, who, according to their custom, had retreated immediately after the attack. Schuyler continued the pursuit as far as the Hudson, and would have overtaken the enemy had not a severe storm of snow and wind prevented his crossing the river. As it was, he succeeded in recapturing about fifty of the prisoners, with whom he returned to Albany. The sufferings of those engaged in this expedition were so great that the Indians fed upon the dead bodies of the enemy, and the French were compelled to eat their own shoes.[1]

Although the contest between the French and English continued several years longer, this was the last expedition of any importance which entered the valley of Lake Champlain during this war. The peace of Ryswick, in 1697, was soon followed by a formal treaty between the French and the Five Nations.

---

[1] Gordon.

CHAPTER III.

The history of events connected with Lake Champlain brings us down to the year 1709. During Queen Anne's War, which commenced in 1702, the frontier towns of New England were severely scourged by marauding parties from Canada. Deerfield was destroyed in 1704 by a party of three hundred French and Indians under command of the inhuman de Rouville.[1] In 1708, a party of four hundred men, including savages, crossed the almost impracticable mountains of Vermont and New Hampshire, and attacked the little fort and village of Haverhill, which, after a sharp defence, they carried and reduced to ashes.

These and other repeated and unprovoked aggressions at length aroused the British ministry, who, in 1709, at the earnest solicitation of the colonists, adopted a plan for the conquest of the French possessions in America. This plan contemplated an attack by water upon Quebec, whilst fifteen hundred men, from New York and the New England provinces, were to attempt Montreal by the way of Lake Cham-

---

[1] This expedition followed the route up Lake Champlain to the Winooski, and then ascended that river and crossed the mountains to the Connecticut. On their return they secreted the bell of St. Regis in the sands of Burlington, where it remained until the following spring, when it was taken to Canada.

plain. The inhabitants of New York entered cordially into
the scheme. They not only furnished their quota of troops,
but several volunteer companies were organized to join the
expedition. The Five Nations, through the exertions of Col.
Peter Schuyler, were induced to take up the hatchet and to
send five hundred warriors into the field. New York also
at her own expense, opened a road from Albany to Lake
Champlain, which greatly facilitated the movements of the
troops and the transportation of supplies.

This road commenced near the present village of Schuylerville, and ran up the east side of the river to Fort Edward,
and thence by the way of Wood Creek to the head of Lake
Champlain, leading all the way through a dense forest.
Along the route three forts were erected; one on Wood
Creek near the present village of Fort Ann, another at the
commencement of the carrying place between the Hudson
River and the head of Wood Creek, which was at first
called Fort Nicholson, and a third on the summit of one
of the hills opposite Schuylerville. These forts were built
of timber and were surrounded by palisades so constructed
as to protect the garrisons from the fire of musketry. One
hundred bateaux and a large number of canoes were built at
the mouth of Wood Creek for the transportation of the troops
across Lake Champlain. All the arrangements for the campaign being complete, the army left Albany under the command of Col. Nicholson and encamped at Fort Ann, where
they awaited intelligence of the arrival of the expedition
destined for the attack on Quebec.

These demonstrations on the part of the English colonists
created great alarm among the inhabitants of Canada, who
were but ill-prepared to resist the large force which threatened both extremes of the colony. M. de Vaudreuil called
a council of war, under whose advice a force of fifteen hundred
men was sent to Lake Champlain to oppose the advance of

Nicholson's army; but a misunderstanding between the governor general and some of his principal officers embarrassed the enterprise, and ultimately caused the army to return.

The two expeditions against Canada proved equally abortive. The fleet destined for the attack of Quebec was sent to Lisbon instead, to support the Portuguese against the power of Castile; while Nicholson's army, discouraged by delays and almost decimated by a malignant and fatal malady which broke out in the camp,[1] returned to Albany, where it was soon afterwards disbanded.

In 1711 preparations were again made by the colonists for the invasion of Canada. Colonel Nicholson, under whom served Colonels Schuyler, Whitney and Ingoldsby, mustered at Albany a strong force, comprising two thousand English, one thousand Germans and one thousand Indians, who, on the 28th of August, commenced their march towards Lake Champlain, taking the Lake George route, instead of the unhealthy one by the way of Wood Creek, which had proved so fatal to the troops on the former expedition. At the same time an army of six thousand four hundred men, under Brigadier General Hill, sailed from Boston on board of sixty-eight transports under convoy of Sir Hovedon Walker, for a simultaneous attack on Quebec.[2]

As soon as M. de Vaudreuil received intelligence of these movements he hastened to Quebec, and having strengthened its defences, confided to M. de Boucourt the responsible duty

---

[1] This sickness is said to have been caused by the Indians, who poisoned the waters of the Creek. But Doctor Fitch in his *Survey of Washington County* questions the truth of this accusation, and presumes the malady to have been a malignant dysentery, brought on by the troops drinking the stagnant water which flowed into the creek from the surrounding marshes.

[2] Gordon.

of resisting the debarkation of the English troops, and then
returned to the defence of Montreal. But the plans of the
invading army were destined to be again defeated. The
British admiral had neglected the warnings of an experienced
French navigator named Paradis who accompanied him,
and approached too near a small island in the narrow and
dangerous channel of the Traverse. While embarrassed
amid its rocks, a sullen squall scattered the fleet, driving
eight of the vessels on the shore, where they were wrecked.[1]
Charlevoix says nearly three thousand men were drowned,
whose bodies were afterwards found scattered along the
banks of the river. After this severe disaster the admiral
bore away for Cape Breton, and the expedition was abandoned. The advance corps of Nicholson's army had scarcely
reached the head of Lake George, when intelligence arrived
of the failure of the northern expedition. Orders were at
once given for their return to Albany.

These two attempts upon Canada cost the province of
New York alone, more than thirty thousand pounds sterling.
Their failure disheartened the inhabitants, and chilled for a
time the affections of the Five Nations, who began to look
upon the English as a weak and cowardly people. The
situation of the New York colonists was now most critical,
clouds of adversity lowered darkly over the province. The
river Indians became restless, and evinced a strong and growing disposition to break their allegiance; the Five Nations
listened favorably to the renewed propositions of peace from
the French, who threatened an invasion of the province
by sea and land. Happily these impending evils were
averted by the treaty of Utrecht, which was concluded
in the spring of 1713. By this treaty the French king released his nominal sovereignty over the Iroquois, and recog-

---

[1] Warburton, vol. I.

nized their country as subject to the dominion of Great
Britain.

As yet no settlement had been permanently established
in the valley of Lake Champlain. Fort St. Anne, built in
1699, had been occupied for a few years and then abandoned.
The Little Stone Fort mentioned by Schuyler in 1690, was
a structure of no importance except as it served for the immediate protection of those by whom it was erected. Fort
Ann, erected by Colonel Nicholson on Wood Creek in 1709,
was burned by him on the return of his army to Albany in
1711. Kalm saw the remains of the burnt palisades
when he passed there thirty-eight years afterwards. In
1713 Fort Saratoga was the nearest post to the lake on the
south, and Forts Laprairie and Chambly on the north. No
settlements were commenced within the present limits of
Vermont until after the erection of Fort Dummer, on the
Connecticut river, in 1724.

We have already seen that from the first settlement of
the country, Lake Champlain had been used as a thorough-
fare through which predatory excursions were directed
against both the French and English frontiers. Its control
was therefore a matter of great importance. No movement
was however made to obtain the command of this important
avenue until the year 1731, when the Marquis de Beauharnois, governor general of Canada, erected a fort at Crown
Point, which he called St. Frederic,[1] in honor of Frederic

---

[1] The proposition to erect a fort at Crown Point was submitted
to the French King in February 1730, who on the 8th May, 1731,
instructed Messrs. de Beauharnois and Hocquart to erect a stockade until a stronger work could be constructed and to make grants
of lands to such farmers as would settle in that vicinity. This
stockade was a small work and could accommodate a garrison of
30 men only. In 1734 a "redoubt à machicoulis" was erected
sufficient for a garrison of 120 men. The work was subsequently

Maurepas, the French secretary of state. The English
claimed the title to the territory on both sides of the lake,
by virtue of their treaties with the Five Nations, and strongly remonstrated against, but took no steps to prevent its
unauthorized occupation by the French.

Fort St. Frederic, says a celebrated traveler, " is built on
a rock consisting of black lime slates,[1] and is nearly quad-
rangular, has high and thick walls, made of the same limestone, of which there is a quarry about half a mile from the
fort. On the eastern part of the fort is a high tower, which
is proof against bomb shells, provided with very thick and
substantial walls, and well stored with cannon from the
bottom almost to the very top, and the governor lives in the
tower. In the *terre plaine* of the fort is a well built little
church and houses of stone for the officers and soldiers.
There are sharp rocks on all sides towards the land beyond
cannon shot from the fort, but among them are some which
are as high as the walls of the fort and very near them.
Within one or two musket shots to the east of the fort is a
windmill, built of stone, with very thick walls, and most of
the flour, which is wanted to supply the fort, is ground here.
This windmill is so constructed as to serve the purpose of a
redoubt, and at the top of it are five or six small pieces of
cannon."[2] Subsequently a trench or wide ditch was dug
around the fort, on the land side, enclosing the hill referred
to by Kalm. "This trench," says Captain Rogers, who
reconnoitered the place in 1755, " begins at the south-west
corner of the fort, and tends south-westerly; about two
rods wide at the fort, and widens to about fifteen at the

strengthened and enlarged, and in 1742 was, with the exception of
Quebec, the strongest work held by the French in Canada.—*Paris
Documents in Colonial History of New York.*

[1] Chazy limestone—*Emmons.*
[2] Kalm's *Travels,* 1749.

other end." An enclosure was also erected about twenty-five rods north-west of the fort which reached the water's edge and surrounded several buildings used for soldiers' quarters.[1]

Soon after the erection of the fort a settlement was formed about it, on both sides of the lake, composed, principally, of the families of old soldiers who had been paid off and discharged from service. The houses of some of the settlers were convenient and comfortable, but the majority lived in mere cabins built of boards. To each soldier in service was allotted a small piece of ground near the walls of the fort, which was cultivated as a garden, and occasionally occupied as a summer residence.[2]

A small village stood about a half a mile south-west of the fort, and one half mile further south was a hamlet, containing four houses, surrounded by wheat fields.[1]

The boats used by the inhabitants were of three kinds; bark canoes, dugouts or canoes made of logs of wood hollowed out, and bateaux. The last mentioned were constructed with flat bottoms of oak and sides of pine, and were used for the transportation of troops or supplies upon the lake. When Kalm visited the fort, in 1749, a yacht or large sail vessel made regular trips between that place and St. Johns, in Canada.[3]

Until 1659 St. Frederic was the seat of French power on the lake. Here was a rallying point for the fierce Abenaquis of the St. Francis, the Arundacks of the fertile Ottawa, and the warlike Wyandots of the west — drawn together by a common love of revenge or the hope of plunder. Here the ferocious Outagamis, the restless Algonquin and the vindictive Huron met to recount their deeds of barbarity.

---

[1] *Journal of the New Hampshire Scout.*

[2] Kalm's *Travels*, 1749.

[3] Kalm says this was the first sail vessel built on the lake.

It was a strange and varied scene often presented at this frontier post. At one moment would be heard the vesper bell of the little chapel calling the rude but virtuous husbandman, the scarred veteran of France and the voluble Canadian to their evening prayers; while at the next the rocky shore would echo to the loud whoop of the merciless savage, returning from some successful attack upon the neighboring settlements. Long had the English colonists cause to regret that want of vigilance and forecast on the part of their rulers, which permitted the French to seize and retain this controlling position on the lake.

We have no data by which to ascertain the exact population of the French settlements around St. Frederic: but it probably at no time exceeded six or eight hundred, exclusive of the garrison at the fort.[1] The period of the existence of these settlements was confined to the twenty-eight years of French ascendency on the lake. Prior to 1731, the borders of the lake, in every direction, were wild and uncultivated; no buildings stood upon its shores, not an acre of its majestic forests had been cleared, nor had its fertile soil been touched by the hand of the husbandman.

---

[1] In August, 1747, Col. Johnson wrote Gov. Clinton that one of his parties of Indians had just returned from Crown Point, where, "they could see very few French and but about forty Indians round the fort, having built of logs six little houses for that use, *which is all that has been done there yet.*" In 1750 M. de la Galissonniere, in a memoir on the French colonies, urges the importance of settling a French village at Fort St. Frederic. And Captain Robert Rogers, who made several reconnoissances to the walls of the fort in 1755–6, describes the settlements on the west side of the lake as small villages or hamlets, which he burned. The settlements about St. Frederic were much exposed, and at the time of Kalm's visit in 1749, had been once abandoned; the settlers being ordered to remove to Canada "or to settle close to the fort and to lie in it at night." They still continued to sleep within the enclosure of the fort at the time of Rogers' visit in 1755–6.

The governor of Canada did not confine the encroachments
on Lake Champlain to the vicinity of Crown Point, for soon
after the erection of Fort St. Frederic, he issued grants for
large tracts of land lying on both sides of the lake, to several
persons holding office under the French king. The first of
these grants was made to Sieur Penn, major of the town
and castle of Quebec, on the 10th day of April, 1733, and
embraced a tract " two leagues or two and a half in front,
by three in depth along the river Chambly and Lake Champlain, together with the river Chazy included therein and
Isle a la Motte."[1]   Two days afterwards another grant was
issued to Sieur St. Vincent, ensign of foot, for "two leagues
in front, by three leagues in depth on Lake Champlain,"[2] and
another, on the 20th of the same month, to Sieur la Ganch-
etiere, captain of marines, of " two leagues front by three
leagues deep on said lake."[3]

On the 7th of July, 1734, a grant was issued to Sieur
Contrecœur, Jr., ensign of infantry, for a tract of land which
was described as "beginning at the mouth of the *Rivière aux
Loutres* (Otter Creek, Vt.), one league and a half above and
one league and a half below, making two leagues in front by
three in depth, together with so much of said river as is
found included, with three islets which are in front of said
concession and depend thereon."   On the 20th of the same
month, another grant was made to Sieur de Beauvis of lands
"two leagues in front and three in depth on Lake Champlain
together with the peninsula which is found to be in front of
said land."[4]   In the same month another was issued to
Sieur de la Periere, " beginning at the mouth of the river
Ouynouski (Winooski) one league above and one league
below, making two leagues front by three leagues in depth,

---

[1] Now northern part of the town of Champlain, N. Y.
[2] Remainder of Champlain.
[3] In town of Chazy, N. Y.
[4] Now parts of Swanton and Highgate, Vt.

with the extent of said river which will be found com-
prehended therein, together with the islands and *battures*
adjacent." Also one to Sieur Douville, on the 8th of
October, 1736, for lands on the east side of the lake,
"two leagues front by three leagues deep;"[1] and another
on the 13th of June, 1737, to Sieur Robart, king's store-
keeper at Montreal, "three leagues front by two leagues
in depth on the west side of Lake Champlain, taking in
going down one league below the River Bouquet, and in
going up, two and a half above said river." The Island
of North Hero or *Isle Longue* was granted to Contrecour,
captain of infantry, and M. Raimbault received a large
concession north of and adjoining the lands granted to
M. de la Periere.

These grants were issued subject to forfeiture in case the
lands were not settled and improved within a certain time.
This condition not having been fulfilled, all but the two
last mentioned were reunited to the king's domains by
an ordinance of the governor and intendant of Canada
of the 10th of May, 1741. The grantees gave various
reasons why their lands had not been settled within the
prescribed time. Pean could find no farmers to place
upon his seigniory; St. Vincent had been absent on the
king's service, and Contrecour had offered very advantageous inducements to settlers, including a bonus of three
hundred livres, but without success. Sieur Robart had
surveyed his lands and had offered every inducement for
young men to settle upon them. These excuses were not
satisfactory to the government officers. They, however,
declared that patents would be reissued to any who should
place settlers on the land within one year from that
time. This was not done; but soon afterwards settlements

---

[1] In town of Georgia, Vt.

MAP OF FRENCH GRANTS ON LAKE CHAMPLAIN.

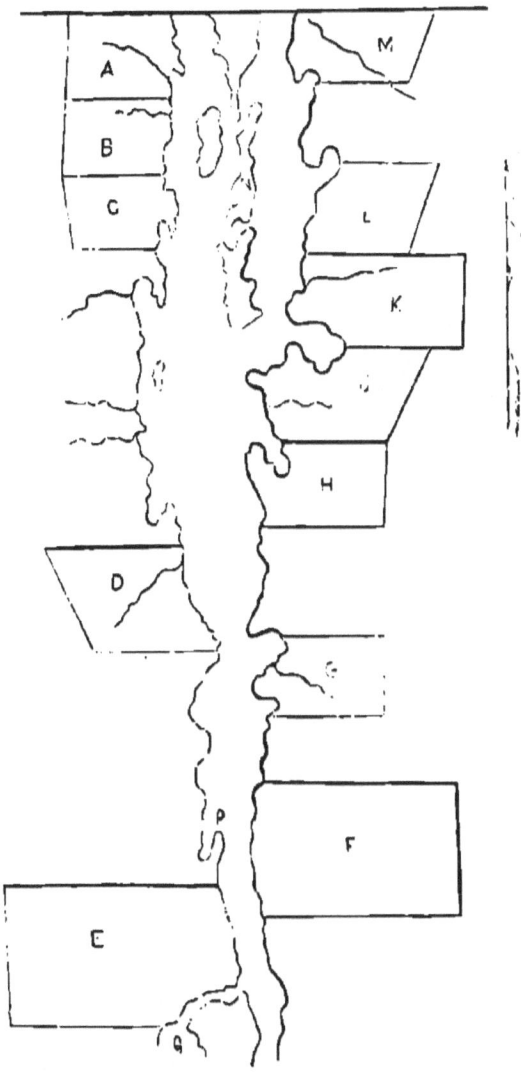

REFERENCES. — A, Sieur Pean. — B, Sieur St. Vincent, Jr. — C, M. de la Gauchetiere. — D, M. Robart. — G, M. Contrecour, Jr. — H, La Manaudiere. — J, M. de la Periere. — K, M. Rahnboult. — L, M. Douville. — M, M. de Beauvois, Jr. — N, M.Contrecour. — E, Alainville. — F, Hocquart. — P, Crown Point. — Q, Lower End of Lake George.

were formed near the mouth of the Big Chazy River and at Windmill Point,[1] which were occupied for a short time and then abandoned.

The lands originally granted to Pean were, in 1752, conceded to Sieur Bedou, councilor in the superior council of Quebec, and by him afterwards transferred to M. de Beaujeu, who owned a seigniory adjoining on the north. In April, 1734, and again in 1745, patents of concession were issued to Sieur Hocquart, councilor of state and intendant of the naval forces at Brest, for a large tract embraced in the present towns of Panton, Addison, and Bridport, Vt., which Hocquart conveyed to Michael Chartier de Lotbiniere in 1764, and in November, 1758, the Marquis de Vaudreuil, governor general of Canada, granted to the same de Lotbiniere the seigniory of Alainville, embracing upwards of four leagues front by five leagues depth, and lying partly on Lake George and partly on Lake Champlain.

The aggregate of these concessions embraced over eight hundred square miles of territory. No permanent settlements were made however under any of the grants, except of parts of the seigniories of Hocquart and Alainville, in the immediate vicinity of Crown Point and Ticonderoga. After the conquest of Canada the grantees petitioned for a confirmation of their titles, but this the British government refused, at the same time, however, declaring that the claim-

---

[1] The first houses I saw after leaving Fort St. Frederic were some on the western side of the lake, about ten French miles from St. Johns, in which the French lived before the last war, and which they then abandoned. * * * A windmill, built of stone, stands on the east side of the lake, on a projecting piece of ground. Some Frenchmen lived near to it. From this mill to Fort St. Johns they reckon eight French miles. The English, with their Indians, have burned the houses here several times, but the mill remained unhurt. — *Kalm* in 1749.

ants should be entitled to so much of the concessions as should be proportionate to the improvements made on them, at the rate of fifty acres for every three acres improved, provided they took out new grants for the same under the seal of the province of New York, subject to the usual quit-rents. No new grant to one person was to exceed twenty thousand acres, nor did this privilege extend to the grants of La Gauchetiere and others, annulled by the ordinance of the 10th of May, 1741.

The claimants refused the smaller grants from the province of New York, and declined to pay the required quit-rents. They fell back upon the original title of the French king, who, they contended, first discovered the country, and had held undisturbed possession of it to the year 1758. To this the authorities of New York replied, that the country south of the St. Lawrence River belonged originally to the Five Nations, from whom it passed to the English by virtue of a treaty made as early as 1683; that the treaty of Utrecht recognized the sovereignty of Great Britain over these nations, and that the possession of the French at Crown Point was an encroachment on British soil, which could confer no title to the French king. They also referred to an ancient grant (1696) to Godfrey Dellius of a large tract along the head of the lake, extending upwards of twenty miles to the north of Crown Point, as proof that the English had claimed the lake to be within their jurisdiction. But the strongest position taken against these claims, and which, considering the weakness of the French title, induced the British government to disaffirm them, was the fact that a large portion of the lands covered by the French grants was then held by old officers and soldiers of the provincial army, under patents issued under the seal of the province of New York.[1]

---

[1] For interesting documents relating to the French Grants on Lake Champlain see *Documentary History of New York*, vol. I.

New York was the central point of English influence in
America. It held the keys of Canada and of the great
western lakes. Within its limits burned the council fire
of the Six Nations,[1] the most powerful confederacy ever
formed among the Indians, whose sway extended west to
the Mississippi, and beyond the Ohio on the south. But
though strong in position, New York was weak in power.
Its history, from the death of Governor Montgomery in
1731, to the close of Mr. Clinton's administration in 1753,
is one of almost continued distrust and contention between
the executive and the assembly. In this war of party the
public business of the province was neglected and the security of the inhabitants disregarded. Occasionally, however,
the government would awake from its lethargy, and for a
moment return to the performance of its legitimate duties.
During one of these periods of quiet, a plan was projected
for the settlement of the wilderness between Lake Champlain and the Hudson River, to serve as a check upon the
French positions on Lake Champlain. The governor issued
a proclamation describing in glowing language the beauty
and fertility of the country, and offering the most liberal
terms to those who might settle there.

Seduced by this proclamation, Captain Laughlin Campbell
came from Scotland in 1737 to examine the land, and was
so well satisfied with its appearance that he returned to Isla,
sold his estate and brought over, at his own expense, eighty-
three protestant families, comprising four hundred and
twenty-three adults. The governor of New York had pro-

---

[1] The Tuscaroras joined the Confederacy in 1712. It is of them
that the fable was narrated that Chapelain, in 1619, saved himself
from their hands, when they were about to scalp him, by speaking
in his Gaelic mother tongue. Physiognomists pretend to have discovered in the countenances of the Tuscaroras evidence of a mixed
race between the ancient Welsh and the American aboriginal tribes.

mised Campbell a grant of 30,000 acres, free of all charge except those of survey and the usual quit-rents. But on his arrival, the mercenary officers of government refused to fulfill this engagement, unless they were allowed a share in the grant. A dispute arising between Campbell and the government on this account, in which the assembly joined with the emigrants, the negotiations were broken off. The emigrants were saved from starvation by enlisting in an expedition to Carthagena, while Campbell, broken down in spirits and fortune, sought a home elsewhere.

The colonists soon had reason to regret the folly of the government in not securing, at this time, the settlement of their northern frontier. The protestant Highlanders, brought over by Campbell, were a race of hardy and industrious people, indued by nature and habit with great power of endurance. They would have formed a bulwark against the French, who, for twenty years afterwards, retained absolute control of the lake, and sent out from their stronghold at Crown Point, bands of marauders to plunder and devastate the frontier settlements.

CHAPTER IV.

In the month of April, 1755, the governors of the several English colonies met in conference at Alexandria, in Virginia, and determined on a plan of military operations, by which to repel the encroachments of the French upon the northern frontier. The campaign contemplated three separate expeditions; one under Sir William Johnson against Crown Point,[1] another under Governor Shirley, of Massachusetts, against Niagara, while Major General Braddock, the commander-in-chief, with a third, was to move upon the French fort on the Ohio.

The expedition against Crown Point was to be composed of provincial troops and Indians. But the Six Nations did not enter into the scheme with their usual spirit and alacrity. They were dissatisfied with the long-continued inaction of the English, which contrasted unfavorably with the activity and vigilance of the French. Nor had the Indians been backward to express their disapprobation. "You are desirous that we should open our minds and our hearts to you," said the celebrated Mohawk sachem, Hendrik, at one of their councils, "look at the French : they are men, they

---

[1] Sir William Johnson's commission bears date the 16th of April, 1755, and recites that the troops are placed under his command "to be employed in an attempt to erect a strong fortress upon an eminence near the French fort at Crown Point, and for removing the encroachments of the French on his majesty's land there."

arc fortifying everywhere ; but, we are ashamed to say it, you are like women, bare and open, without fortifications."[1] This difference in the condition of the two countries was the natural result of the peculiar character and genius of their respective inhabitants. The English colonists were bold, intelligent and self-dependent. They understood and cherished the principles of self-government. Jealous of their rulers, they kept a constant watch upon their conduct, refused to vote supplies unless they knew the money would be appropriated for the public good, and opposed the erection of forts on the frontier, least their guns might be used to overawe the people. On the other hand, France kept her colonists in a state of dependence upon the mother country. They were allowed neither freedom of thought nor action ; and thus had they become more loyal and obedient but less independent than their English neighbors.[2] France directed forts to be built in the wilderness, and her orders were obeyed. England also required forts, but, instead of building them, the colonists questioned their necessity, objected to the expense and neglected to provide the means necessary for their erection.

The words of the Mohawk sachem were true. When the governors met at Alexandria, England had no works of defence upon her frontier, while the French were fortified at du Quesne, Niagara, Crown Point and Beau-Sejour. But notwithstanding their avowed reluctance to support their

---

[1] *Documentary History of New York*, vol. II.

[2] "Let us beware how we allow the establishment of manufactures in Canada, she would become proud and mutinous like the English. So long as France is a nursery to Canada, let not the Canadians be allowed to trade, but kept to their wandering, laborious life with the savages, and to their military exercises. They will be less wealthy, but more brave and more faithful to us."—*Montcalm to M. de Berryer*, 1757.

ancient allies, the Six Nations at length renewed their cove-
nant of friendship, and promised to aid the colonies in the
approaching struggle.

Considerable land carriage had to be encountered in passing from the Hudson River to Lake Champlain. The
portage commenced at the Hudson, near the present village
of Fort Edward, from whence two routes diverged : one
leading by the way of Fort Ann to the mouth of Wood
Creek, a distance of twenty-four miles; the other passing
by the way of Glen's Falls to the head of Lake George, a
distance of fourteen miles. From the first route a third
diverged near Fort Ann, which led to the waters of Lake
Champlain at the head of South Bay. By the aid of boats
on Wood Creek the portage on the first route was usually
reduced to from six to ten miles. This portage was called
the Great Carrying Place, and was selected as the point of
rendezvous for General Johnson's army, from whence it
was to move to Lake Champlain.

Early in July Major General Phinehas Lyman arrived at
the carrying place with about six hundred New England
troops, and commenced the erection of a fort, which was
afterwards called Fort Edward, in honor of Edward, Duke
of York, the grandson of the English sovereign.   Johnson
reached the camp on the 14th day of August, and found the
army increased to two thousand eight hundred and fifty men,
fit for duty. New recruits continued to arrive so that the
general found himself, by the end of August, at the head of
three thousand one hundred provincials and two hundred
and fifty Indians.[1] By the 3d of September the main army
had reached the head of Lake George, while a great number
of teamsters were engaged in dragging six hundred boats from
the Hudson River to be used for the transportation of troops
across the lake.   At Lake George Johnson halted for the

---

[1] Johnson to Lt. Gov. De Lancey.

boats to come up, and to announce the plan of his future
operations. "I propose," said he, "to go down this lake
with a part of the army, and take post at the end of it, at a
pass called Ticonderogue, there to wait the coming up of the
rest of the army and then attack Crown Point."[1] While the
English commander was thus planning his advance upon
Fort St. Frederic, the French general had left that post and
was hastening towards South Bay.

When General Lyman stopped on the banks of the Hudson to await the arrival of the main army, the whole
available French force on Lake Champlain did not exceed
eight hundred men, exclusive of Indians. Early in the summer, however, the Baron Dieskau, a brave old officer, who
had distinguished himself under the celebrated Marshal
Saxe, arrived at Quebec, accompanied by several veteran
regiments from France. These troops were immediately
ordered to Lake Ontario, but Dieskau, hearing that the English were in motion towards Lake George, changed his route
and passed rapidly forward towards Crown Point, where he
arrived about the 1st of August. For the defense of this
fortress Dieskau brought with him seven hundred regulars,
sixteen hundred Canadians and seven hundred savages.[2]

Dieskau left a strong garrison at Fort St. Frederic,
encamped a portion of his army at Ticonderoga, and with six
hundred savages, as many Canadians and two hundred regular troops, ascended the lake to the head of South Bay,
and after four days march, arrived within four miles of Fort
Edward, on the Lake George road. The Indians now refused
to proceed further in the direction of the fort, but were
willing to go against the open camp of the English at Lake
George. The head of the column was therefore turned
towards the lake.

---

[1] Johnson to the Board of Trade.
[2] Bancroft's *History of the United States*, vol. IV.

As soon as the English commander learned that the French had left South Bay, he determined with the advice of a council of war, to send a strong party to reinforce Fort Edward, then guarded by two hundred and fifty New Hampshire troops and five companies of the New York regiment.[1] This reinforcement consisted of one thousand provincial troops, under command of Colonel Ephraim Williams of Massachusetts,[2] and two hundred Indian warriors led by Hendrik, the Mohawk sachem. They started from the camp about nine o'clock on the morning of the 8th of September expecting to find the French at or near Fort Edward. When Dieskau learned from his scouts, the approach of Williams's party, he extended his line on both sides of the road in the form of a half moon, and in this order continued slowly and cautiously to advance. Colonel Williams, in the mean time, pushed forward with rash confidence, and had proceeded about four miles from the lake, when he suddenly found himself in the very centre of the half circle. At that moment the French opened a fire of musketry in front and on both flanks. Thus attacked on all sides by an unseen enemy the provincials offered but a slight resistance. For a short time the slaughter of the English was dreadful. Williams fell dead at the head of his regiment, and the brave and faithful Hendrik was mortally wounded; but the troops were withdrawn with great skill and coolness by Lieut. Colonel Whitney, who succeeded to the command on the death of Williams.

---

[1] Johnson to the Governors of the several Colonies.

[2] Before joining Johnson, Colonel Williams made a will by which he bequeathed his property to the town of Williamstown, Massachusetts, on condition that the money should be used for the establishment and maintenance of a free school. This school was incorporated as a college in 1773, by the name of Williams College.

Johnson lay at Lake George without intrenchment or defense of any kind. Aroused by the noise of the firing, he sent Lieutenant Colonel Cole with a reinforcement of two hundred men to the aid of Williams, and hastened to form a sort of breastwork with fallen trees, drawing up a few pieces of cannon which had been left five hundred yards distant from the front.[1] At ten o'clock the defeated troops began to arrive at the camp in large bodies, and at half-past eleven the French appeared in sight, marching in regular order against the centre of the breastwork.

It had been Dieskau's purpose to rush forward and to enter the camp with the fugitives, but the Iroquois (Caughnawagas) took possession of a rising ground and stood inactive. At this the Abenakis halted also, and the Canadians became intimidated.[2] A few shots from the artillery drove them all to the shelter of the neighboring swamps, and left the French commander and his handful of veteran troops unsupported. As the regulars advanced against the centre they suddenly halted for several minutes about one hundred and fifty yards from the breastwork, and then again advanced, firing by platoons.[3] Finding it impossible to break the centre, Dieskau moved to the right and attacked Williams's Ruggles's and Titcomb's regiments, where a warm fire was kept up for nearly an hour.

---

[1] *Review of Military Operations in North America.*

[2] Bancroft's *History of the United States*, vol. IV. Baron Dieskau had no confidence in the Iroquois. After his defeat he writes M. de Vaudreuil: "I prophesied to you, sir, that the Iroquois would play some scurvy trick. It is unfortunate for me that I am such a good prophet."—*Paris Doc.*

[3] "This halt," says the author of *A Review of Military Operations in North America from 1753 to 1756*, "was the Baron's chief error, for amidst the consternation of the camp, had he followed up the retreating detachment, he had easily forced the lines and gained a complete victory."

About four o'clock in the afternoon the English suddenly leaped over the slight breastwork and charged upon the assailants, who precipitately retreated, leaving almost all the regular troops dead on the field. The Canadians and Indians retired, in small parties, to the scene of Williams's defeat in the morning, where they were surprised and defeated by a party of one hundred and twenty New Hampshire and ninety New York troops, who, under command of Captain Mc Ginnes, had been sent from Fort Edward to reinforce the army at Lake George. The loss of the English this day was about two hundred and sixteen killed and ninety-six wounded; of the French the loss was much greater.[1] Dieskau was found, after the retreat, leaning against the stump of a tree, thrice wounded and helpless. Early in the action General Johnson received a painful wound in the thigh and retired to his tent; the command then devolved on General Lyman, who actually fought the battle and was entitled to all the glory of the day. Yet Johnson, by this victory, became a baronet, and received a gratuity of five thousand pounds; while Lyman is not mentioned in the official bulletin.

A rapid movement upon Crown Point would have forced the French to evacuate that post, but Johnson did not profit by his success. Instead of following up his victory by a quick and well directed blow, he wasted the rest of the season in building Fort William Henry, a useless pile of wooden barracks, surrounded by an embankment and ditch, which stood on an elevated spot about three hundred yards from the temporary breastwork attacked by Dieskau.

While the army remained at the head of Lake George, in timid inaction, Captain Robert Rogers and Captain Israel

---

[1] Johnson in his official report of this battle estimates the loss of the French at from five to six hundred. Warburton states it as a " little short of eight hundred."

Putnam, two daring and active officers belonging to the New England troops, made repeated demonstrations against the French, cut off many of their working parties and obtained correct information of all their proceedings. Upon one of these occasions Rogers and his men spent the night in the trench under Fort St. Frederic, and at another time, surprised a Frenchman within gun-shot of its walls.[1]

The season of 1756 passed without any military movement of importance being made by either party, in the vicinity of Lake Champlain. The English completed the defenses of Fort William Henry, and at one time contemplated building a fort at the head of South Bay; but this last work was at first delayed and ultimately abandoned. On the other hand the French were busily engaged in fortifying the peninsula of Ticonderoga. After the defeat of Dieskau the remnant of his army sought shelter there, where they established a camp and commenced building a fort, afterwards called Fort Carillon. During the season of 1756 upwards of two thousand French were constantly engaged upon the work. The lake now presented a most lively appearance. Canoes, bateaux and schooners were constantly passing and repassing between Canada, Crown Point and Ticonderoga, transporting troops from point to point, or loaded with supplies and ammunition.

Small scouting parties would occasionally leave Fort William Henry and penetrate as far as the French works, to gather information and beat up the outposts of the enemy.

---

[1] *Journal of the New Hampshire Scout.* Rodgers was born in Dumbarton, New Hampshire. He was appointed to the command of a company of rangers in 1755, and served until the conquest of Canada in 1760. He afterwards served in the Cherokee war, and took up arms for the king at the time of the revolution. In 1777 he went to England, where he died. His name is now generally spelled *Rogers.*

On one occasion Capt. Robert Rogers was sent on a scout with a party of fifty men and five whale-boats. Rogers drew his boats over the mountain into Lake Champlain, and passing Ticonderoga in the night, on the morning of the 7th of July secreted his party on the east side of the lake, about twenty-five miles north of Crown Point. While lying here, Rogers counted thirty boats passing towards Canada, and about three o'clock in the morning, discovered a schooner of thirty-five or forty tons at anchor a short distance below. As he was preparing to attack this vessel, two lighters with twelve men on board approached the shore, into which his party fired, killing three of the Frenchmen and wounding two others. The lighters were taken and found loaded with wheat, flour, rice, brandy and wine. Destroying all but the two last, Rogers hastened back, his men rowing none the less stoutly when the prisoners informed them that a party of five hundred men were only two leagues below, on their way to Crown Point.[1]

The campaign of 1757 opened early and briskly on the northern frontier. While the strong ice yet covered the surface of the lake and the snow lay in heavy drifts along its shores, eleven hundred French and four hundred Canada Indians, under Vaudreuil and the Chevalier Longueuil, marched from Ticonderoga to surprise the garrison of Fort William Henry. During the night of the 16th of March the party lay upon the snow behind Long Point, and early the next morning, appeared suddenly before the fort, expecting to carry it by surprise; but Stark — the same who, twenty years later, was ready to make his Molly a widow for the cause of liberty[2] —

---

[1] Rogers's Journal, *Documentary History of N. Y.* IV, 286.

[2] John Stark was born in Londonderry, New Hampshire, on the 17th of August, 1728. He was appointed captain of a company of rangers in 1755, and was with Lord Howe when he was killed near Ticonderoga, in July, 1758. At the close of the French war,

was there with his rangers, and the assailants were forced back; not however until they had burned several sloops, a large number of bateaux and some store houses which stood beyond reach of the guns of the fort.

Soon after the return of the French, Colonel Parker was sent from Fort William Henry with a command of four hundred men, to attempt the works at Ticonderoga. The detachment crossed the lake in whale-boats and bateaux, but before reaching Ticonderoga, were decoyed in an ambuscade, and the whole party, with the exception of two officers and seventy men, either killed or taken prisoners.

The French still urged forward the defenses of Fort Carillon. Montcalm, brave, sagacious and active, was at Montreal preparing to carry out his favorite project of reducing Fort William Henry. Everything favored the enterprise. The Indians, including many stern warriors of the Six Nations, gathered around the little fort of St. Johns on the Richelieu, and there danced their war dances beneath the white banner of France. Six days afterwards they landed from two hundred canoes, upon the rock-bound shores of Ticonderoga, where they were met by Marin, returning from a foray near Fort Edward, his canoes decorated with the bleeding scalps of forty-two Englishmen. Six thousand French and Canadians, and seventeen hundred Indians were now collected at

he retired with the reputation of a brave and vigilant officer. Immediately after the battle of Lexington Stark repaired to Cambridge where he received a colonel's commission. Feeling aggrieved by the promotion of several junior officers, he resigned in 1777, but soon afterwards returned to the field in command of a body of New England militia, which had been raised to oppose the advance of Burgoyne. He commanded the American force at the battle of Bennington. It was immediately before that engagement that he made the well-known speech to his men, "Boys, those are your enemies, the red-coats and tories. We must conquer them, or to night Molly Stark will be a widow."

Ticonderoga, armed to the teeth, and anxious to be led against the enemy. Montcalm needed no persuasion. On the last day of July M. de Levy was sent forward by land, under the guidance of the Indians, with two thousand five hundred men, and Montcalm followed the next day, with the main body of the army, in two hundred and fifty boats.

Gen. Webb, a man of weak, irresolute and timid character, was in command of the provincial troops, and had five thousand men with him at Fort Edward, while a body of one thousand garrisoned Fort William Henry. It so happened that Webb started for Lake George, with an escort of two hundred men, under command of Major Putnam, at the very time Montcalm was embarking his army at the lower end of the lake. On his arrival at the fort, Putnam was sent to reconnoitre as far as Ticonderoga, and had proceeded part of the way, when he discovered the boats of the French moving slowly up the lake. Returning to the fort, Putnam informed Webb of the approach and strength of the enemy; and urged that the whole army should be brought forward immediately to repel their attack; but to this Webb would not consent. Enjoining secresy upon Putnam he returned, with dastard haste, to Fort Edward, from whence he sent Colonel Monro, with one thousand men, to reinforce and take command of the garrison at the lake.

Montcalm landed about the time of Colonel Monro's arrival, and immediately laid siege to the fort, at the same time sending proposals for its surrender. " I will defend my trust to the last," was the spirited reply of the brave Monro. The siege lasted six days, in the course of which the French general pushed his advances within musket shot of the fort, while a body of over five thousand regulars, Canadians and Indians, under de Levy and de la Corne, held the road leading to Fort Edward in rear of the English works. Then it was that Monro, finding his provisions and ammunition nearly exhausted, and having received a letter from his pusillanimous chief declining to send him further assistance, consented to surrender. By the terms of capitulation the English were to march out with their arms and baggage, and were to be escorted by a detachment of French troops as far as Fort Edward; the sick and wounded remaining under Montcalm's protection until their recovery, when they were to be allowed to return to their homes.

At the time of the capitulation four hundred and fifty-nine English occupied the fort, while seventeen hundred and fifty were posted in a fortified camp standing on an eminence to the east, now marked by the ruins of Fort George. The troops marched out of the works on the morning of the 10th of August, and had scarcely passed the gates, when they were attacked by a large party of Indians attached to the French army. The savages rushed on with the fury of demons. Men, women and children were murdered in cold blood, and in the most barbarous manner.[1] The massacre continued until the English had proceeded half way to Fort Edward, when the scattered and terrified troops were met by an escort of five hundred men sent out for their protection. The French officers endeavored in vain to arrest the

---

[1] Major Putnam, who had been sent forward to watch the movements of Montcalm, thus describes the awful scene which he beheld after the departure of the French from Fort William Henry. "The fires were still burning, the smoke and stench offensive and suffocating. Innumerable fragments, human skulls and bones, and carcasses half consumed, were still frying and broiling in the decaying fires. Dead bodies, mangled with scalping knives and tomahawks in all the wantonness of Indian fierceness and barbarity, were every where to be seen. More than one hundred women, butchered and shockingly mangled, lay upon the ground, still weltering in their gore."

terrible onslaught. "Kill me," cried Montcalm, baring his breast, "but spare the English who are under my protection." The appeal was in vain. The vindictive savages had tasted blood, and neither prayers, nor menaces, nor promises availed while a victim was to be found.[1] Immediately after the victory the fort was leveled to the ground; the cannon and stores were removed to Ticonderoga, and the boats and vessels taken to the lower end of the lake. Thus closed the military operations of the year. The French returned to resume their labor upon the walls of Carillon, Webb shrank back to Albany, and the timid deer again drank, undisturbed, of the cool waters of the silver Horicon.

The British government decided to press the campaign of the succeeding year (1758) with extraordinary vigor. Twelve thousand troops were to attempt the reduction of Louisburg on the Island of Cape Breton; sixteen thousand were to march against Ticonderoga and Crown Point; and eight thousand were to attack Fort du Quesne. The command of the troops destined for Lake Champlain was entrusted to Major General Abercrombie, who had succeeded the imbecile Loudon to the chief command in America.

On the first of July, six thousand three hundred and sixty-seven regulars and nine thousand and twenty-four provincials were collected around the decaying ruins of Fort William Henry. Four days later the whole armament struck their tents, and in nine hundred bateaux and one hundred and thirty-five whale-boats embarked on the waters of Lake George; a large number of rafts, armed with artillery and loaded with provisions, accompanied the expedition. That night the proud host rested for five hours on Sabbath Day Point, and early on the morning of the 6th, reached the landing at the lower end of the lake.

---

[1] Bancroft's *History of United States*, vol. IV; *Conquest of Canada*, vol. II; Williams's *Hist. Vermont*, vol. II.

A PLAN OF FORT WILLIAM HENRY, 1757,

And the English camp and retrenchment, with the French camps and the attack thereupon.

A. Dock.
B. Garrison Gardens.
C. Fort William Henry.
D. Morass.
E. Montcalm's 1st Battery of 9 guns and 2 mortars.
F. Montcalm's 2d Battery of 10 guns and 3 mortars.
G. Montcalm's approaches.
H. Two intended Batteries.
I. Place where Montcalm landed his artillery.

K. Montcalm's camp, with the main body of the army.
L. M. de Levy's camp; 4,000 Regulars and Canadians.
M. M. de la Corne, with 1500 Canadians and Indians.
N. English encampment before the retrenchment was made.
O. The bridge over the Morass.
P. The English retrenchment.

10

Fort Carillon, against which the English were now advancing, stood near the point of the peninsula formed by the junction of the outlet of Lake George with Lake Champlain. This peninsula contains about five hundred acres, and is surrounded on three sides by water. One half of the western or land side was then covered by a swamp. The fort was nearly one hundred feet above the water, and stood on the south side of the peninsula adjoining the outlet, which here expands into a bay of considerable size. On the extreme easternmost point of the peninsula, at a short distance from the main work, was a strong redoubt of earth and stones, which commanded the narrow part of the lake. A battery also stood on the bank of the bay, a short distance west of the fort, while the low land to the north was covered by two batteries, standing behind its walls. The road from Lake George to Ticonderoga crossed the river or outlet twice, by bridges. Near the lower bridge, and less than two miles from the fort, the French had built saw-mills, which were defended by a slight military work. They had also built a log camp near the landing at the foot of Lake George.

To oppose the powerful army now advancing against them, the French had only twenty-eight hundred regulars and four hundred and fifty Canadians. But Montcalm was not the man to despond. The apparent hopelessness of resistance excited him to action. With consummate judgment he marked out his lines, half a mile west of the fort, and pushed the work with such ardor that, in ten hours, a wall as many feet high had been thrown up across the high ground which lay between the swamp and the bank of the outlet. On the 1st of July, three regiments under M. de Bourlemaque, occupied the log camp at the foot of the lake, while the battalion of La Sarre was posted near the mills. When the English first appeared in sight, Bourlemaque fell

back upon the mills, leaving Captain de Trepezéc, with three
hundred men, to watch the approaching column.

Immediately on landing, Abercrombie, leaving his baggage,
provisions and artillery in the boats, formed his men into
three columns and advanced towards Ticonderoga. The
route lay through a thick and tangled wood which prevented any regular progress, and the troops, misled by the
bewildered guides, were soon thrown into confusion. While
thus pressing forward in disorder, the head of the advance
column, under Lord Howe, fell in with a party of the French
troops, who had lost their way likewise, and a warm skirmish ensued. At the first fire the gallant Howe fell and
instantly expired. He was the idol of the army and had
endeared himself to the men by his affability and virtues.
Infuriated by the loss of their beloved leader, his men
rushed forward and swept the French from the field. Abercrombie's bugles now sounded the retreat, and the fatigued
soldiers returned to the landing place, where they encamped
for the night.

Early on the morning of the 7th, Lieutenant Colonel
Bradstreet moved forward with a strong party and took
possession of the saw-mills, while Abercrombie again formed
his men in order of battle, and prepared to advance against
the French works. But the attack was not made until the
morning of the 8th, when the whole army was brought up,
except a small detachment left to guard the boats, and a
provincial regiment stationed at the saw-mills. Montcalm
had that morning received a reinforcement of four hundred
men, under M. de Levy, which increased his force to about
thirty-six hundred. Behind the newly erected lines, which
were now strengthened by a wide and difficult abattis, he
posted the tried battalions of La Reine, La Sarre, Bearn,
Guyenne, Berry, Languedoc and Roussillon, and calmly
awaited the onset.

PLAN OF ATTACK BY GEN. ABERCROMBIE, AT TICONDEROGA,
8th JULY, 1758.

As the English approached, the rangers, light infantry, bateau men, and Ruggles's, Dotey's, Partridge's, Williams's and Bagley's regiments of provincials, with a battalion of the New York regiment, took post in front, out of cannon-shot of the French works. Next came the regulars destined for the assault, while the Connecticut and New Jersey troops were drawn up in the rear. At one o'clock the English bugles sounded the attack. When the regular battalions moved forward with quick and steady step—the veteran fifty-fifth leading, closely followed by the gallant Colonel Graham, at the head of Murray's highlanders. As the columns approached, and when the ranks became entangled among the logs and fallen trees which protected the breastwork, Montcalm opened a galling fire of artillery and musketry, which mowed down the brave officers and men by hundreds. For four hours the English vainly strove to cut their way through the impenetrable abattis, until Abercrombie, despairing of success, and having already lost one thousand nine hundred and forty-four men in killed and wounded, ordered a retreat. Montcalm did not pursue. Having refreshed his exhausted soldiers, he employed the night in strengthening his lines — a useless labor, for the frightened Abercrombie did not stop until he reached the head of Lake George, and even then he sent his artillery and ammunition to Albany for safety.[1]

Soon after the retreat of the English, Majors Putnam and Rogers were sent, with their rangers, towards the head of Lake Champlain, to watch the movements of a party of five hundred Canadians and Indians, who, it was understood, intended to pass up the lake from Ticonderoga, under com-

---

[1] Abercrombie's dispatch — *Conquest of Canada.* Bancroft's *History of the United States.* Williams's *Vermont,* &c. The loss of the English on that day was as follows: Regulars, 464 killed, 29 missing, and 1117 wounded; Provincials, 87 killed, 8 missing, and 239 wounded ; Montcalm reported his loss at 110 killed, and 248 wounded.

mand of the famous Marin. Rogers, with the main body took a position near Wood Creek, about twelve miles from its mouth, while Putnam, with thirty-five men, took post on the bold, rocky shore of the lake about half a mile north of the creek. Near the edge of these rocks he constructed a wall of stones, and placed young trees before it in such a manner as completely to hide the defense from the water below. Learning, four days afterwards, that the enemy were approaching, under cover of the night, Putnam called in his sentinels and stationed his men where their fire would prove most effective; commanding them to remain perfectly quiet until they received his orders. The canoes advanced in solemn silence, and had passed the wall of stone, when they became alarmed by a slight noise, caused by one of Putnam's men carelessly striking his gun against a stone. Crowding together beneath the rocks, a brief consultation ' was held by the party, when the canoes were turned back towards Ticonderoga. As they turned, Putnam gave the order to fire. This fire was returned from the lake, and for a short time the contest was warmly kept up on both sides. Great was the carnage among the canoes, which lay exposed upon the smooth surface of the water. Marin at length withdrew and landed his men a short distance below, intending to surround the rangers; but Putnam was upon the alert and immediately withdrew towards Fort Edward. While retreating through the thick forest an unexpected enemy fired upon the party, and wounded one man. Putnam instantly ordered his men to charge, when his voice was recognized by the leader of the other party, who cried out, "Hold, we are friends." "Friends or foes," answered Putnam, "you deserve to perish for doing so little execution with so fair a shot." The party proved to be a detachment sent out to cover his retreat.

A few days afterwards, Putnam was taken prisoner by

some of the Indians attached to Marin's command. The Indians bound Putnam[1] to a tree. A young savage then amused himself by seeing how near he could throw a tomahawk to his prisoner's head without touching it — the weapon struck into the tree a number of times, at a hair's breadth from the mark. When the Indian had finished this novel, but, to one of the parties, not very agreeable sport, a Canadian came up, snapped his fusee at Putnam's breast, then violently and repeatedly pushed the muzzle against his ribs, and finally gave him a severe blow on the jaw with the butt end of the gun. Putnam was then stripped of his clothes and taken to the place selected for their night encampment, where the Indians determined to roast him alive. For this purpose they bound him to a tree, piled dried bushes in a circle around him, and then set fire to the pile. At the moment when Putnam began to feel the scorching heat, and had resigned himself to the keen agonies of certain death, Marin rushed through the crowd, opened a way by scattering the burning brands, and unbound the victim.[2]

---

[1] Israel Putnam was born at Salem, Massachusetts, January 7th, 1718. He was distinguished for his bravery, enterprise and perseverance, and for the most undeviating principles of honor, humanity and benevolence. He first joined the provincial army in 1755, as captain of a company of rangers, and was rewarded for his services in the campaign of 1756 by promotion to the rank of major. In 1760 he was a lieutenant colonel, and served under Amherst in the conquest of Canada. It was said of him that *"he dared to lead where any dared to follow."* At the commencement of the revolutionary war, Putnam was appointed a major general in the American army, where he served with distinction. In December, 1779, he was prostrated by a paralytic affection, under which he languished until the 19th of May, 1790, when his honorable and useful life was brought to a final close.

[2] Thacher's *Military Journal.*

This humane officer, having reprimanded the savages in severe terms, took Putnam under his own protection and delivered him to Montcalm, by whom he was sent to Montreal. Thus, through hardships, privations and blood, were the sturdy provincials schooled for the great and heroic deeds of the American revolution.

CHAPTER V.

Notwithstanding the great importance attached by the provincial and home governments to the control of Lake Champlain — the key of Canada — three campaigns, under three different generals, had been undertaken without any progress towards the attainment of that object. Johnson was inefficient, Webb pusillanimous, and Abercrombie wanting in firmness and military skill. The first halted his army to build a fort when he should have captured one ; the second, with four thousand men under his immediate command, abandoned the brave Monro to the tomahawk of the merciless savage ; while Abercrombie, by a false move and " the extremest fright and consternation," allowed less than four thousand men to repel the advance of fifteen thousand troops, " the largest and best apportioned army in America." Success however, had attended the British arms in other quarters. Louisburg capitulated to General Amherst in July, and in November General Forbes was in possession of Fort du Quesne.

Pitt, the English secretary of state, had long desired the conquest of Canada. Fully appreciating the skill, bravery and activity of Amherst, he appointed him to the chief command in America. Amherst entered upon his work with zeal. Wolfe was placed in command of one expedition destined to the attack of Quebec ; Prideaux was sent with

another against Niagara, while the commander-in-chief led a
third in person, against the French posts on Lake Champlain.

Montcalm was indefatigable in his preparations for the
approaching struggle. Three armed vessels were built to
command the navigation of Lake Champlain, and the strong
walls of Carillon again echoed with the noise of workmen.
Still the French general, sorely pressed on every side,
feared for the safety of that post. He could spare but few
troops for its defense, and besides he well knew that its
batteries were commanded by the controlling summit of
Mount Defiance. "Had I to besiege Fort Carillon," said
he the year before, while wondering at the retreat of Abercrombie, "I would ask but six mortars and two pieces of
artillery."[1] Bourlemaque was sent forward to protect the
fort with three battalions of regulars and a body of Canadians and Indians, but he received instructions, at the same
time, to blow up the works on the approach of the English,
if he judged it expedient, to retire to Isle aux Noix on the
Richelieu, and there make a strong resistance.

About the 1st of July, Amherst reached the head of Lake
George with an army of six thousand men, where he remained
for a month, waiting for the remainder of the troops to come
up. On the 21st he embarked with fifty-seven hundred and
forty-three regulars and five thousand two hundred and
seventy-nine provincials, and crossing the lake in four
columns, landed the next day, near the spot where Abercrombie had disembarked the year before. That night his
army lay under arms at the saw-mills, while the French held
their old lines in force. On the night of the 23d, de Bourlemaque withdrew his men, and leaving a party of four hundred in Fort Carillon to mask his retreat, embarked with

---

[1] Bancroft's *History of the United States.*

PLAN OF FORT CARILLON, 1759.

A. Stone Battery.
B. The Fort.
C. Earth Battery.
D. Wharf.
E. Stone houses for naval stores.
F. Redoubt.
G. Battery.

H. Stone houses for provisions.
I. Lime kilns.
K. Nine ovens.
L. Gardens.
M. Batteries in the lines.
N. French lines.

the main body for Crown Point. The English grenadiers immediately occupied the deserted intrenchments.[1]

During the 24th and the 25th, the French kept up a continuous fire upon the English camp, which was warmly returned. In the meantime, Amherst advanced his approaches within six hundred yards of the fort, and was preparing to assault the works, when the French, having now held their opponents at bay long enough to secure the retreat of M. de Bourlemaque, determined to blow up and abandon them. Several mines were constructed under the walls, and a fuse connected with the powder magazine. At ten o'clock on the night of the 26th, they sprung the mine and hastily retreated to their boats.[2] The explosion scattered the flames in every direction — breastworks, barracks and store-houses were consumed, while the report of the bursting guns, following each other in quick succession, announced to the retreating French the progress of the work of destruction.

Amherst immediately commenced repairing the fort, the stone work of which remained mostly uninjured. He also sent forward Major Rogers, with two hundred rangers, to examine the position of the French at Crown Point, and to seize, and at all hazards hold some strong post near the fort. But this haste was useless, for before the rangers could reach their post, the French had destroyed the fort, burned the surrounding settlements and retreated to Isle aux Noix. The glory of St. Frederic was gone.[3]

---

[1] "In the centre of these remarkable lines the French had, in celebration of the victory of Carillon, erected a lofty cross, which still remained; a deep grave was sunk before it, and on the cross was affixed a plate of brass, with this inscription.

'Pone principes eorum sicut Oreb et Zebee et Zalmanna.' "— *Warburton*, vol. II.

[2] *Conquest of Canada*, vol. II.

[3] Mr. Lossing (*Field Book of the Revolution*, I, 120) says Amherst

On the 4th of August, Amherst reached Crown Point with the main army, and immediately traced out the lines of a new fort, about two hundred yards west of the old French works. This fort, although never completed, is said to have cost the English government more than two millions of pounds sterling. The ramparts were about twenty-five feet thick and nearly the same in height, and were built of solid masonry. The curtains varied in length, from fifty-two to one hundred yards, and the whole circuit, measuring around the ramparts and including the bastions, was eight hundred and fifty-three yards. A broad ditch surrounded the work. On the north was a gate, and from the north-east bastion a covered way leading to the water.

While engaged upon this work, Amherst directed Captain Loring, who superintended the naval operations on the lake, to build with the greatest dispatch a sloop of sixteen guns, a radeau or raft eighty-four feet long, capable of carrying six large cannon, and a brigantine. These were completed by the 11th of October, when the English commander embarked his whole army in bateaux and started for Canada. Towards the evening of the next day the wind commenced blowing a gale, and the general was obliged to anchor his bateaux under the west shore of the lake. Captain Loring, however, kept at sea with his armed vessels, and at day-light in the morning discovered the French about forty-five miles down the lake. He immediately gave chase and drove a schooner and three sloops under shelter of Valcour Island. Two of the sloops were here sunk, while the other was run

moved "cautiously along Lake Champlain, crossed the outlet of Lake George, and appeared before Ticonderoga on the 26th of July." He also says that "not a gun was fired or a sword crossed." This is a mistake. Sixteen soldiers were killed or wounded by an attack of the French upon the British advance guard on the 23d. Between the 22d and 26th, seventy-seven of the British forces were killed or wounded.

aground by her crew, who escaped into the woods.[1] The schooner got away during the night.

Amherst, after remaining wind-bound for several days, again started for Canada; but he had scarcely reached Val-cour Island, when the autumn winds threatened to swamp his vessels. Satisfied that he could accomplish nothing at that late and inclement season of the year, he now abandoned the enterprise and returned to winter quarters at Crown Point, where he arrived on the 21st of October.

While Amherst was at Crown Point he opened a road from that place to Number Four on the Connecticut River, and also planned an expedition against the St. Francis In-dians, who lived on the east side of the St. Lawrence, near Three Rivers. The command of this expedition was entrust-ed to Major Rogers of the New Hampshire troops, who in October, left Crown Point in bateaux with two hundred men. This number was afterwards, by an accident, reduced to one hundred and forty-two, with whom Rogers proceed-ed to Missisco Bay, where he concealed his boats and a portion of his provisions, and started by land for the Indian village. After reducing the village to ashes, Rogers and his men returned to Crown Point by the way of the Con-necticut River.

In August, 1760, Colonel Haviland left Crown Point at the head of fifteen hundred regular troops, eighteen hundred provincials and some Indians, and on the 16th of that month encamped opposite the French post at Isle aux Noix, and on the 24th, opened a fire of mortars upon it. Three days afterwards, M. de Bougainville, the commandant, withdrew from the island, leaving a garrison of only thirty men, who

---

[1] See Brasier's map of Lake Champlain, where the north end of Valcour Island is designated as the place where "the French sunk their vessels in 1759."

immediately surrendered.[1] On the 8th of September, Colonel Haviland joined Amherst and Murray, under the walls of Montreal. That same day the city was surrendered by Vaudreuil. By this act the French dominion in Canada ceased, and by the treaty of peace signed in Paris on the 10th day of February, 1763, that province was formally ceded to Great Britain. This, says Mr. Smollet,[2] "was a conquest the most important of any that ever the British army achieved, whether we consider the safety of the British colonies in America, now secured from invasion and encroachment, the extent and fertility of the country subdued, or the whole Indian commerce thus transferred to Great Britain."

When the French army retreated to Canada, it was accompanied by the few inhabitants then residing upon the borders of the lake. There was, however, at this time, a settlement of French and Indians at Swanton Falls, in Vermont, several miles east of the lake, containing a small church, a saw-mill and about fifty huts, which was not abandoned until the year 1775.[3]

In the course of the year 1760, the New England troops frequently passed over the road opened by Amherst from the lake to the Connecticut, and thus became acquainted with the fertility and value of the lands in that section. These lands were soon sought out and settled upon.

The lands north of Crown Point, although equally fertile, were more remote and did not as early attract the attention of the pioneer or speculator. They however, came into notice gradually, so that several permanent settlements were made along the borders of the lake, during the fifteen years which intervened between the expulsion of the French and the commencement of the revolutionary war.

---

[1] *Conquest of Canada.* Williams's *History of Vermont.*
[2] *History of England.*
[3] Thompson's *Gazetteer.*

In 1766, Colonel Ephraim Doolittle, Paul Moore, Marshall Newton and others settled in the town of Shoreham, and in the same year, Donald McIntosh, a native of Scotland, moved into the town of Vergennes. A saw-mill was erected at the lower falls of Otter Creek as early as 1769, and shortly afterwards a grist-mill was built at the same place.

Some years before the commencement of the revolutionary war, two Germans by the name of Logan and Pottier settled upon the points of land in the town of Shelburne, known as Pottier's Point and Logan's Point. They were engaged in getting out timber for the Canadian market, and are said to have been murdered near the north end of the lake, by a party of soldiers sent out from Montreal to escort them home, on their return with the avails of a raft which they had sold. Soon after their death, about ten families settled in the town, among whom were Thomas and Moses Pierson.

John Strong, Zadock Everest and a Mr. Ward commenced a settlement in the town of Addison, on the opposite side of the lake from Crown Point, in 1769 or 1770. A settlement was also commenced in 1770, in the town of Panton, by John Pangborn and Odle Squires, who were afterwards joined by Timothy Spaulding, Peter Ferris and others. Ferris resided at the bay in which Arnold burned his vessels during the revolutionary war.

The town of Bridport was first settled in 1768, by Philip Stone, of Groton, Massachusetts. About the same time, two families by the name of Richardson and Smith moved into the township and commenced a settlement, under New York titles, and were followed by Towner, Chipman and Plumer, who held grants from the governor of New Hampshire. In 1773, Samuel Smith moved his family into the town and was followed during the following winter by Mr. Victory.

A settlement was begun at the lower falls on the Winooski River, by Ira Allen and Remember Baker, in 1773.[1]

These settlements were all on the eastern border of the lake. A few improvements had also been commenced on the New York side, which were principally confined to the grants made by the colony of New York to the officers and soldiers who had served in the wars against the French and Indians. The most important of these, lying north of Crown Point, was at the Bouquet River, where William Gilliland had erected a saw-mill, and where several persons, including Gilliland, Watson, Scarr, Cross, Blood and McAuley, resided.[2]

William Hay and Henry Cross lived on a tract of land granted, in 1765, to Lieutenant Friswell. Hay's house stood near the shore of the lake opposite Valcour Island. From this house his family watched the progress of the naval engagement between the American and British fleet, 11th Oct., 1776, and witnessed Arnold's masterly retreat during the following night. Before the revolution, the few inhabitants residing at the north end of the lake received their supplies from Montreal, which they were in the habit of visiting several times in the course of the summer months. About

---

[1] For further information in relation to the first settlement of the towns on the eastern border of the lake, see Thompson's *Gazetteer of Vermont.*

[2] Mr. Gilliland took posession of his lands on the Bouquet in the summer of 1765, and the same season built a frame house near the falls, two miles above the mouth of that river. The saw-mill was erected the next year. In 1775, Milltown as it was then called, contained from 20 to 30 houses, and was the largest and most flourishing settlement on the western borders of the lake. It was abandoned during the war of the revolution.

For a very full and interesting account of the early settlement of Willsborough, Essex County, N. Y., by Mr. Gilliland, the reader is referred to Mr. Watson's *Pioneer History of the Champlain Valley.*

the 1st of June, 1775, Mr. Hay went to Montreal to purchase
a supply of flour, and was there arrested and thrown into
prison by order of General Carleton. He remained in
prison several days, but was at length liberated at the solicitation of the merchants of that city. On his return home
he repaired to Crown Point, and gave information to the
American commander as to the strength and plans of the
Indians, which was considered of great importance at the time.
He also brought the first news of Carleton's efforts to enlist
the Caughnawagas on the side of the English. For some
reason he was afterwards suspected of holding communication with the enemy, and in July, 1776, while his wife
and children lay sick of the small pox, was arrested
and sent to Crown Point, by order of General Sullivan ;
Cross accompanied him. "These men are suspected of
being inimical to us and have it in their power to give
intelligence to the enemy," was the reason assigned for
their arrest.

As early as 1763, one John la Frombois, a native of
Canada, accompanied by two men named Goude and Swarte,
visited the shores of the lake, and remained a short time in
the present town of Chazy, Clinton county. La Frombois
returned to Canada in 1768, and obtained permission from
Francis McKay to settle on a tract which McKay pretended
to claim by virtue of an assignment of the old French grant
to La Gauchetiere.[1] Under this license La Frombois took
possession of what are now lots numbers seventy and seventy-
two, in Dean's Patent, and built a house on number seventy-

---

[1] See Chap. III. La Gauchetiere assigned to Estebe, in 1746, who
sold to de Pontbriant, Bishop of Quebec, in December, 1757.
Pontbriant afterwards conveyed to de Montgolfier, Superior of the
Seminary of St. Sulpice, who in 1768, released to McKay, as one
of the heirs at law of the Bishop de Pontbriant.

two, where he remained until 1776, when he was driven off by the English and his house burned. He returned in 1784, after the war, rebuilt his house and remained in possession of the lot until his death in 1810. Joseph la Monte (now Monty) moved on to a lot near La Frombois, in 1774, which he abandoned two years afterwards, and reclaimed after the war. His descendants still reside upon the same land.

After the first visit of La Frombois, but before his actual location, Charles de Fredenburgh, a needy German nobleman, who, in 1766, had received from the English government a warrant for thirty thousand acres of land, lying on the river Saranac, moved on to the tract and built a house and sawmill there. De Fredenburgh remained on this tract until about the time of the commencement of the revolution, when he removed his family to Montreal. He soon after returned to protect his property, and had been back but a short time, when the house and mill were burned down. Fredenburgh disappeared at the same time and was supposed to have been murdered. The saw-mill stood on a fall of the Saranac, two miles above its mouth.

In 1761, Philip Skene, an English major under half pay, who had been with Amherst in 1759, established a large colony near the mouth of Wood Creek. In the autumn he accompanied an expedition against Havana, and on his return, in 1763, found the settlement reduced to fifteen persons. He immediately set about reestablishing the colony, and in 1765 obtained patents for twenty-five thousand acres of land lying on and near the creek. Here he built a stone mansion forty feet by thirty, and two stories and a half in height. In 1770 he erected a large stone building one hundred and thirty feet long, which was used for a military garrison and depot. He also built at this place a stone forge of about the same dimensions as his house, where he commenced the manufacture of iron. This was the first forge erected on the borders of the lake. Skene owned a sloop, with which he kept up a regular communication with Canada, and at his own expense he cut a road through the wilderness as far as Salem, a distance of about thirty miles, from which point it was continued by others to Bennington. This road was used during the season when the navigation on the lake was closed by ice. In 1773, Skenesborough contained a population of 379.[1]

The causes which had formerly prevented the occupancy of the fertile lands of the Champlain Valley were removed when the whole country came into the possession of the English government, by the conquest of Canada, in 1760. But other difficulties almost immediately sprang up to retard the growth of this section of country, originating in the conflicting claims of the English colonists to the sovereignty of that portion of the valley lying east of the lake. The colony of New York claimed jurisdiction as far east as the Connecticut River, while New Hampshire asserted her right as far west as the shores of the lake, and south of the lake, to a line running parallel to and twenty miles east of the Hudson River. Both colonies frequently issued grants for the same territory, causing much confusion in the land titles, and creating great animosity between the rival claimants.

Prior to the close of the year 1763, the governor of New Hampshire had granted charters to different persons for fourteen towns lying along and adjoining the east shore of the lake, and by similar grants, had asserted the right of

---

[1] See a petition to Governor Tryon, praying that Skenesborough might be made the shiretown of Charlotte county. The petition is signed by thirty-eight "inhabitants of Crown Point district and Ticonderoga." These thirty-eight probably included all the settlers in the vicinity of those posts, on both sides of the lake.— *Documentary History of New York*, vol. IV.

that colony to the whole territory claimed to be within her
jurisdiction. On the other side, the colony of New York
issued grants of land on the lake to eighty-one or more reduced officers, who had served in the French and Indian
wars ; nearly one-half of which were located on the east
side of the lake. New York had also appropriated a large
tract, lying between Otter Creek and Mallet's Bay, for the
disbanded soldiers of those wars. A county had also been
organized by New York, called Charlotte county, which
extended, on the north, from Lake Memphremagog to the
St. Regis River, and stretched south, on both sides of the
lake, far beyond its southern extremity; the county seat was
fixed at Skenesborough.

The efforts of New York to extend its jurisdiction to the
east was met, from the first, by a most decided opposition on
the part of the people. Conventions were called to devise
means to protect the New Hampshire claimants in their
rights, committees of safety were organized, and the law
officers and land surveyors of New York were driven by
force from the disputed territory. These disputes were
generally confined to the southern part of Vermont. Occasionally, however, they extended as far north as the grants upon
the lakes.

In 1761, the governor of New Hampshire granted a tract
of land, lying around the lower falls of Otter Creek (Vergennes), to several persons who settled there, and as early
as 1769 had erected a saw-mill at the falls. Soon after the
erection of the mill, Lieutenant Colonel John Reed, who had
formerly commanded the Forty-second Royal Highland regiment, and who held a claim to the same land under the
colony of New York, forcibly drove off the New Hampshire
settlers, and put about fifteen families, his own tenants, in
possession. These last extended the settlements and had
erected several log houses and a grist-mill, when they were

in turn driven off by a party of Green Mountain Boys, who burned the houses, destroyed the grist-mill and put the New Hampshire claimants again in possession.

In June, 1773, Colonel Reed persuaded a number of Scotch emigrants who had lately arrived at New York, including John Cameron, James Henderson, Donald McIntosh, John Bardans and Angus McBean, to accompany him to Otter Creek for the purpose of retaking possession of these lands. On their arrival they found Joshua Hyde and several other persons in possession, with whom Reed entered into an arrangement by which Hyde and his associates were to give up quiet possession of the lands and to allow Reed's tenants to retain the same until the dispute as to title should be decided by the English government. Colonel Reed paid £61, 16s. for the crops and improvements, repaired the grist mill, and also purchased a quantity of provisions and some cows for the use of his tenants. He then left them and returned to New York.

This arrangement, although made with the consent of the New Hampshire claimants, was disapproved by the committee of safety, who sent Ethan Allen, Seth Warner and Remember Baker, with a party of about one hundred Green Mountain boys to Otter Creek for the purpose of driving off the Scotch occupants. On the 11th of August, Allen's party, attended by Hyde—the same person who two months before had sold his claim to Colonel Reed—arrived at the settlements, drove the Scotch from their dwellings, burned the hay and corn and five houses, and then tore down the grist-mill, breaking the mill-stones in pieces and throwing them over the bank into the creek. Cameron and his companions remained at Otter Creek about two weeks longer, and then returned to New York. After their departure a small block house was erected at the falls, which was garrisoned and afterwards used as a protection to the New

13

Hampshire claimants.   Another block house was soon afterwards built near the falls of the Winooski River.

During the controversy between the settlers under the New Hampshire grants and the colony of New York, a project was started by Major Skene and others to form that part of New York, lying east of the Hudson River, into a new province.   To effect this object, Skene visited England, and in March, 1775, wrote back that he had been appointed governor of Crown Point and Ticonderoga, and should soon call on the people for an address to show their loyalty to the king.   During the absence of Skene the troubles on the grants had increased to an alarming extent, and it is extremely doubtful what would have been the result of the contest, had not the commencement of the American revolution turned the attention of all parties to the common cause of the country.

CHAPTER VI.

War of the Revolution — Surprise of Ticonderoga — Arnold at St. Johns — Sentiments of the Canadians — Invasion of Canada — Siege of St. Johns — Death of General Montgomery at Quebec — Retreat of the Army of Canada.

"We conjure you by all that is dear, by all that is sacred, that you give all assistance possible in forming an army for our defense," was the appeal of Massachusetts, while the first blood of the revolution yet moistened the field of Lexington. Every section of the country responded to the call. Liberty poles were raised throughout Massachusetts and the adjoining provinces, and everywhere the militia took up arms and hastened to the scene of action.

"Putnam was at work in the field when the news came that blood had been shed; he immediately dropped his implements and started for Cambridge, without waiting to change his apparel. Stark was sawing logs, without his coat; he shut down the gate of his mill, and commenced the journey to Boston in his shirt sleeves." The same spirit was displayed throughout the country. Occasionally, however, a few persons were found who were inimical to the common cause. These were called *Tories*, and were often subjected to the most rigorous discipline. "When a disaffected tory renders himself odious," says Doctor Thacher, "he is seized by a company of armed men, and conducted to the liberty pole, under which he is compelled to sign a recantation, and give bonds for his future good conduct."

Upon one occasion a divine of Long Island pronounced, from his pulpit, a severe philippic against the *Patriots*, stigmatizing them as rebels, robbers and assassins. Information of the high tory character of the discourse was carried to

Captain Nathaniel Platt, a most zealous patriot, who commanded a company of Long Island militia. Capt. Platt immediately called out his men, seized the minister and carried him to the liberty pole, around which the company were formed. The minister was there severely reprimanded, and forced to walk up and kiss the pole as a punishment for his political heresy. On the next sabbath Captain Platt was at the church, to see what effect his *discipline* had produced upon the man of God. The discourse was unexceptionable until the minister reached the conclusion of his sermon, when while portraying the enjoyments of heaven to the true Christain, he gave expression to his feelings by turning towards the Captain and exclaiming, "there are no rebels in heaven, my brethren.— No! and you will find no Nathaniel Platts there, nor any accursed liberty poles to kiss."

The great body of the clergy, however, were firm and zealous patriots, who daily offered the most fervent prayers in behalf of their bleeding and afflicted country. Upon one occasion a zealous divine, who had been compelled to abandon his congregation in Boston, used the following emphatic language : "Oh! Lord, if our enemies will fight us, let them have fighting enough. If more soldiers are on their way hither, sink them, O Lord, to the bottom of the sea." " Amen," responded his congregation, " Yea, Lord, let them have fighting enough."

Among the men brought out by the revolution to meet the exigencies of the times, were Ethan Allen and Benedict Arnold. Arnold, a native of Connecticut, was indued with qualities which characterized him, at once, as the best of warriors and the meanest of men. In battle he was " the bravest among the brave." No enterprise was too daring for him to undertake, no obstacle too great for him to surmount. Whether among the unexplored forests of Maine, upon the decks of a little vessel on Lake Champlain, before the muskets of a platoon at Danbury, or under the fire of Burgoyne's veterans at Bemis's Heights, he was firm, daring and unterrified. But in every other respect the man was despicable. In early life he had been, by turns, a half-bred apothecary, a retailer, a skipper and a jockey, and had marked his course by hypocrisy, falsehood and crime. To escape the grasp of his creditors, he committed perjury, and to relieve himself of pecuniary embarrassments, occasioned by a life of extravagance and profligacy, he practised every dirty act of peculation, and ultimately aimed a traitor's dagger at the bosom of his country.

Ethan Allen was also a native of Connecticut, and possessed all the impetuous daring of Arnold, but without his vices. Associated in early life with the pioneers of Vermont, he soon became one of the leading men in that quarter, and by his bold, unyielding spirit, repelled the repeated attempts of New York to extend her jurisdiction over the New Hampshire grants. As a political writer he was clear and forcible, but uncultivated ; as a leader, bold and decided but often rash; as a man, frank, generous and unassuming.

Such were the two men who, on the 7th of May, 1775, met at Castleton to lead an expedition to the surprise of Ticonderoga. Allen, furnished with funds by Dean, Wooster and Parsons, in behalf of the assembly of Connecticut, had collected a band of two hundred and seventy men, all but forty-six of whom were his own well tried and faithful Green Mountain boys, led by Brown and the cool and cautious Warner. Arnold came attended by a single servant, but bringing with him a colonel's commission from the committee of safety of Massachusetts, authorizing him to raise a regiment of four hundred men. As soon as the two leaders met, Arnold pompously drew forth his commission and claimed the right to lead the expedition, but Allen refused to yield the command. The dispute was at length referred to a committee of officers, by whom it was decided that

Allen should retain the command, while Arnold was to act as his assistant. The main body now left Castleton to proceed by land to a point opposite Ticonderoga. At the same time, Captain Herrick was sent against Skenesborough with thirty men, with orders to seize the small fort at that place, to take the vessels collected there, and meet Allen and transport his party across the lake.

The forts at Ticonderoga and Crown Point had been abandoned soon after the conquest of Canada, and were now in a ruinous condition. Within the year a garrison had been sent there, at the request of the governor of New York, to protect the public property, and to secure that section from the threatened encroachments of the New Hampshire claimants. The garrison was, however, small and weak; Crown Point being held by a sergeant and twelve men, while a company of only forty-eight men, under command of Captain de la Place, was stationed at Ticonderoga.

Early on the evening of the 9th of May, Allen's party reached the shore of the lake opposite Ticonderoga. Herrick not having yet arrived from Skenesborough, it became necessary to procure a supply of boats in the neighborhood in order to cross to the fort. This was a work of no small difficulty. Douglass, one of the party, was sent to Bridport for a scow. A large oar-boat belonging to Major Skene, which lay at anchor near by, was decoyed ashore and seized by James Wilcox and Joseph Tyler, while several smaller boats were procured from other quarters.

As these boats were not sufficient to ferry the whole party at once, it was arranged that Allen and Arnold should first cross with eighty-three men, and that the boats should return for the rest of the party, who were to remain behind under command of Warner.[1] The little band, guided by

---

[1] The party embarked from the farm next north of Larabee's Point, in Shoreham, about three fourths of a mile below the fort.

Nathan Beman, a lad of fifteen years, was soon drawn up on the low ground below the fort, where an altercation again commenced between the two leaders, each claiming the right to lead the advance. Again the subordinate officers interfered, and decided that they should go in together— Allen on the right hand, and Arnold on the left. As the day began to break, it was deemed prudent to make the attack without waiting for the arrival of Warner, who had not yet crossed the lake with his party.

Allen now advanced to the front and adressed his men, as follows : "Friends and fellow Soldiers—You have, for a number of years past, been a scourge and terror to arbitrary power. Your valor has been famed abroad and acknowledged, as appears by the advice and orders to me from the general assembly of Connecticut, to surprise and take the garrison now before us. I now propose to advance before you, and in person conduct you through the wicket gate; for we must this morning either quit our pretensions to valor, or possess ourselves of this fortress in a few minutes ; and inasmuch as it is a desperate attempt, which none but the bravest of men dare undertake, I do not urge it on any contrary to his will. You that will undertake voluntarily, *poise your firelocks.*" "Each man," says Allen, "poised his firelock. I ordered them to face to the right, and at the head of the centre file, marched them immediately to the wicket gate."[1]

When they approached, the sentinel snapped his gun, and immediately retreated through the covered way, closely followed by the assailants, who were thus guided within the fort. As the patriots rushed into the parade ground,

This farm is the birth place of the Hon. A. C. Hand, of Elizabethtown, one of the justices of the New York supreme court, and has been in the possession of his family since the year 1789.

[1] Allen's *Narrative.*

they formed in the centre, facing the barracks, and gave a loud cheer, while Allen ascended a flight of steps leading to the commandant's quarters, and in a loud voice ordered him to appear, or the whole garrison would be sacrificed.

In this affair the patriots captured forty-eight men, one hundred and twenty pieces of cannon, several swivels and howitzers, together with a large number of small arms and ammunition of every description, and also a warehouse filled with materials for boat building. Colonel Warner arrived, with the remainder of the party, just after the surrender of the fort, and was immediately sent, with one hundred men, to take possession of Crown Point; but a strong head-wind drove his boats back, and he returned to Ticonderoga. The next morning a more successful attempt was made, and the fort at Crown Point was captured without blood-shed. Warner was there met by Captain Remember Baker, who had left the small fort on the Winooski to join Allen's party, and who, on his way up the lake, had intercepted two boats, which had been sent from Crown Point to carry intelligence of the reduction of Ticonderoga to St. Johns and Montreal.

It will be remembered that when the patriots left Castleton, Captain Herrick was sent with thirty men against Skenesborough. Herrick approached the place unobserved, and captured young Major Skene, twelve negroes and about fifty dependants or tenants, without firing a gun. He also took a large schooner and several small boats belonging to Skene, in which he embarked his men and prisoners, and passing down the lake, joined Allen at Ticonderoga. The history of the surprise of Skenesborough is embellished by an account of a singular discovery made there by the patriots. It is said that some of Herrick's men, while searching Skene's house, found the dead body of a female deposited in the cellar, where it had been preserved for many years. This was the body of Mrs. Skene, the deceased wife of the elder Skene, who was then in Europe, and who was in the receipt of an annuity, which had been devised to his wife

" while she remained above ground." Like a good patriot, Herrick crippled the resources of the enemy, by burying the body in the garden at the rear of the house.

In order to accomplish their plans, and to obtain absolute control of the lake, it was now only necessary that Allen and Arnold should get possession of an armed sloop, of about seventy tons, which lay at anchor in the Richelieu River, near the fort of St. Johns. After consultation and a dispute between the two officers, who were mutually jealous of each other, it was agreed that Arnold should fit out and arm the schooner which Herrick had captured at Skenesborough, and sail for St. Johns, accompanied by Allen, who was to take command of several long-boats which lay at Crown Point.

The schooner having been brought to Crown Point, Arnold embarked on the evening of the 14th of May, with fifty men under Captains Brown and Oswald, and on the 17th arrived within thirty miles of St. Johns, where his vessel was becalmed. Leaving the schooner, he manned two small boats with thirty-five men, and started to row down the river. At six o'clock the next morning he arrived at St. Johns, and surprised a sergeant and twelve men who garrisoned the fort. He also seized the sloop, in which he found seven men and two brass six-pounders. From the prisoners he learned that the commanding officer of the fort was hourly expected to return from Montreal, with a large detachment of troops for Ticonderoga, and a number of guns and carriages for the sloop. A company of forty men was also momentarily expected from Chambly.

Arnold had at first intended to await the arrival of Allen, who had been left far behind by the schooner while crossing the lake, but this information induced him to hasten his departure. Having destroyed three row-boats he immediately set out on his return, taking with him the sloop, four boats loaded with stores, and twenty prisoners. The party had proceeded about fifteen miles when they met Allen with one hundred

14

men, hastening down the river. Arnold informed Allen of the expected arrival of troops at St. Johns, and urged him to return. But this Allen refused to do, declaring that he should push on to St. Johns, and hold possession of it with the men under his command.[1]

When Allen reached St. Johns, he learned that the English troops were within two miles of the fort. He therefore crossed to the opposite side of the river, where he encamped for the night. Early the next morning the English commenced a fire upon the party, with six field pieces and two hundred small arms. Allen returned this fire for a short time, but finding he could make no resistance against the superior numbers opposed to him, he hastily reëmbarked, leaving three of his men behind.[2]

As soon as Arnold reached Crown Point, on his return, he fitted up the sloop with six cannon and ten swivels, fixed four guns and six swivels on the schooner, and prepared to resist an expected attack against that place from Canada. Also wrote to the committees of safety of Massachusetts and New York, urging them to send forward a large body of men to rebuild the fort at Ticonderoga.

The fortunate issue of the movement against the British possessions on Lake Champlain was of the utmost importance to the cause of the country, as it created a confidence among the people in the ultimate success of the struggle, and at the same time, placed the colonists in possession of the key of Canada, effectually preventing any sudden attack from that quarter.

The feelings of the Canadians in regard to the approaching struggle were not known, nor could it yet be determined which side of the question they would take. Sir Guy Carleton, governor of Canada, used every exertion to enlist them on the side of the government, while the American

---

[1] Arnold to Committee of Safety of Massachusetts.

[2] Arnold to General Assembly of Massachusetts.

congress, on its part, endeavored to conciliate their friendship, and induce them to make common cause with the colonists, or at least, to stand neutral during the approaching struggle. The efforts of congress were so far successful as to secure their neutrality.

Disappointed in not receiving the cöoperation of the Canadians, Gen. Carleton next attempted to rally the royalists, and for that purpose organized a corps to which he gave the name of the Royal Highland Emigrants. He also entered into negotiations with the Indians. Towards the last of July, Colonel Guy Johnson, superintendent of Indian affairs, arrived at Montreal, accompanied by a number of the chiefs and warriors of the Six Nations. Here a solemn council was held, and the assembled Indians swore, in the presence of the governor, to support the cause of the king against the colonists. A great number however, who had not attended the council, declared they would not intermeddle in the dispute, nor would they consent to aid or oppose either party.

The American congress was informed of these attempts on the part of General Carleton, to enlist the Canadians and Indians on the side of the king. It was also advised that the Canadians had refused to enter into the contest; but there was no assurance that they would long preserve their neutrality. Carleton had obtained great influence over this class, and might ultimately succeed in drawing them over to his side. To prevent this, and in the hopes that the *habitans* might be persuaded to embrace the opportunity to attempt the vindication of their political rights, congress determined to fit out an expedition for the invasion of Canada. For this purpose three thousand New York and New England troops were ordered to assemble at Crown Point and Ticonderoga, under the command of Major General Schuyler and Brigadier General Montgomery, while an expedition was organized to march against Quebec, by the way of the Kennebec River.

A large number of flat bottomed boats were built at Skenesborough, Ticonderoga and Crown Point, for the transportation of the army across the lake, and congress, by great exertions, raised the sum of fifty thousand dollars in specie, for the support of the army while in Canada. The arrangements for the expedition were conducted by General Montgomery, while General Schuyler remained at Albany to close negotiations for a treaty of peace with the Mohawk Indians, over whom he had great influence.

General Carleton, in the meantime, was actively engaged in preparations to oppose the advance of the American army. He placed the works at St. Johns in good repair, and directed a large vessel to be constructed there, which he intended to station near the north or lower end of the lake.

The American generals deemed it important by an immediate movement, to prevent Carleton from getting possession of the passage down the Richelieu River. Montgomery, therefore, on the 4th of September, embarked what men he had collected at Crown Point and sailed for Canada, leaving orders for the rest of the troops to follow, as soon as they should arrive. Schuyler left Albany in great haste, and following rapidly, joined Montgomery near Isle la Motte. From that place the two generals moved to Isle aux Noix, where they issued an address to the Canadians, assuring them that the army was not designed to act against their country, but was directed only against the British garrisons and troops, and exhorting them to join the Americans, in order to assert and defend their liberties. Copies of this address were distributed by Colonel Allen and Major Brown, who were sent among the people of the adjacent country for that purpose.

The army, although not over one thousand strong, now moved forward, and soon afterwards landed about one and a half miles above the Fort of St. Johns. At this point the ground was marshy, and covered with thick woods, through which the men had to pass in order to reach the fort. While advancing to reconnoitre the works, the left wing was attacked by a party of Indians, who killed three and wounded eight of the Americans. The Indians were however repulsed with some loss. Schuyler then advanced to within sight of the fort, where he commenced a breastwork; but finding the work strongly fortified and garrisoned, and learning that the armed sloop was preparing to sail from St. Johns towards his boats, which had been left with only a slight guard, he determined to retire to the Isle aux Noix, and there await the arrival of the artillery and the rest of the troops, who were daily expected. Schuyler fortified Isle aux Noix, and to prevent the passage of the sloop into the lake, constructed a *chevaux-de-frise* across the channel of the river, which is very narrow at that point. As soon as these arrangements were completed, he returned to Albany to conclude his treaty with the Indians, where he was attacked with a severe illness which disabled him from duty. The conduct of the Canada expedition then devolved upon General Montgomery, who retained the sole command until he fell under the walls of Quebec.

A small detachment of recruits, with a few pieces of artillery, having arrived at Isle aux Noix, Montgomery determined again to push forward and undertake the siege of St. Johns. This fort was garrisoned by five or six hundred regulars and two hundred Canadians, under Major Preston, and was well supplied with stores, ammunition and artillery. The American army, on the contrary, was undisciplined and disorderly, the artillery was too light, the mortars were defective, the ammunition scarce, and the artillerists unpractised in their duties. Still these difficulties did not abate the ardor or zeal of the commanding officer.

On the 18th of September, Montgomery led a party of five hundred men to the north of the fort, where he met a detachment from the garrison, with which he had a slight skirmish. Proceeding a little further north, he formed an intrenched camp at the junction of the roads leading from Montreal and Chambly, and then hastened back to bring up his artillery. A few days afterwards the camp was moved to higher ground, north-west of the fort, where a breastwork was thrown up.

Although the Americans had now encompassed the fort, they could do but little towards a regular siege for the want of ammunition and heavy guns to breach the works; but fortune soon opened a way through which to supply this deficiency. A little below St. Johns, and upon the same river, is Fort Chambly, which then contained several pieces of cannon, one hundred and twenty-four barrels of gunpowder and a large quantity of military stores and provisions. The fort was garrisoned by six officers and eighty-three privates. On the 18th of October, a strong detachment of Americans and Canadians — many of the latter having by this time joined the army — were placed under command of Majors Livingston and Brown, and ordered to attack the fort. The detachment passed down the river in boats during a dark night, and surprised the fort, which made but a feeble resistance. The stores and ammunition were sent to Montgomery, who now supplied with the necessary munitions, pressed the siege of St. Johns with vigor. A strong battery of four guns and six mortars was erected within two hundred and fifty yards of the fort, and a block-house was built on the opposite side of the river, mounting one gun and two mortars.

While Montgomery was thus employed at St. Johns, detachments of his army were scouring the country between the Richelieu and the St. Lawrence. One of these detachments, numbering about eighty men, under command of

Colonel Ethan Allen, passed through all the parishes east of the Richelieu as far as its mouth. From this point, Allen moved up the east bank of the St. Lawrence to Longueuil, where he crossed the river, and on the morning of the 25th of September, appeared unexpectedly before the city of Montreal. He was there met by General Carleton, and his whole party taken prisoners. A few days later, Carleton left Montreal with one thousand regulars, Canadians and Indians, for the purpose of raising the siege of Fort St. Johns. He embarked upon the St. Lawrence and attempted to land at Longueuil, but was driven back by Colonel Seth Warner, who with three hundred Green Mountain boys, lay secreted on the east bank of the river.

When Montgomery heard of Colonel Warner's success, he sent a flag to Major Preston informing him of Carleton's repulse, and demanding the immediate surrender of the fort. Preston asked for a delay of four days, which was denied, and the demand renewed. The next morning (Nov. 3d) the whole garrison surrendered as prisoners of war. Among the spoils found in the fort were seventeen pieces of brass ordnance, two howitzers, seven mortars, twenty-two iron cannon and eight hundred stand of arms, with a quantity of shot and small shells. The prisoners were treated with great kindness, and were conveyed by the way of Ticonderoga, into the interior of New England for safe keeping.

Montgomery received great praise for the energy and perseverance with which he had, for six weeks, urged the siege against obstacles of the most difficult and embarrassing character. Not only did he lack proper implements and munitions of war, but his army was composed of young and raw troops, unused to the privations of the field, or to military restraint. Indeed his camp at times resembled a great political assembly. Prompt and implicit obedience to orders was unknown. Each man claimed a right to canvass, debate and decide upon all the plans and movements of the campaign. This insubordination extended through all the grades of the army. The colonels would dispute with the general, to be themselves opposed by their captains; and when these last were convinced, the whole subject must again be debated with the rank and file, who claimed an equal right of judging for themselves whether the proposed plan was expedient. It required the kind temper, patriotic zeal and winning eloquence of Montgomery to restrain such turbulent and disaffected spirits from acts of open mutiny.

After the capitulation of Fort St. Johns, Montgomery marched against Montreal, and entered that city on the 13th of November. He then moved down the St. Lawrence, and on the 1st of December arrived at Point aux Trembles, about twenty miles above Quebec, where he found Colonel Arnold, who with seven hundred and fifty men had crossed to the St. Lawrence, through the thick forest and the almost impassible mountains of Maine. On the 5th, the united forces, even yet less in number than the British, arrived within sight of the walls of Quebec, and at two o'clock on the morning of the 31st, advanced to the assault of the city.

Captains Brown and Livingston, with ninety-four men, were directed to lead a feint against the upper town, while Montgomery was to advance by the way of Cape Diamond, and Arnold through St. Roche, to assault the lower town, on opposite sides. The morning was cold and stormy; the snow fell fast, and was piled in heavy drifts by a furious northwest wind. Cautiously Montgomery led his men in the dark from the plains of Abraham to Wolfe's Cove, and along the margin of the river to a point under Cape Diamond, where the British had erected a strong stockade extending from the precipice to the brink of the river. On the approach of the Americans, the men posted behind the stockade retreated to a block-house, which stood a short distance to the north, and which was pierced with loop-holes for musketry and cannon. In the second story of the block-house were some cannon charged with grape and canister shot, and so pointed as to sweep the narrow cartway above.

As the assailants advanced, and when they were within forty paces of the block-house, a single gun loaded with grape was discharged, which killed Montgomery, his two aids, Captains McPherson and Cheeseman, and every man in front except Captain Aaron Burr and a French guide. The brave and gallant Montgomery fell into Burr's arms and expired. The rest of the party, appalled at the fearful havoc and the death of their general, retired in confusion.

The attack upon the opposite side of the town was equally unsuccessful. The detachment passed through St. Roche towards a two gun battery, which was captured by Morgan's riflemen after an hour's severe struggle. At the commencement of the attack Arnold received a severe wound in the leg, and was carried helpless from the field. Morgan continued the fight, until one half of his men were killed and the rest were benumbed and helpless from cold, when he surrendered.

Montgomery was endeared to the army and to his country, by the possession of every noble virtue. With intrepid bravery he led his little band of half clothed and undisciplined men under the walls of Quebec, and fell upon a soil already hallowed by the blood of a Wolfe and a Montcalm. His death was a great public calamity. America acknowledged his worth and paid public honors to his memory, while the eloquence of England's purest statesmen proclaimed his praise upon the floor of the British parliament. "Happy would it have been for Arnold," exclaimed a celebrated American,[1] "if instead of being wounded, he too had died, since by his subsequent treason at West Point, he blasted forever the glory of his gallant conduct on that occasion."

After the death of Montgomery, the remains of the little

Colonel Trumbull.

army retired to a point about three miles up the river, where they remained during the winter. On the 1st of May, General Thomas arrived and took command of the troops which, by reinforcements from time to time, now numbered about nineteen hundred men. The army was soon afterwards increased to three thousand, but the small pox breaking out in the ranks with great severity, not over nine hundred were fit for duty. General Thomas in a few days retired as far as the mouth of the Richelieu, where he was taken down with the small pox. He was removed to Chambly, and died there on the 2d of June. About the time of Thomas's death, General Sullivan arrived in Canada with a reinforcement of several battalions, and assumed the chief command.

Early in the spring of 1776, the British force in Canada was augmented by the arrival from England of thirteen thousand men, a large portion of whom were sent into camp at Three Rivers. Against this place an unsuccessful attack was made, in which General Thompson and two hundred men were taken prisoners. Other reverses followed, until General Sullivan, finding his numbers greatly diminished by sickness, desertion and death, determined to evacuate Canada. He therefore, on the 14th of June, abandoned his position at the mouth of the Richelieu, and leisurely moved up its banks towards St. Johns. Arnold, who had been promoted to the rank of brigadier general, and who then commanded at Montreal, withdrew from that city on the 15th, and marching across the country, joined Sullivan's division at Chambly.

The American general conducted the retreat in good order, and saved all the baggage, artillery and military stores, which were dragged up the rapids of the Richelieu in boats. The army reached St. Johns towards the last of June. The sick were immediately sent to Isle aux Noix, Point au Fer and Isle la Motte, when the boats returned and took the remainder of the troops to Isle aux Noix.

Here the men fit for duty remained for eight days, waiting for the boats to take the sick to Crown Point and to return. It is difficult to conceive a degree of misery greater than that suffered by the invalids during their voyage through the lake. The boats were leaky and without awnings, and the men, lying upon the bottom, were drenched with water, and exposed to the burning sun. Their only sustenance was raw and rancid pork and hard biscuit or unbaked flour. "The sight of so much misery, privation and distress," says Doctor Meyrick, "broke my heart, and I wept till I had no more power to weep."

When the boats returned to Isle aux Noix they were loaded with the baggage, while the men were sent by land to Point au Fer, which had been fortified by order of General Sullivan. At that place they found a supply of boats awaiting them, in which they embarked, and on the 3d of July, reached Crown Point.

The broken fragments of the army of Canada presented one of the most distressing sights witnessed during the whole war. Of the five thousand two hundred men collected at Crown Point, twenty-eight hundred were so sick as to require the attentions of the hospital, while those reported as "fit for duty," were half naked, emaciated and entirely broken down in strength, spirits and discipline. Some few lay in tents, others in half built sheds, but by far the greater number occupied miserable bush huts, which afforded a slight shelter from the burning sun, but were no protection against the damp and unhealthy night air. Among these tents and huts the men were scattered in indiscriminate confusion, without regard to comfort or health, or to the distinction of companies, regiments or corps. "I found the troops totally disorganized by the death or sickness of officers," says Colonel Trumbull, "and I can truly say, that I did not look into tent or hut in which I did not find either a dead or dying man." The troops remained about ten days at Crown Point, and when they left for Ticonderoga, over three hundred new made graves attested the frightful ravages that death had made among their broken ranks.[1]

---

[1] Botta's *American Revolution* — *American Archives, Fifth Series* — Trumbull's *Reminiscences of his own Times* — Thacher's *Military Journal* — Davis's *Memoirs of A. Burr* — *Journal of the New York Provincial Congress* — Allen's *Narrative.*

CHAPTER VII.

The plan of the campaign of 1776, as formed by the British ministry, contemplated a separate movement against Ticonderoga and New York, and the conjunction of the two armies at Albany. General and Lord Howe were sent with a large military and naval force against New York, while the thirteen thousand troops collected in Canada were placed under the command of Sir Guy Carleton, who had under him Generals Burgoyne, Phillips, Fraser, Nesbit and Riedesel; all men of acknowledged skill and ability. Several vessels were built in England, and sent over to be used on Lake Champlain.

During the summer of 1776, the English were busily engaged in preparing a fleet for the lake service. Seamen, ship carpenters and laborers were collected at St. Johns in numbers. The vessels built in England were taken to pieces, carried over the rapids of the Richelieu and reconstructed. Several other vessels were brought up from the St. Lawrence, and a great number of transports were framed and launched at St. Johns. The fort at St. Johns was repaired and strengthened, and garrisoned with three thousand men; an equal number was stationed at Isle aux Noix. The rest of the troops were reserved to man the armed vessels and transports, and to form the army of invasion. Six hundred and ninety-seven seamen were also drafted from the Isis and the other ships of war lying at Quebec, and sent forward to Lake Champlain.[1]

While the English were thus engaged, the Americans were actively employed at the other extremity of the lake, in preparations to repel the threatened invasion. On the 17th of June, Congress appointed Major General Gates to the command at Ticonderoga and Crown Point. Gates found those posts in a very reduced condition. The small pox was still prevalent among the troops, not a cannon was mounted, nor were any preparations made for defense. The first efforts of the commander-in-chief were directed to recruiting the ranks, restoring the men to health, and providing them with clothing and necessary accommodations. Those sick of the small pox were sent to a general hospital established at the head of Lake George. Reinforcements were earnestly solicited from the Eastern states, and requisitions made for ship carpenters to be employed at Skenesborough in building the hulls of galleys and boats. Crown Point was reduced to a mere post of observation, while the most active efforts were made to enlarge and strengthen the defenses at Ticonderoga. Mount Independence was carefully examined by Colonels Wayne and Trumbull, who reported that the ground was finely adapted for a military post. A portion of the troops were ordered to clear away the wood and to encamp upon this eminence. The Pennsylvania regiments, the *elite* of the army, were posted at the French lines, which they were ordered to repair; and the old works were strengthened at all points.

The small fort at Skenesborough was also repaired, and that place selected as the point of rendezvous for the ex-

---

[1] The number of seamen detached for this service was as follows : From the Isis, 100; Blood, 70; Triton, 60; Garland, 30; Canceaux, 40; Magdelen, Brunswick and Gasper, 18; Treasury and several armed brigs, 90; Fell, 30; Charlotte, 9; from transports, 214; Volunteers, 9; besides 8 officers and 19 petty officers.

TICONDEROGA AND ITS DEPENDENCIES, AUGUST, 1776.

From a plan drawn by Col. John Trumbull.

pected reinforcements. The lake above Ticonderoga soon presented a scene of busy activity, as boats were constantly passing and repassing, loaded with men, provisions and munitions of war. By the month of September an army of from eight to ten thousand men had been collected at Ticonderoga. Each regiment had its alarm post assigned, to which it was ordered to repair at daylight every morning, and every means was taken by the officers to bring the whole body to a state of high discipline.[1]

The superintendence of the construction of the fleet was confided to General Arnold, who entered upon the work with his characteristic energy, but in its progress, found himself surrounded by great and complicated difficulties, occasioned by want or limited supplies of nearly all the materials necessary for boat building, or a naval equipment. These embarrassments only excited the men to greater exertions. By the middle of August Arnold was prepared to take the lake with a naval force carrying fifty-five guns and seventy-eight swivels, and manned by three hundred and ninety-five men. His fleet consisted of the sloop Enterprise, Captain Dickson; the schooner Royal Savage, Captain Wynkoop; schooner Revenge, Captain Seaman; schooner Liberty, Captain Premier; and the gondolas New Haven, Providence, Boston, Spitfire, and Philadelphia.[1]

With this force Arnold sailed from Crown Point on the 20th of August, and cruised between that place and the mouth of the Bouquet River until the 2nd of September. On the evening of the 2nd he proceeded north as far as Schuyler Island, and the next day reached Windmill Point,

---

[1] Trumbull's *Reminiscences of his own Times.*

[1] The Enterprise had been captured by Arnold at St. Johns; the Liberty by Herrick at Skenesborough. The other vessels were built at Skenesborough and then taken to Ticonderoga and Crown Point, where they received their sails, military stores and equipments.

eight miles below Isle la Motte. It was his first intention to have gone as far down as Isle aux Tetes, but finding that island already occupied by the British, he anchored off Windmill Point, in a line from shore to shore, and he sent his lookout-boats about one mile below, with orders to keep a sharp eye upon the movements of the enemy.

On the morning of the 6th, several boats were sent on shore for fascines to fix on the bows and sides of the gondolas, to prevent the enemy from boarding, and to protect the men from the fire of musketry. One of the boats reached the shore before the others, and was attacked by a party of Indians who occupied the adjoining woods. Before the men could row off, three of their number were killed and six wounded. Arnold immediately ordered his vessels to discharge their broadsides towards the woods, when the Indians precipitately retreated.[1] The same morning the fleet was reinforced by the arrival of the galley Lee, of six guns, and the gondola Connecticut of three guns.

The noise of the firing on the morning of the 6th was distinctly heard at Crown Point, fifty miles distant. Lieutenant Colonel Hartly, the commanding officer there, immediately wrote to General Gates, at Ticonderoga, that an engagement had undoubtedly taken place between Arnold and the enemy. Gates sent the letter, by express, to General Schuyler, then at Albany, who ordered out the Ulster and Dutchess County, and a portion of the New England, militia. This order was revoked on the 18th, when the true account of the affair reached Albany.[2]

On the night of the 7th, the English sent strong parties up the river, and commenced preparations to erect batteries on both sides of Arnold's position. This movement induced Arnold to retire as far back as the Isle la Motte, where he

---

[1] Arnold to Major General Gates, Sept. 7, 1776.

[2] *American Archives,* fifth series.

came to anchor about two o'clock on the afternoon of the 8th. There the fleet remained until the 19th, when it removed to Bay St. Amand, which lies on the west side of the lake, a few miles north of Cumberland Head. As the schooner Liberty was on her way to this anchorage, she was hailed by a Canadian, who came down to the water's edge and requested to be taken on board. Captain Premier sent a boat towards the shore, with orders to approach with caution, and to keep her swivels pointed and the matches ready to fire in case everything was not right. The man on shore waded about a rod into the water and stopped, entreating the boat's crew to come to him. Finding he could not decoy them into shallow water, he made a signal, when about three hundred Canadians and Indians, who were secreted in the woods near the shore, uncovered and fired into the boat, wounding three of the crew. The boat returned the fire with her swivels and small arms, and the schooner discharged several broad-sides of grape, when the party retreated, having apparently suffered some loss.[1]

While Arnold lay at Bay St. Amand he sent two boats to sound the channel between Valcour Island and the main shore, who reported that they found the anchorage exceedingly fine and secure. To this harbor the fleet moved on the 23d of September. A few days afterwards the galley Trumbull, Captain Warner, arrived, and on the 6th of October, Brigadier General Waterbury came up with the galleys Washington, Captain Thacher, and Congress, Captain Arnold. The entire naval force of the Americans was now collected at Valcour Island, with the exception of an eight gun galley, then receiving her armament at Ticonderoga, and the schooner Liberty, which had been sent to Crown Point for supplies. The fleet consisted of the sloop Enterprise mounting ten guns and ten swivels; the schooner Royal Savage,

---

[1] Arnold to Gates, Sept. 21, 1776.

twelve guns and ten swivels; the schooner Revenge, eight guns and ten swivels; the galley Lee, six guns and ten swivels; the galleys Trumbull, Congress and Washington, each eight guns and sixteen swivels; and the gondolas New Haven, Providence, Boston, Spitfire, Philadelphia, Connecticut, Jersey and New York, each mounting three guns and eight swivels. There were therefore fifteen vessels in all, mounting eighty-four guns and one hundred and fifty-two swivels. The number of men and sailors detached to serve on these vessels was eight hundred and eleven, but of this number at least one hundred had not yet joined the fleet. Arnold trained his men daily at the guns, and used his best endeavors to reduce them to the proper discipline. He however, complained frequently of their inefficiency. " The drafts from the regiments at Ticonderoga," he writes General Gates, "are a miserable set; indeed the men on board the fleet in general are not equal to half their number of good men." Again he says, " We have a wretched, motley crew in the fleet; the marines, the refuse of every regiment, and the seamen, few of them ever wet with salt water; and we are upwards of one hundred men short of our complement."

At this time, the British naval force in the Richelieu consisted of the ship Inflexible, Lieutenant Schank, of eighteen guns; The schooner Maria, Lieutenant Starke, fourteen guns; schooner Carleton, Lieutenant Dacres, twelve guns; radeau Thunderer, Lieutenant Scott, twelve guns and two howitzers; the gondola Loyal Convert, Lieutenant Long-craft, seven guns; twenty gun-boats, mounting one gun each, and four long-boats, mounting one carriage gun each.[1] The whole force was twenty-nine vessels, mounting eighty-nine guns, and manned by six hundred and ninety-

---

[1] Letter of Captain Douglass, of the Isis. The Inflexible, Maria and Carleton, were brought from England and reconstructed at St. Johns.

seven picked seamen, besides a number of soldiers and artillerists.

The route taken by vessels passing up the lake from Canada, lies along and nearly parallel to the west shore of Grand Isle. Opposite Cumberland Head the lake is two miles wide, but as soon as that point is passed, it increases in width to five miles, and does not again contract until you approach the mouth of the Bouquet. On the western side of the lake, about four miles south-west of Cumberland Head, and nearly two miles to the right of the track of vessels sailing directly up the lake, is the island of Valcour, which is separated from the main shore by a channel about one half mile in width. This channel is deep enough for the largest vessels, and is hid from the view of boats sailing up the lake, until they have passed some distance south of the Island. Midway of this channel, and where it is most contracted, Arnold anchored his vessels in a line extending from shore to shore. "We are moored," he writes to General Gates, "in a small bay on the west side of the island, as near together as possible, and in such form that few vessels can attack us at the same time, and those will be exposed to the fire of the whole fleet."

At eight o'clock on Friday morning, October 11th, the English were discovered passing Cumberland Head with a strong north or north-west wind, and bearing in the direction of Crown Point, towards which it was supposed Arnold had retired. The fleet at this time was under the command of Capt. Thomas Pringle, of the Lord Howe, who made the schooner Maria his flag ship.[1] General Carleton was also on board the Maria, but took no command of the fleet. As the English appeared in sight, off Cumberland Head, General Waterbury went on board the Congress galley, and urged

---

[1] The fleet was accompanied by twenty-four long-boats loaded with baggage and provisions. A small party of Indians had been placed on board the smaller vessels.

that they should immediately set sail and fight the enemy on the retreat in the broad lake; but Arnold declined, at that late hour, to change his plan of defense.

Capt. Pringle was some distance ahead of Valcour when he first discovered the Americans. He immediately changed his course towards the island, with a view to engage, but found great difficulty in bringing any of his vessels into action. About eleven o'clock, however, the gun boats were enabled to sweep to windward and take a position to the south of the American fleet, when they opened a fire upon the Royal Savage, which, with the galleys, had advanced a short distance in front of the line. The British schooner Carleton soon afterwards came to the assistance of the gun-boats. The Royal Savage sustained the fire of the British vessels for some time, and until her mast was crippled and much of her rigging shot away. She then attempted to return to the line, but running too far to the leeward, grounded near the south-west point of the island, and was abandoned by her men, who succeeded in reaching the other boats in safety. At night the British boarded the schooner and set fire to her.[1]

At half past twelve o'clock the Carleton and the gun-boats had approached within musket shot of the American line, when the action became general, and continued without cessation until about five in the afternoon. During the engagement Arnold was on board the Congress, Waterbury on the Washington, and Colonel Wigglesworth on the Trumbull. The Congress and Washington suffered severely. The latter was hulled in several places, her main-mast shot through, and her sails torn to pieces. Waterbury fought

---

[1] Arnold's account of the engagement. The hull of the schooner lies on the spot where she was sunk, and her upper timbers can yet be seen during low water in the lake. Arnold's papers were on board the schooner and were lost.

bravely on the quarter deck of his vessel, and towards the close of the action was the only active officer on board, the captain and master being severely wounded, and the first lieutenant killed. The gondola New York lost all her officers except Captain Lee, and the gondola Philadelphia, Captain Grant, was so badly injured that she sank about one hour after the engagement. Arnold fought the Congress like a lion at bay, pointing almost every gun with his own hands, and cheering his men with voice and gesture. His vessel was hulled twelve times, and received seven shot between wind and water; the main-mast was injured in two places, the rigging cut to pieces, and many of the men killed and wounded.

On the side of the English, the battle was sustained by the gun-boats and the schooner Carleton, and by a party of Indians who were landed on the island and main shore, and who kept up an incessant fire of musketry during the engagement. The English vessels suffered considerably. On board the Carleton eight men were killed and six wounded. Two of the gun-boats were sunk, and one was blown up with a number of men on board.[1] About five o'clock in the afternoon, Captain Pringle, who had made several unsuccessful attempts to bring his larger vessels into action, called off those engaged, and anchored his whole fleet just out of reach of the American guns. The Thunderer lay at the right of the line, a little south of Garden Island,[2] the schooner Maria on the left near the main shore, while the Loyal Convert and the Inflexible occupied intermediate positions. The Carleton and gun-boats were anchored near and among the other vessels. By this arrangement, Captain Pringle

---

[1] Arnold states the loss sustained (by the blowing up of this gun-boat) at sixty.—*Letter to General Schuyler*, Oct. 15.

[2] This is a small island about 600 yards south of Valcour.

hoped to prevent the escape of the American fleet during the night.

MAP OF BATTLE AT VALCOUR ISLAND.

REFERENCES.— A, American Fleet drawn across the Channel.— B, British Gun-Boats and Schooner Carleton.— C, Anchorage of British Vessels after the Battle.— D, Point where the Royal Savage was lost.— E, Cumberland Head.— F, Saranac River.— G, Grand Island.— H, Island of North Hero.

Arnold was well satisfied that he could not successfully resist the superior force with which the English were prepared to attack him on the following morning. His men had fought with the most daring bravery and resolution, but he had only succeeded in retaining his position by the direction of the wind, which had prevented the larger vessels of the British fleet from joining in the action. Even under equally favorable circumstances, he could not resist a renewed attack, for his boats were already badly crippled, sixty of his men, including several officers, killed or wounded, and nearly three-fourths of each vessel's ammunition spent. A council of war was immediately called, when it was determined that the fleet should retire during the night towards Crown Point.

At seven o'clock in the evening. [1] Colonel Wigglesworth got the Trumbull under way, and bearing around the north end of Valcour, directed his course towards the upper end of the lake, passing outside of the British line. The Trumbull was soon followed by the Enterprise and Lee, with the gondolas; and about ten o'clock, Waterbury started in the Washington galley, followed by Arnold, in the Congress. In this order, with a light at the stern of each vessel, the fleet passed to Schuyler Island, about nine miles distant, where it arrived early the next morning. On examination, Arnold found two of the gondolas too badly injured to repair. These he sank near the island, and having fitted up the other vessels as well as his limited time and means would permit, again set sail for Crown Point.

While Arnold was repairing his vessels, the British fleet weighed anchor and commenced beating up the lake in pursuit; the wind blowing gently from the south. Early on the morning of the 13th, the American fleet was off the Bouquet, and the English lay a little above Schuyler Island. Arnold now had the wind in the south, while the fresh north-east wind, blowing in the broader part of the lake, favored the English commander, who brought up his leading vessels soon after the former had passed Split Rock. On this occasion Captain Pringle led in person in the Maria, closely followed by the Inflexible and Carleton. The Maria and Inflexible at first attacked the Washington galley, which

---

[1] Arnold's account of the battle. Mr. Cooper, in his *Naval History*, erroneously states that Arnold got under way at 2 o'clock, p. m. He also states that the American fleet, on the morning of the 11th, "was lying off Cumberland Head," and includes in the fleet the schooner Liberty, which was then at Crown Point.

was too much shattered to keep up with the rest. The galley struck after receiving a few shots. The two vessels then joined the Carleton, and for several hours[1] poured an incessant fire into the Congress galley, which was briskly returned. Arnold kept up a running fight until he arrived within ten miles of Crown Point, when he ran the Congress and four gondolas into a small bay, in Panton, on the east side of the lake, and having removed the small arms, burned the vessels to the water's edge.[2] In this action the Congress lost her first lieutenant and three men.

As soon as the boats were consumed, Arnold led his party through the woods to Crown Point, where he arrived at four o'clock the next morning. The sloop Enterprise, the schooner Revenge and the galley Trumbull, with one gondola, had reached that place the day before, in safety. The galley Lee, Captain Davis, was run into a bay on the east side of the lake above Split Rock, where she was blown up. The only vessels taken by the enemy were the Washington galley and the gondola Jersey. The loss of the Americans in both engagements was between eighty and ninety, including the wounded. The English stated their loss in killed and wounded at forty, but according to the American accounts, it must have exceeded one hundred, as at least sixty men were on board the gun-boat which was blown up on the 11th.

Immediately after the action of the 13th, Sir Guy Carleton gave orders for his surgeons to treat the wounded prisoners with the same care as they did his own men. He then directed all the other prisoners to be brought on board the ship, where he treated them to a drink of grog, praised the bravery of their conduct, regretted that it had not been

---

[1] Captain Pringle says the action commenced at twelve and lasted two hours. Arnold says it continued "for about five glasses."

[2] See Arnold's and Pringle's account of this engagement in Appendix.

displayed in the service of their lawful sovereign, and offered to send them home to their friends, on their giving their parole that they would not again bear arms against Great Britain until they should be exchanged. On the 14th, Captain, afterwards Sir James Craig, accompanied the prisoners to Ticonderoga, where he dismissed them on parole. The generous manner in which they had been treated filled the prisoners with the highest emotions of gratitude, and they returned proclaiming the praise of the British general. The feelings and sentiments expressed by these men were such, that it was not considered safe to allow them to land, or to converse with the American troops. They were therefore sent forward to Skenesborough the same night.[1]

The humanity of Governor Carleton's course was somewhat tinctured with policy. He well knew the great dissatisfaction which had prevailed among the American troops, and with a profound sagacity, that distinguished his whole administration, took advantage of every opportunity to direct this feeling into a channel favorable to the British cause, and to impress upon the minds of the half clothed and destitute troops, a high opinion of the generosity, kindness and liberality of their opponents.

Although the results of the two engagements of the 11th and 13th had been so disastrous, yet the Americans gained great credit for the obstinacy of their resistance. Even the English acknowledged that no man ever manœuvred with more dexterity, fought with more bravery or retreated with more firmness, than Arnold did on both of these occasions. Such gallantry converted the disasters of defeat into a species of triumph. Several American officers, however, were found ready to censure Arnold, whom they called "our evil genius to the north,[2]" but General Gates, who under-

[1] Trumbull's *Reminiscences of his own Times.*

[2] General Maxwell to Governor Livingston.

stood perfectly all the details of the affair, always speaks of him in the highest terms of praise. " It would have been happy for the United States," he writes to Governor Trumbull, " had the gallant behavior and steady good conduct of that excellent officer been supported by a fleet in any way equal to the enemy's. As the case stands, though they boast a victory, they must respect the vanquished."

On the 14th of October the works at Crown Point were destroyed and the troops and military stores removed to Ticonderoga. As soon as the Americans left, Carleton landed his army and occupied the shores on both sides of the lake. It had been his intention to march immediately against Ticonderoga, but on the 15th the wind commenced blowing so hard from the south that, for eight days, the English vessels could not sail up the lake. This delay was of great importance to the Americans, as it afforded them time to receive reinforcements of militia and to prepare for a vigorous defense. In that short interval they made carriages for, and mounted forty-seven pieces of cannon; they also surrounded the works with a strong abattis. General Gates had about twelve thousand men under his command, all of whom were desirous of an opportunity to display their prowess before the enemy.

General Carleton, finding he could not advance immediately, proceeded to establish himself at Crown Point, and to repair the fort at that place. He also occupied Chimney Point with a portion of his army, and placed three of his largest vessels at anchor near Putnam's Point, a little below which the light infantry, grenadiers, and a body of Canadians and Indians were encamped. Reconnoitering parties filled the woods in every direction, and frequently penetrated as far south as Lake George, where one or two slight skirmishes occurred with straggling parties of the militia, who were passing from Fort George to Ticonderoga. Boats were also sent to sound the channel of the lake above Crown

Point. On one occasion, one of these boats approached within shot of the lower battery of Ticonderoga, when it was fired into, and two men killed and one wounded.

On Monday, the 27th of October, between eight and nine o'clock in the morning, the advance guard-boat lying below Ticonderoga, made signal that the English fleet was approaching, and about an hour afterwards, five of their largest transport boats appeared in sight of the fort, and landed a number of troops upon Three Mile Point. Soon afterwards, two armed boats stood over to the east side of the lake and appeared to be reconnoitering. As soon as they approached near enough, they were fired upon from the lower battery, and from a row-galley stationed near by, when they retired. In the meantime other British troops were landed upon the point, and a body of men were sent across the lake into a small bay about four miles below the works.

As these movements indicated an attack upon Ticonderoga, General Gates ordered the lines and redoubts to be manned, and brought three regiments from Mt. Independence to reinforce those on the western side. "Nothing," he says, "could exceed the spirit and alertness which was shown by all the officers and soldiers in executing every order that was given." The display made on this occasion convinced Carleton that Gates's means of defense were sufficient to resist an assault. At four o'clock in the afternoon he withdrew his forces and returned to Crown Point, where he made immediate preparations to retire into winter quarters, in Canada. The rear-guard of the English army left Crown Point on the morning of the 3d of November, and the place was on the same day occupied by a detachment sent forward from Ticonderoga. As soon as it was ascertained that the English had retired to Canada, Gates dismissed the militia and soon afterwards left with the greater part of the regular troops to join Washington, who was then in New Jersey.

CHAPTER VIII.

The British ministry still adhered to the scheme of opening a communication between Canada and the city of New York, by way of Lake Champlain. This project had acquired new favor at the English court from the representations and sanguine promises of General Burgoyne, who had visited England in the winter of 1776-7, and urged upon the government its importance, and the certainty of its success. Dissatisfied, without just cause, with the proceedings of Governor Carleton, the ministry formed their arrangements for the new campaign without his counsel or advice, and assigned to General Burgoyne the command of the army in Canada, and the direction of all its operations.

The regular force allotted to Burgoyne numbered seven thousand one hundred and thirteen men, among whom were three thousand two hundred and seventeen Brunswick troops, commonly known as Hessians. A large and complete train of brass artillery was sent to Canada, together with a full supply of arms, ammunition and military accoutrements of every description. Major General Philips, and Brigadier Generals Fraser, Powell and Hamilton served under Burgoyne. The Brunswick troops were commanded by Major General Riedesel and Brigadier General Specht.

Burgoyne arrrived at Quebec in the month of May, 1777, and immediately commenced preparations for the prosecution of the campaign. Two thousand Canadians were employed upon the fortifications at Sorel, Chambly, St. Johns and Isle aux Noix, and boats were constructed on the Richelieu, for the conveyance of the troops and supplies through the lake.

To favor the opperations of the army, Col. St. Leger was sent against the American posts on the Mohawk River, with a force of about eight hundred men, and a large body of Indians under Sir John Johnson. St. Leger was to proceed by the way of Oswego, and having reduced the posts on that route, was to rejoin the main army at Albany.

Early in the month of June, the army left St. Johns in boats, and after several delays occasioned by contrary winds, reached Cumberland Head, where it halted to await the arrival of the ammunition and stores. The naval part of the expedition was under the command of Captain Lutwidge, and consisted of the armed vessels built during the preceding year. Seven hundred carts were brought on with the army, to be used in transporting baggage and provisions across the portages between the lakes and the Hudson River, and fifteen hundred Canadian horses were sent by land up the west side of the lake under a strong escort.

As soon as the supplies arrived, Burgoyne left Cumberland Head and advanced as far as the Bouquet River, where he again halted. He was there joined by four hundred Iroquois, Algonquin, Abenaquis and Ottawa Indians, to whom he gave a war-feast on the 21st of June, at their encampment near the falls of the Bouquet. On this occasion he made a speech to the assembled Indians, in which he humanely endeavored to soften their ferocity and restrain their thirst for blood. He spoke of the abused clemency of the king towards the colonies, and explained to them that the present war was carried on against a country where the faithful were intermixed with rebels, and traitors with friends. He released them from restraint, but cautioned them not to violate the rules of civilized warfare or disregard the dictates of religion and humanity. "Be it our task," he said, "from the dictates of our religion, the laws of our warfare, and the principles and interest of our policy, to regulate your passions when you overbear, to point out where it is nobler to spare than to revenge, to discriminate degrees of guilt, to suspend the uplifted stroke, to chastise, and not destroy." He then called their attention to the rules which they should observe during the campaign. "I positively forbid bloodshed where you are not opposed in arms. Aged men and women, children and prisoners must be held sacred from the knife or hatchet, even in the time of actual conflict. You shall receive compensation for the prisoners you take, but you shall be called to account for the scalps." The Indians pledged obedience to his orders, and Burgoyne had the credulity to believe them. Little did he understand the unappeasable appetite for blood of those by whom these fine promises were made.

While the English were slowly approaching Ticonderoga, the Americans were busily engaged in strengthening its defenses. The northern department, including Albany, Ticonderoga, Fort Stanwix and their dependencies, was now under the charge of Major General Schuyler, while the immediate command of the works on Lake Champlain was confided to Major General St. Clair, an officer of great military experience and reputation.[1] Both generals were advised of the

---

[1] Arthur St. Clair was a soldier from his youth. At an early age, while the independent states were yet British colonies, he entered the Royal American army, and was commissioned as an ensign. He was actively engaged, during the French war, in the army of General Wolfe, and was carrying a pair of colors in the battle in which that celebrated commander was slain, on the Plains of Abraham. He was highly esteemed by the distinguished commanders under whom he served, as a young officer of merit, capable of obtaining a high grade of military reputation. After the peace of '63, he sold out and entered into trade, for which the generosity of his

plans of the British government for the present campaign, and used every exertion to prevent its success. The old French lines, to the west of the fort, had been repaired and were guarded by a strong block-house; an outpost was established at the saw-mills on the falls of the outlet, and another just above that point, and a block-house and hospital were erected at the foot of Lake George. Redoubts and batteries were established upon the low lands below the fort, and the extreme left was protected by a small fort on Mount Hope, an eminence about half a mile in advance of the old French lines.

A star-fort, in the centre of which was a convenient square of barracks, had been built on the summit of Mount Independence, which was well supplied with artillery, strongly picketed, and its approaches guarded with batteries. The foot of the hill, towards the lake, was protected by a breastwork which had been strengthened by an abattis, and by a strong battery standing on the shore of the lake near the mouth of East Creek. A floating bridge connected the works of Mount Independence and Ticonderoga, and served as an obstruction to the passage of vessels up the lake. This bridge was supported on twenty-two sunken piers, formed of very large timber; the spaces between the piers were filled with floats, each about fifty feet long and twelve feet wide, strongly fastened together with iron chains and rivets. A boom made of large pieces of timber, well secured together

---

nature utterly disqualified him: he soon became disgusted with a profitless pursuit, and having married, after several vicissitudes of fortune, he located himself in Ligonier valley, west of the Alleghany mountains, and near the old route from Philadelphia. In this situation the American revolution found him, surrounded by a rising family, in the enjoyment of ease and independence, with the fairest prospects of affluent fortune, the foundation of which had been already established by his intelligence, industry and enterprise.

by riveted bolts, was placed on the north side of the bridge, and by the side of this was a double iron chain, the links of which were one and a half inches square.[1]

Opposite Mount Independence is the lofty eminence of Mount Defiance, which rises abruptly from the water to the height of about seven hundred and fifty feet, and is separated from Ticonderoga by the mouth of the outlet of Lake George. The American works formed an extensive crescent, of which this eminence was the centre. The entire lines required at least ten thousand men and one hundred pieces of artillery, for its defense. But at the time of Burgoyne's approach, St. Clair's whole force did not exceed two thousand five hundred and fifty-six continental troops and nine hundred militia; the latter badly equipped, worse armed, and most of them raw and undisciplined. They however, were zealous and determined, and were ready to oppose any force that might be brought against them.

The works about Ticonderoga were, by many. considered impregnable; but in fact they were weak and untenable, for every position, whether at the old French lines, at the fort or on Mount Independence, was commanded by the summit of Mount Defiance, which had hitherto been neglected by the engineers of all parties. In 1776, Colonel John Trumbull, adjutant general under Gates, made several experiments which proved the controlling position of the eminence, and he afterwards, in company with General Arnold, Colonel Wayne and others, ascended its rocky sides. "The ascent " says Trumbull, " was difficult and laborious, but not impracticable, and when we looked down upon the outlet of Lake George, it was obvious to all that there could be no difficulty in driving up a loaded carriage.

While Ticonderoga was thus poorly garrisoned and its defenses exposed, Burgoyne was moving against it at the

---

[1] Thacher's *Military Journal.*

head of a well disciplined army, numbering seven thousand nine hundred men. On the 30th of June, the whole force reached Crown Point, where the English general halted to issue a proclamation, by which he expected to intimidate the patriots and to strengthen the hopes of the disaffected. In this paper he extolled the strength and number of the British forces, and portrayed, in vivid language, the horrors which would result from an opposition to their arms. He offered encouragement and employment to those who should assist the king in redeeming the colonies, and restoring to them "the blessings of British liberty," while against those who should disregard his offers of mercy and forgiveness, he threatened the merciless vengeance of the whole Indian force under his command. Of the patriots, he says, "The messengers of justice and of wrath await them in the field; and devastation, and famine, and every concomitant horror that a reluctant but indispensable prosecution of military duty must occasion, will bar the way to their return." These thundering anathemas were received, in every quarter, with derision and ridicule. Their only effect was to call forth a reply, written by a young officer, which created much amusement in the ranks of the American army, by its admirable imitation of the pompous style of the proclamation.

Burgoyne's army moved from Crown Point on the 1st of July, in three divisions; the Germans under Riedesel, taking position on the east shore of the lake, at Richardson's opposite Putnam Creek; the right wing under Fraser, advanced as far as Three Mile Creek; and the centre, commanded by Burgoyne in person, moved up the lake in transports, accompanied by the ships Royal George and Inflexible, and anchored in a position just out of reach of the American guns. The following day, a party of Indians approached the outposts at Lake George, and were soon followed by a large detachment under Major General Phillips. On the approach of this column, the Americans evacuated and burned the block-houses, and abandoning the saw-mills, retired within the lines. In the course of the night General Phillips took possession of Mount Hope, which the next morning was occupied in force by Fraser's corps, consisting of the 1st British brigade and two brigades of artillery. Phillips now held the ground west of Mount Hope, and Fraser's camp at Three Mile Creek was occupied by a body of men drawn from the opposite side of the lake. The column under Riedesel was pushed forward as far as East Creek, from which it could easily stretch behind Mount Independence.

During all these movements the American troops kept up a warm fire against Mount Hope, and against Riedesel's column, but without effect. On the 4th, the British were employed in bringing up their artillery, tents, baggage and provisions, while the Americans, at intervals, continued the cannonade. The same evening the radeau Thunderer arrived from Crown Point with the battering train.

The British line now encircled the American works on the north, east and west. The possession of Mount Defiance would complete the investment, and effectually control the water communication in the direction of Skenesborough. Burgoyne's attention had, from the first, been attracted towards this eminence, and he had directed Lieut. Twiss, his chief engineer, to ascertain whether its summit was accessible. On the 4th, Lieutenant Twiss reported that Mount Defiance held the entire command of Ticonderoga and Mt. Independence, at the distance of about fourteen hundred yards from the former, and fifteen hundred yards from the latter, and that a practicable road could be made to the summit in twenty-four hours. On receiving this report, Burgoyne ordered the road to be opened and a battery constructed for light twenty-four pounders, medium twelves and eight-inch howitzers. This arduous task was pushed with such

activity, that during the succeeding night, the road was completed, and eight pieces of cannon were dragged to the top
of the hill.

On the morning of the 5th, the summit of Mount Defiance
glowed with scarlet uniforms, and the guns of its batteries
stood threateningly over the American forts. "It is with as-
tonishment," says Doctor Thacher in his *Military Journal*,
"that we find the enemy have taken possession of an eminence called Sugar-loaf Hill or Mount Defiance, which, from
its height and proximity, completely overlooks and commands
all our works. The situation of our garrison is viewed as
critical and alarming; a few days will decide our fate. We
have reason to apprehend the most fatal effects from their
battery on Sugar-loaf Hill." General St. Clair immediately
called a council of war, by whom it was decided to evacuate
the works, before Riedesel should block up the narrow
passage south of East Creek, which with the lake to Skenesborough presented the only possible way of escape.

The decision of the council was concealed from the troops
until the evening order was given. About twelve o'clock
at night, directions were issued to place the sick and wounded and the women on board two hundred long-boats, which
had been collected for this purpose. The boats were then
loaded deep with cannon, tents and provisions, and at three
o'clock in the morning started for Skenesborough, accompanied by five armed galleys and a guard of six hundred
men, under command of Colonel Long, of the New Hampshire troops. The boats reached Skenesborough about three
o'clock on the afternoon of the same day, where the fugitives
landed to enjoy, as they fancied, a temporary repose; but in
less than two hours they were startled by the reports of the
cannon of the British gun-boats, which were firing at the
galleys lying at the wharf. By uncommon effort and industry, Burgoyne had broken through the chain, boom and
bridge at Ticonderoga, and had followed in pursuit with the

Royal George and Inflexible, and a detachment of the gun-boats under Captain Carter. The pursuit had been pressed with such vigor that, at the very moment when the Americans were landing at Skenesborough, three regiments disembarked at the head of South Bay, with the intention of occupying the road to Fort Edward. Had Burgoyne delayed the attack upon the galleys until these regiments had reached the Fort Edward road, the whole party at Skenesborough would have been taken prisoners. Alarmed however, by the approach of the gun-boats, the Americans blew up three of the galleys, set fire to the fort, mill and store-house, and retired in great confusion towards Fort Ann. Occasionally the overburdened party would falter on their retreat, when the startling cry of "March on, the Indians are at our heels," would revive their drooping energies, and give new strength to their weakened limbs. At five o'clock in the morning they reached Fort Ann, where they were joined by many of the invalids who had been carried up Wood Creek in boats. A number of the sick, with the cannon, provisions and most of the baggage were left behind at Skenesborough.

On the 7th, a small reinforcement sent from Fort Edward by Schuyler, arrived at Fort Ann. About the same time a detachment of British troops approached within sight of the fort. This detachment was attacked from the fort, and repulsed with some loss; a surgeon, a wounded captain and twelve privates were taken prisoners by the Americans. The next day Fort Ann was burned, and the garrison retreated to Fort Edward, which was then occupied by General Schuyler.

As soon as Colonel Long had started for Skenesborough, St. Clair with the main army retired by land towards Castleton. The garrison of Ticonderoga crossed the bridge about three o'clock in the morning, and at four o'clock the rear guard, under Colonel Francis, left Mount Independence. Up to this time a continued cannonade from one of the batterics was kept up in the direction of Mount Hope, in order to allay any suspicions of the movement on the part of the enemy. The whole army would have departed unobserved, had not General De Fermoy, who commanded on Mount Independence, foolishly and regardless of express orders, set fire to the house he had occupied. The light of this conflagration revealed the whole scene to the British, and at the same time threw the Americans into great disorder; many of them now pushing forward without any regard to discipline or regularity. At Hubbardton the stragglers were collected and the ranks again organized. After a halt of two hours at, this place, the main army proceeded toward Castleton, leaving Colonels Francis, Warner and Hale behind with a rearguard of about thirteen hundred men.

As soon as the retreat from Ticonderoga was discovered by the British, General Fraser started in pursuit with his brigade, and was soon followed by Riedesel. The British troops continued the pursuit during the day, and at night lay on their arms near the position occupied by the American rear-guard, at Hubbardton. Early on the following morning, Fraser, with eight hundred men, advanced to the assault without waiting for the arrival of Riedesel, who was approaching with his column. On the appearance of Fraser's corps Colonel Hale fled with his regiment towards Castleton, leaving Colonels Francis and Warner, with seven hundred men, to resist the attack.

The battle between the two parties was severe and bloody, and at one time the British grenadiers recoiled before the galling fire of Francis's and Warner's men, but Riedesel coming up at that moment, the grenadiers rallied, and sustained by the whole British line, returned to the charge with fixed bayonets. The American troops now broke and fled in every direction. In this action the Americans lost three hundred and twenty four men, in killed, wounded and prisoners. Among the killed was the gallant Colonel Francis who fell at the head of his regiment. On the part of the English the loss was one hundred and eighty-three, including Major Pratt and about twenty inferior officers. Hale, who retired so prpiteiately in the morning, was intercepted on the road to Castleton, and surrendered without firing a shot. St. Clair, as soon as he had been joined by the remnant of Warner's men, retreated to Fort Edward, where he arrived on the 12th of July.

The loss to the Americans, by the evacuation of Ticonderoga, was very great; no less than one hundred and twenty-eight pieces of cannon, together with all the boats, provisions, stores and magazines were either destroyed or fell into the hands of the British. Among the trophies of the day was the continental standard, which the Americans had neglected to take with them on their retreat.

The evacuation of Ticonderoga and Mount Independence was condemned throughout the country. The people were not prepared for so disastrous an event, for it was generally believed that the works on Lake Champlain were in a condition to resist any attack of the enemy. Both Schuyler and St. Clair were severely and unjustly censured; the former for not sending on reinforcements, when he had none to send, and the latter for omitting to fortify Mount Hope and Mount Defiance, when his whole force was insufficient to man the defenses of the forts themselves. That a great error was committed, in relying too much upon the supposed strength of the positions at Ticonderoga, cannot be denied, but there were no just grounds for attaching blame to either of the officers in command.

The attention of the government had been directed to the exposed situation of this post, and St. Clair had repeatedly called for more troops for its defense. As late as the 25th of June, he addressed a letter to General Schuyler, in which he vividly portrayed his want of men, and his fears that he might not be able to resist Burgoyne, who was known to be approaching with a large force. In the letter, he says : " I cannot help *repeating* to you the disagreeable situation we are in, nor can I see the least prospect of our being able to defend the post unless the militia come in; and should the enemy protract their operations, or invest us and content themselves with a single blockade, we are infallibly ruined."

On the 28th of June, General Schuyler writes to General Washington, at the same time enclosing St. Clair's letter of the 25th, and says, " Should an accident happen to the garrison of Ticonderoga, and General Burgoyne makes a push to gain the south part of the lake, I know of no obstacle to prevent him : comparatively speaking, I have not a man to oppose him : the whole number at the different posts at, and on this side of the lake, including the garrisons of Fort George and Skenesborough, not exceeding seven hundred men, and these I cannot draw away from their several stations, in every one of which they are already too weak."

These letters show the real state of the frontier at the time. Burgoyne was approaching with an army of over seven thousand veterans, while St. Clair had three thousand four hundred men to defend a circle of works which could not be properly manned with less than ten thousand, and Schuyler had not troops enough with him to defend the posts in the rear. It had been said that, considering his want of men, St. Clair should have evacuated the works before the approach of the British army. Such a course would have been considered inexcusable. Besides the question, whether all or even a part of these works should be abandoned, had already been presented to the consideration of the provincial congress of New York, and that body, on the 6th of May preceding, had passed a resolution declaring that, in their opinion, the abandoning of any part of the works of Ticon-

19

deroga, would be productive of great evils. A copy of this
resolution was at the time forwarded to General Gates, who
replied that he saw no reason for abandoning any part of the
post at Ticonderoga, and that he had good ground to hope
there would never be any necessity of evacuating or sur-
rendering any portion of the position, if the body of the
eastern troops arrived in any reasonable time.

When Burgoyne placed his batteries upon the summit of
Mount Defiance, he effectually destroyed all hopes of resistance on the part of the Americans. Their only alternative was to surrender or evacuate the works. By adopting
the latter course, St. Clair saved the greater portion of his
garrison, and preserved the nucleus of an army, which ultimately baffled Burgoyne, and compelled him to capitulate.
At the moment, however, all classes of people were astonished
at the unexpected result. It is "an event of chagrin and
surprise," says Washington, " not apprehended nor within
the compass of my reasoning."[1]   The council of safety of
New York stigmatized it as a measure "highly reprehensible," and "probably criminal."[2]   Among the people, the
most violent charges were made against both St. Clair and
Schuyler. It was even asserted that they were bribed by
Burgoyne, who, it was said, had fired *silver bullets* into the
fort, which were gathered by order of St. Clair, and divided
between him and Schuyler.

---

[1] Letter to Major General Schuyler.

[2] " The evacuation of Ticonderoga appears to the council highly
reprehensible, and it gives them great pain to find that a measure
so absurd and probably criminal should be imputed to the direction
of General Schuyler, in whose zeal, vigilance and integrity the
council repose the highest confidence"—*Letter to Major General
Putnam, July* 11, 1777.   To this letter from the council of safety,
General Putnam replied," I am greatly astonished at the evacuation
of Ticonderoga in the manner it is represented ; think there is
great fault somewhere."

This report would seem too ridiculous to gain credit with any one, and yet we have the authority of Wilkinson, who was adjutant general to Gates, that respectable men questioned him, with much gravity, as to its truth.[1] Time softened the disappointment of the people, and when the true condition of the case was known, both officers were fully reinstated in the confidence of the nation.

When St. Clair joined Schuyler at Fort Edward, their united force, including recent arrivals, did not exceed four thousand four hundred men, who were immediately employed in obstructing the roads leading to Lake Champlain, and in placing impediments to the navigation of Wood Creek. So thoroughly was this work accomplished that, when Burgoyne afterwards led his army on this route, he was often unable to advance more than one mile in twenty-four hours. Schuyler remained at Fort Edward until the latter part of the month of July, when he fell back as far as Saratoga, and subsequently retired to Stillwater. While at Fort Edward, he removed the provisions, stores, boats and arms from Fort George, and on the 17th of July, destroyed the fort itself.

We left Burgoyne at Skenesborough, and Fraser and Riedesel at Hubbardton, on the 7th of July. After the retreat of St. Clair towards Fort Edward, these two columns occupied the ground between Castleton and Skenesborough; the English right wing occupying the heights at Skenesborough, in two lines, the right flank to the mountain and the left to Wood Creek; the German troops were stationed at Castleton, with detachments on the roads leading to Rutland and Poultney; the centre was occupied by Fraser's corps. A third column of the English army, under General Phillips was engaged in getting the gun-boats, transports and provisions over the falls of the outlet into Lake George. This

---

[1] See also Doctor Thacher's *Military Journal*, where he gravely denies the truth of the absurd report.

was accomplished after great labor and fatigue. Phillips then advanced as far as Fort George, where he established a depot and erected magazines for the army.

While Burgoyne was at Skenesborough, he issued a proclamation addressed to the inhabitants on the New Hampshire grants, in which he directed them, under pain of military execution, to send deputations, consisting of ten persons or more from each township, to meet Colonel Skene at Castleton, "who" adds the proclamation, "will have instructions not only to give further encouragement to those who complied with the terms of my late manifesto, but also to communicate conditions upon which the persons and property of the disobedient may yet be spared." As soon as General Schuyler saw this proclamation, he issued an order that every person who had taken or might take a protection from Burgoyne, should be secured and sent to jail; at the same time he gave notice, by a counter proclamation, that all who should join with, or in any manner assist or hold correspondence with the English, should be considered and dealt with as traitors.

Burgoyne had placed great reliance upon the discontent of the inhabitants on the New Hampshire grants, and supposed that large numbers, if not the whole population, would join his army. But in this he was destined to be most sorely disappointed, for not over four hundred royalists or disaffected persons joined him, and at least half of these he represented as "trimmers, merely actuated by interest," in whom he could place no dependence. He also declared, in a letter to Lord George Germain, that the New Hampshire grants abounded in the most active and most rebellious race on the continent, who hung like a gathering storm upon his left. This opinion had not been formed without good reasons, as we shall now see.

When the column under General Phillips moved up Lake George, the posts at Ticonderoga and Mount Independence were left with a guard of nine hundred and ten men, composed of the 53d British regiment, four hundred and sixty-two strong, and a German regiment numbering four hundred and forty-eight men, rank and file. About the time that Burgoyne had collected his troops at Fort Edward, General Lincoln, who had commanded a strong detachment of militia, stationed at Manchester, Vt., determined to make a diversion in the rear of the British line, in the hopes of recovering the Fort of Ticonderoga, and thus cutting off Burgoyne's communication with Canada.

General Lincoln ordered Colonel Warner, with a detachment of the Massachusetts militia, to move in the direction of Mount Independence, in order to make a diversion, and an attack in that quarter, if the occasion should favor one. Another detachment was sent, under Colonel Woodbridge, against Skenesborough and Fort Ann, while Colonel Brown, with Herrick's regiment of rangers and some militia and volunteers, was to cross the lake at the narrows, pass through the woods and take the outposts of Ticonderoga, and the works at the landing of Lake George. These places were to be attacked at the same time. Captain Ebenezer Allen, with his rangers, was to leave Brown and Herrick at a certain point and take Mount Defiance, and then rejoin them to attack Ticonderoga, in conjunction with General Warner. The plan thus arranged, they set out from Pawlet for their different places of destination. Brown had to cross the lake in the night and to pass, for fourteen miles, over rugged mountains, which he accomplished, reaching the head of Lake George the day before the attack. Before it became dark, sentinels were placed at different points on Mount Defiance and in the direction of the other British posts, with directions, from time to time, to give "*three hoots of an owl,*" as a signal to guide the main party on their way through the darkness of night. Colonel Brown took possession of Mount Hope and of a block house near the old French lines.

He also seized two hundred long-boats, an armed sloop and several gun-boats stationed to defend the carrying-place, and captured two hundred and ninety-three soldiers, at the same time releasing one hundred American prisoners.

But the most difficult task was the capture of the British works on the summit of Mount Defiance, which could be reached only by a cut way well defended and guarded. Captain Allen and his men had after great difficulty and labor, nearly reached the top of the mountain, when they found a cliff they could not climb in the ordinary way. Allen therefore ordered one of his men to stoop, and stepping on his back, clambered to the top, which was only large enough to hold eight men without their being discovered by the enemy. As soon as the men had reached the top, he rushed upon the garrison, already alarmed by the firing at the landing, closely followed by his little party, who says Allen, "came after me like a stream of hornets to the charge." The garrison immediately fled, with the exception of one man who attempted to fire a cannon at the assailants. "Kill the gunner," cried Allen, at the same time discharging his musket. At this the man ran away with the match in his hand, leaving the Americans in full possession of the works. The terrified soldiers rushed down the cut way and were captured by Major Wait, who had been stationed at the bridge to intercept their retreat. The only resistance offered, during the night, was by Lieutenant Lord, of the 53d regiment, who commanded at the block house, and who did not yield until several pieces of ordnance, taken from the sloop, had been brought against it.

Colonel Warner did not arrive near Mt. Independence until early the next morning. "He moved so extremely slow," says Ira Allen,[1] "that he saved his own men and hurt none

---

[1] *History of Vermont*, London, 1798.

of the enemy." When he came up, his force was united with
Colonel Brown's and the fortress of Ticonderoga summoned,
but Brigadier General Powel, who commanded there, refused
to surrender, declaring that he was resolved to defend himself to the last. Brown and Warner continued a cannonade
against the fort for four days, when finding the guns made
no impression upon the walls, they abandoned the siege and
withdrew their forces to the lower end of Lake George.
There they embarked on the gun-boats which they had captured, and on the 24th sailed against and attacked Diamond
Island. On this island a large quantity of public property
had been stored, which was guarded by two companies of the
47th regiment, under Captain Aubrey. In this attack the
Americans were repulsed with a small loss, and retreated to
the east shore of the lake, pursued by several gun-boats
which were stationed at the island. As soon as the Americans landed, they burned their boats, crossed over the mountains to Lake Champlain and returned to Lincoln's camp at
Pawlet.[1]

The fate of Burgoyne's army, after it left the lake is well
known. On the 30th of July, the three divisions were united at Fort Edward. On the 16th of August, Colonel Baum
was defeated at Bennington, by a body of New England militia
under General Stark. St. Leger raised the siege of Fort
Stanwix on the 28th of that month, and passing through
Canada and Lake Champlain, soon after joined Burgoyne,
between whom and General Gates a battle had been fought
at Stillwater, on the 18th of September, in which the advantages were decidedly in favor of the latter. After the action
Burgoyne retired as far as Saratoga, where another severe
action was fought on the 7th of October. On the 17th of

---

[1] In this expedition the Americans recovered the continental
standard which had been left behind when St. Clair's army evacuated the fort in July.

that month " articles of capitulation" were signed and five thousand seven hundred and ninety-one British and German troops were surrendered as prisoners of war.

As soon as the news of Burgoyne's surrender reached Ticonderoga, the troops stationed in that vicinity prepared for an immediate retreat to Canada. A few open boats now held what remained of the proud host who three months before had ascended the lake with all the pomp and panoply of war. Then, their banners floated gaily in the breeze, and the clear notes of the bugle startled the echoes of the surrounding hills; now, with watchful eyes they hurried silently along, and carefully avoided the shores, lest the thick and tangled forest might contain some bold and unseen foe. Nor were their fears of an attack without foundation; for as they passed the mouth of the Bouquet they were overtaken by a party of Green Mountain boys, led by Captain Ebenezer Allen, who cut off the rear division of boats and captured fifty men, besides a large quantity of baggage and military stores.

Thus closed the military operations of the year on Lake Champlain. The works at Ticonderoga were not reoccupied by the Americans, nor was this section of country the scene of any important military movement during the remainder of the war. In the fall of 1777, Gates, who had been placed at the head of the board of war, conceived the project of directing a descent upon Canada, in mid-winter, by the way of Lake Champlain, for the purpose of destroying the stores and shipping at St. Johns, on the Richelieu. The conduct of the expedition was entrusted to the Marquis de La Fayette, who repaired to Albany, full of high hopes, and panting for an opportunity to distinguish himself in a separate command. But the project failed from the want of trooops. Scarcely twelve hundred men could be mustered, and the greater part of these were half naked and unarmed. " The generals only," says Marshall, " were got in readiness."

Lafayette was much annoyed, but the obstacles were insuperable.

In 1780 Sir John Johnson made a descent upon Johnstown, near the Mohawk, for the purpose of recovering the silver plate, which he had secreted in the cellar of his house, at the time of his flight in 1776. Having accomplished this object, Johnson retired to Canada by the way of Lake Champlain, taking with him about forty prisoners.[1] He was pursued by Governor Clinton at the head of a body of militia. At Ticonderoga Clinton was joined by a party of Green Mountain boys, but from a want of boats the pursuit was discontinued. In the fall of the same year a party of two hundred and three Indians, led by seven tories and refugees, passed the Winooski and attacked the flourishing settlement of Royalton, Vt., burning twenty-one houses and taking fourteen of the principal inhabitants prisoners.

In October Major Carleton was sent up the lake from St. Johns, with a fleet of eight large vessels and twenty-six long-boats, containing upwards of one thousand men, in order to create a diversion in favor of Sir John Johnson, who directed an attack upon the Schoharie and Mohawk country. On the 10th and 11th Major Carleton surprised Fort George and Fort Ann, and took the garrisons prisoners. In the two assaults the British lost four officers and twenty-three privates killed; while the loss of the Americans in killed and prisoners, was two captains, two lieutenants and one hun-

---

[1] Among the prisoners captured by Sir John Johnson, were two brothers, named Jacob and Frederick Sammons, who resided in the valley of the Mohawk, near the confluence of that river with the Cayadutta. A very interesting account of the escape of the brothers from the fort at Chambly, and of their subsequent adventures in the wilderness on the east side of Lake Champlain, is given by Colonel Stone, in his life of Brant (Thayendanegea).

dred and fourteen privates. Carleton remained at Ticonderoga until the 1st of November, when he returned with the boats and shipping to St. Johns.

In the spring of 1781, the Iroquois chief Thayendanegea (Brant), meditated an expedition against the Oneidas who had been driven for safety to a position about fifteen miles west of Saratoga. This enterprise received the sanction of Sir Frederick Haldimand, then governor of Canada, who proposed to send a party of sixty loyalists under Major Jessup, the commandant at Point au Fer, towards Fort Edward to coöperate with Brant's Indians, who were to rendezvous on Carleton Island[1] in Lake Champlain. For some cause now unknown, the project was never executed.

In the course of the summer, the British, upon several occasions, entered the lake with their whole fleet, but attempted nothing beyond landing at Crown Point and Ticonderoga. The mysterious, and at the time inexplicable movements of the enemy in this quarter, kept the northern frontier in a state of ceaseless inquietude and alarm. The army about Albany was small and weak, and the American generals were greatly perplexed at these strange manœuvers of the fleet. Whenever it ascended the lake, an attack was expected in the direction of Fort Edward, but when, a few weeks afterwards, the fleet would withdraw without making any hostile demonstration, the idea prevailed that the movement was intended to create a diversion, while the actual blow was to be struck in another quarter. The mystery of these singular proceedings was not fully explained until several years afterwards, when it became publicly known that the leaders of the people on the New Hampshire grants had been, during the years 1780 and 1781, in frequent and secret correspondence with the authorities of Canada in relation to the political destiny of the grants.

---

[1] This is a small island near the south end of Grand Isle. It is now called Stave Island.

It is not my purpose to enter into an investigation as to the character or effect of this correspondence. The subject properly belongs to the history of Vermont, and has already been ably reviewed by her historians. It is enough here to say, that on the part of the British the negotiation consisted of repeated endeavors to persuade the leaders on the grants to abandon the American cause, and to declare the country a British province, and on the other side, of evasive and ambiguous answers, calculated to keep alive the hopes of the British authorities, but not intended to pledge the leaders or the people to any certain action. It is very evident that if the leaders were really serious in their intentions, the people were prepared for no such arrangement.

When the remnant of Burgoyne's army retreated to Canada in 1777, the British retained possession of Point au Fer, which they occupied as a military post. They also held a small block-house on the west side of the island of North Hero. These places were not given up until some time after the close of the war.[1]

---

[1] Botta — Burgoyne's *Narrative* — Thacher's *Military Journal* — Trumbull's *Reminiscences of his own Times* — Stone's *Life of Joseph Brant* — *Journal of the New York Provincial Congress* — Lossing's *Field Book of the Revolution*, &c., &c.

CHAPTER IX.

We have now traced the history of Lake Champlain, from its first exploration by the Europeans in 1609, to the close of the war of the revolution; a period of one hundred and seventy-five years. This history, thus far, has been little more than a narrative of continued strife and contention. Champlain was guided to the lake by a war party of Indians, who were seeking their enemies upon the well-known battle ground of that early day. He wrote the name of the lake upon its sands with the blood of the Iroquois, and proclaimed it, for the first time, amid the cries of tortured and dying prisoners. For many years afterwards the French and English colonists crimsoned its waters with each other's blood, and when, after a short interval of comparative quiet, the war of the revolution broke forth, the tide of battle almost instinctively returned to its old channel. It is not surprising that, under such circumstances, but little progress had yet been made towards the settlement and improvement of the country.

In 1783 the settlements near the lake were principally confined to the few towns in Vermont opposite and south of Crown Point. In that year the whole population upon the borders of the lake, on both sides, did not exceed six hundred.

For several years after the declaration of peace, emigration to the north eastern part of Vermont was retarded by the still pending dispute between the claimants under the New Hampshire grants and the state of New York, in regard to land titles. This controversy had however lost much of its acrimony, and all parties were prepared for its final adjustment, which took place in 1790. On the 4th of March, 1791, Vermont was admitted into the Union as a separate and independent state. In this year the population of the lake towns was six thousand seven hundred and seventy three.

In 1782, a party of royalists emigrated from St. Johns on the Richelieu, and commenced several improvements in the town of Alburgh. Soon afterwards Ira Allen obtained a grant of the town from the authorities of Vermont, and brought actions of ejectment against the royalists, which however terminated in their favor. A claim to the township was afterwards advanced by Sir George Young, under color of a grant from the Duke of York, which was also successfully resisted by the settlers.

Isle la Motte was settled in 1785, by Ebenezer Hyde, Enoch Hall and William Blanchard, and was organized as a town in 1790. In 1802 the name of the town was changed to Vineyard, which it retained until 1830, when the original name of Isle la Motte was again resumed. The islands of North Hero and Grand Isle were chartered as a town in the year 1779, but no settlement was commenced there until 1783. In March of that year Ebenezer Allen,[1] Alexander

---

[1] Ebenezer Allen was a native of Massachusetts. At the age of twenty-four he moved into Poultney, and in company with his brother-in-law, Thomas Ashley, commenced the first settlement in that town. He was soon afterwards appointed captain of a company of minute men, and served in Colonel Herrick's regiment of rangers during the revolution. He led the attack against the British post on Mount Defiance in September, 1777, and afterwards captured about fifty of the rear-guard of Burgoyne's army on their retreat to Canada.

Gordon and Enos Wood visited the township for the purpose of locating their respective claims. Wood, who by agreement between the parties was entitled to the first choice, located upon the south end of the north island; Gordon took the north end of the south island, and Allen the south end. In August all three brought on their families and commenced permanent improvements. For the first few years the inhabitants of these islands, in common with those of the neighboring towns, suffered great inconvenience from the want of grist-mills, the most accessible being at Whitehall and Granville, from eighty to one hundred miles distant.

The town of Milton was first settled in 1783, Georgia in 1784, and St. Albans in 1785. In 1784 McClain, Law and Boardman moved on to Colchester Point, and in the same year Ira Allen returned to the lower falls of the Winooski, where he soon after erected mills, a forge and a shop for making anchors.[1]

The first residents in the town of Burlington abandoned their improvements at the time of Burgoyne's invasion in 1777. Stephen Lawrence, Frederick Saxton, Simeon Tubbs and John Collins moved into the town and renewed the settlement in 1783. The first town meeting was held in March, 1787, when Samuel Lane was chosen town clerk. In 1789 Stephen Keyes built a store in the village, which was opened in the fall of that year under the charge of Orange Smith. Another store was soon afterwards started by Zacheus Peaslee.

In the year 1787 there were about twenty families in the town of Shelburn. Charlotte was first permanently settled

---

[1] Ira Allen was the first secretary of Vermont. Subsequently he was state treasurer, member of the council, and surveyor general. He rose to the rank of major general of militia, and in 1795 was sent to Europe to purchase a supply of arms for the state.

in 1784, by Derick Webb and Elijah Woolcut. John Mc-
Neil soon afterwards moved into the town. He was elected
its first town clerk and representative. In 1790 he removed
to the lake shore and established a ferry between that place
and the town of Willsborough (now Essex), N. Y. Ferris-
burgh was settled, after the war, by Abel Thompson, Gideon
Hawley, Timothy Rogers and others. In the year 1783 Amos
Spafford, Shadrack Hathaway, Eben Murry, Ephraim and
Wm. Fisher and John Charter commenced a settlement at
Mount Independence, in the town of Orwell, and the next
year Pliny Smith and others moved into the town with their
families. The same year Barber, Durfee and Noble moved
into the town of Benson.[1]

Let us now cross to the western or New York side of the
lake. In 1784 the county of Washington was organized,
and originally included all the territory lying west of and
adjoining the lake. In 1788 that portion contained in the
present counties of Clinton, Essex and Franklin, was taken
from Washington and formed into a new county, which was
called Clinton. Essex was taken from Clinton in 1799, and
Franklin in 1808. The town of Plattsburgh was organized
as a part of Washington county in 1785, and included all
the territory within the limits of the present towns of Beekmantown, Saranac, Schuyler's Falls, and also portions of Old
Peru and Old Chateaugay. It was the only town on the
west side of the lake until 1788, when Champlain, Willsborough and Crown Point were organized. Willsborough
originally included the present towns of Chesterfield, Essex,
Lewis and a part of Old Peru. Crown Point embraced all
the territory lying between Willsborough and Lake George.

---

[1] For further information in regard to the first settlement of
Vermont, see Zadock Thompson's *Gazetteer of Vermont* — a most able
and elaborate work.

When Burgoyne entered the United States, all the persons residing on the west side of the lake abandoned their habitations, and either joined the American army, or retired to the neighborhood of Albany. They returned immediately after the peace, and were soon followed by others; but the progress of the settlement of the county was very slow for the first ten years. In 1790 the population of Clinton county, which then embraced the whole territory west of the lake, was to be found in the vicinity of the Saranac and the Bouquet rivers, and did not then exceed sixteen hundred and fourteen.

Prior to the revolution William Gilliland had commenced a settlement at the falls of the Bouquet River, from which he was taken and sent to Albany by order of General Gates, in 1776. After the war he returned, accompanied, or soon followed by Aaron Fairchild, Jonathan Lynde, Joseph Sheldon, Abram Aiken, Martin Pope, Melchior and John Hoffnagle, John Morehouse and others, who in 1784 settled at and near the mouth of the Bouquet. In August, 1783, Benjamin Mooers[1] arrived at Point au Roche, and commenced the first permanent settlement within the limits of the present town of Beekmantown.

Mr. Mooers brought with him Francis Monty and son,

---

[1] BENJAMIN MOOERS was born in Haverhill, Massachusetts, on the 1st of April, 1758, and at the age of eighteen entered the army as a volunteer. In 1777 he was appointed ensign in Hazen's regiment, and was afterwards promoted to the rank of lieutenant and adjutant. At the close of the war he removed to Clinton county, of which he was the first sheriff. He was four times elected member of the assembly, and once of the state senate. During the war of 1812 he held the office of major general of militia, and for forty-eight years was county treasurer. He died at Plattsburgh in February, 1838, in the 80th year of his age.

Zacheus Peaslee, Pierre Boilan, Charles Cloutier, Antoine Lavan, Joseph Letournan, Antoine Lasambert, P. Aboir and John Fessie. On the 26th of July he left Poughkeepsie in a bateau, and on the 29th arrived at Albany, where he was joined by John La Frombois, who was returning to his farm on the lake shore in Chazy. On the 31st the party left Albany and proceeded up the Hudson River about five miles, where the boat was partially unloaded and taken over the rapids to Stillwater. On the 2d of August they reached Fort Miller, and at noon of the 3d arrived at Fort Edward. The baggage and bateau were drawn across the country to Fort George, where the party procured another boat, and the same evening sailed nine miles down the lake, and encamped on a small island near its eastern shore. The next day they reached the lower end of Lake George, and on the 6th drew the boats around the falls into Lake Champlain, and sailed down the lake with a fair wind, passing Crown Point about sundown.

On the 8th the party landed on Valcour Island, where they were delayed by headwinds until Sunday morning (10th), when they set sail, and the same day arrived at Point au Roche. The next day, the whole party, except La Frombois, who had gone on to visit his old place a few miles below, commenced work, and in ten days completed a log house and cleared a small patch of land for turnips. It rained almost incessantly while they were at work on the house, and they were not fairly settled when young Monty, Lavan and Cloutier were taken down with the fever and ague.

On the 26th of August, Mr. Mooers, with three others, left Point au Roche to visit the place occupied by Monty before the war. "There have been several persons taking up land there" says Mr. Mooers in his journal. "I found Monty's house burnt all up, and the place where another

21

house was burned. A man has it fenced, and considerable more cleared. He has been there this summer and made two large stacks of hay." One of the first labors of the new settlers, after building the house, was to cut a quantity of grass for the support of the oxen during the winter. This grass grew wild in many places upon the low lands near the shore of the lake, and for several years was the only fodder used in the country. By the 11th of September Mr. Mooers had cleared up a small field near his house, which he sowed to wheat and turnips.

About the year 1783, Jacque Rous emigrated from Canada and settled at Rouse's Point. Pliny Moore lived at Champlain in 1785, and Davis and Cross near King's Bay. About the same time Prisque Ashline commenced a clearing near the Corbeau River. In the year 1787 Robert Cochran and Nathaniel Mallory resided on the lake shore, near the mouth of the Ausable River, Moses Dickson, Jabez Allen and Lot and John Elmore on the rich lands lying between those rivers, and Edward Everett and John Stanton in what is now called the Union in the town of Peru.

In 1781 the legislature of the state of New York, in order to encourage the raising of troops for the defense of the state, passed certain acts offering bounties of unappropriated lands to such officers and soldiers as should enlist within a specified time. These bounties were divided into rights of five hundred acres each, and there was a provision in the act that whenever any number of persons entitled collectively to sixty-one rights, or 30,500 acres, should join in a location, the lands so located should be laid out in a township of seven miles square, and that the remaining 860 acres in such township should be reserved for gospel and school purposes. These rights were sometimes retained by the soldiers, but more frequently a company of land speculators would furnish money to the recruiting officers to be paid as a bounty to those who on enlistment should transfer their certificates to the company. In this way a large portion of the unappropriated lands of the state, subject to location, passed into the hands of a few individuals.

Judge Zephaniah Platt, of Poughkeepsie, and thirty-two other persons, having united in the purchase of the number of rights requisite to entitle the holders to a township, located them, in 1784, upon the lands which had formerly been embraced in the warrant issued by the English government to Charles De Fredenburgh. A survey of the land was made in the same year by Captain Nathaniel Platt and Captain Simon R. Reeves, two of the proprietors, and a patent issued by the state to Zephaniah Platt in 1785.[1]

The proprietors were active in their efforts to secure the immediate settlement of the tract. Ten *gift lots* were set apart for the first ten persons who should move into the town with their families, and arrangements were made, at an early day, for the building of mills, &c.

On the 30th of December, 1784, twelve of the proprietors met at the house of Judge Platt, in Poughkeepsie, where they

---

[1] The following is a list of the original proprietors of Plattsburgh old patent, and of the number of acres allotted to each. Thomas Treadwell, Nehemiah Benedict and Thomas Benedict, 1,120 acres; Nathaniel Platt, 950; Nathaniel Tom, 480; Burnet Miller, 480; Ezra L'Hommedieu, 320; Peter Tappan, 480; John Miller, 640; Benjamin Walker, 320; John Berrien, 480; Jonathan Lawrence, 480; Benjamin Smith, 480; Israel Smith, 960; Melancton Smith, 1,120; Zephaniah Platt, 900; William Floyd, 320; Benjamin Conklin, 500; Andrew Billings, 400; John Adams, 1,600; Thomas Stone, 1,000; Lewis Barton 200; Ebenezer Mott, 200; Zacheus Newcomb, 1,200; Platt Rogers, 1,500; General Schuyler, 950; Benjamin Titus, 400; Charles Platt, 800; John Smith, 400; Albert Adriance, 200; Samuel Smith, 200; Jacobus S. Swartout, 200; Simon R. Reeves, 2,800; Zephaniah and Nathaniel Platt, 4,050; Zephaniah and Nathaniel Platt and S. R. Reeves, 4,300.

agreed to become jointly interested in building a saw-mill, a grist-mill and a forge on the Saranac, near its mouth. They also agreed to furnish twine for a seine, and to build a piragua "of a moderate size." Attached to the agreement was an estimate of the probable cost of the mills, from which it appears that three hundred and sixteen dollars were apropriated for mill-stones, irons, nails, bolting-cloth and saw, and sixty-five dollars for flour and bread. One hundred and sixty dollars were divided equally between pork and New England rum — a pint of rum to a pound of pork being a workman's requisite in those roistering days.

Among those who received the *gift lots* were Jacob Ferris, Thomas Allen, John B. Hartwick, Derrick Webb, Jabez Petit, Moses Soper and Kinner Newcomb. Ferris received a deed for one hundred and twenty acres lying on the south side of the river Saranac at its mouth, which covered all that part of the present village of Plattsburgh, lying east of the river. In 1785, Charles McCreedy, Melancton L. Woolsey and several others moved into the town. Cumberland Head was then supposed to present the most eligible point for business, and the first stores established in the town were located there. After a few years the stores were removed to the present village, but the Head still continued to be a place of some importance. It had a direct communication with Vermont by ferry, and for a long time was the usual landing place for vessels navigating the lake.

Probably few towns in the state of New York can claim among their first inhabitants and proprietors, a greater number of men of talent than Plattsburgh. Conspicuous in this class were Melancton Smith, Zephaniah Platt, Thomas Treadwell and Peter Sailly.

MELANCTON SMITH, one of the proprietors, was a native of Jamaica, Queens County, L. I., where he was born in 1744. While a boy he was placed in a retail store in Poughkeepsie, and resided in that town until his removal to the city of New York in 1784. At the early age of thirty-one he was chosen one of the delegates to represent the county of Dutchess in the first provincial congress of New York, which met in May, 1775, and soon became a leading and distinguished member of that body. He was one of the committee who prepared the celebrated address to the Canadians, at the commencement of the revolutionary struggle. On the 22d of June, 1776, he was appointed captain commandant of three companies of militia raised in Dutchess and West Chester, and the next year was placed on the commission to prevent and subdue insurrection and dissatisfaction in those counties. He was in the same year appointed the first sheriff of Dutchess county, which office he held for four years, and was afterwards made judge of the common pleas.[1]

In 1788, though then a resident of the city of New York, Mr. Smith was chosen by the people of Dutchess county to the convention which met in June of that year to consider the constitution of the United States, as prepared by the convention at Philadelphia in May of the preceding year. In the discussions and deliberations of this body, he exhibited talents and information of the highest order, and was ranked as one of the ablest opponents of Hamilton and Livingston on the floor of the convention. When it was ascertained that a sufficient number of states had so decided as to render the adoption of the constitution certain, Mr. Smith gave up his objections. "This was deemed at the time," says Chancellor Kent, "a magnanimous sacrifice of preconceived principles and party discipline for the national welfare, and the effort was the greater, inasmuch as he had to desert his friend, Governor Clinton, who persevered to the end in his hostility to the constitution."[2]

---

[1] *Journal of the New York Provincial Congress.*

[2] Chancellor Kent, as quoted in appendix to Thompson's *History of Long Island.*

Mr. Smith was twice married. His first wife was Sarah Smith of New Jersey, who died in 1770; his second, Margaret, daughter of Richbill Motte of Long Island, whom he married in 1771 and by whom he had four children, Richbill, Melancton, Sidney and Phœbe, all of whom afterwards resided in Plattsburgh. He died in the city of New York on the 29th of July, 1798, in the 55th year of his age.

"Melancton Smith," says Mr. Dunlap, "was a man of rough exterior, powerful in bodily appearance, and undaunted in expressing his mind, which he did in plain language, but with a sarcasm that was cutting and a humor correct and playful." "He was," says Chancellor Kent, "very amiable in his temper and disposition, of a religious cast, and very fond of metaphysical and logical discussions, in which he was a master." In private life he was kind, affectionate and communicative, and as benevolent as amiable; indeed his charity knew no limits. While the army was encamped near his residence in Dutchess county, the females of the family were constantly employed in making clothing for the soldiers. "I could only make up my bedding by stealth," Mrs. Smith afterwards used to say, "for if the judge came in and found me sewing upon a pair of sheets, he would request the cloth cut into shirts for the half naked soldiers of Washington's army."

ZEPHANIAH PLATT was possessed of a clear, sound and discriminating mind, and was classed among the first men of the state. In 1776, when forty-one years of age, he was chosen a delegate from Dutchess county to the first provincial congress, and occupied a prominent position in that body; he was a member of the committee of safety, and took an active part in the convention called for forming a constitution for the state. He was for a short time commissary for the troops under command of Brigadier General Clinton. In June, 1777, he was appointed a judge of the

Dutchess common pleas, and the same year was elected one of the state senators of the middle district, then composed of the counties of Dutchess, Ulster and Orange. He was also member of the state convention which assembled at Poughkeepsie, in June, 1788, to deliberate on the adoption of the constitution of the United States.

In the spring of 1777 the counties of Dutchess and West Chester were filled with disaffected persons, who it was feared, upon the first advance of the British troops out of New York city, would attack those friendly to the American cause. To prevent this, the provincial convention appointed Mr. Platt and two other members of their body a committee to clear those counties of all dangerous and disaffected persons. "You are," were the instructions to the committee, "on every occasion, by every means in your power (torture excepted), to compel the discovery and delivery of all spies and emissaries of the enemy, who you may have reason to believe are concealed in any part of the country through which you may make your progress, and upon due proof immediately execute them *in terrorem.*"[1] The committee executed the delicate and responsible duty confided to them with firmness, and with the most impartial justice.

After the war Mr. Platt engaged largely in the purchase of military land warrants and located them principally upon Lake Champlain. He removed from Poughkeepsie to Plattsburgh about the year 1801, where he resided until his death, in September, 1807.

THOMAS TREADWELL, another of the original proprietors of Plattsburgh, was born in Smithtown, Long Island, in 1742, and graduated at Princeton in 1764. He was well educated, and highly distinguished for his good sense, prudence and firmness. In 1775 he was a member of the provincial

---

[1] *Journal of the New York Provincial Congress.*

convention. He was also a member of the convention that
framed the state constitution, and was one of the senators
under that constitution. In 1788 he was a member of the
convention which assembled to consider the constitution of
the United States, in which he coöperated with Clinton,
Melancton Smith, Yates and Lansing. He was made judge
of probate of Suffolk county in 1783, and held the office until
surrogates were appointed, when he received the appointment
of surrogate, which he held until 1791.[2] Soon after the
organization of Clinton county he removed to Plattsburgh
and was chosen a senator for the northern district. In 1807
he was appointed surrogate of Clinton county, which office
he held until the spring of 1831. He was for many years
the last surviving member of the venerable assembly that
framed the first constitution of the state, and died on the
30th of January, 1832, enjoying to the last the respect and
confidence of his fellow men.

PETER SAILLY was a native of Loraine, France. He first
visited the United States in 1784 and made a tour of exploration through the valley of the Mohawk and the country
bordering on Lake Champlain. In 1785 he returned to
France for his family, with whom he arrived at the city of
New York in the summer of that year, and having passed
the winter in Albany settled the following spring in the town
of Plattsburgh. Mr. Sailly was a man of great probity,
possessing strong powers of mind and a clear discernment of
character. He was active, enterprising and firm; a master
of order and method and scrupulously exact in his business
transactions. Although educated in a foreign land he brought
to the country of his adoption a mind deeply imbued with
the principles of liberty, which he carefully cherished and
enlarged in after life. He held several offices of public
trust, and to the hour of his death enjoyed the unlimited

---

[1] Thompson's *History of Long Island.*

confidence of his fellow men. In 1804 he was elected a member of congress from the Saratoga, Clinton and Essex district, and by his strict attention to business and a judicious and unostentatious course, won the confidence of Mr. Jefferson, by whom he was soon afterwards appointed collector of customs for the district of Champlain — an office he held through the successive administrations of Madison and Monroe until his death in 1826; a period of over eighteen years.

The duties of collector, during a portion of this time, were most delicate and responsible, as upon the revenue officers devolved the arduous and unpopular service of putting in execution the embargo and non-intercourse laws. In the discharge of this duty Mr. Sailly never hesitated, but upon all occasions enforced the laws with promptness and strict impartiality. Kind and affable in his intercourse with his fellow citizens, he wounded the feelings of none by a rough or unnecessary display of power, while his firmness and determination of character were too well understood for any one to hope by the strongest opposition to deter him from the prompt discharge of his public duties.

The first court of common pleas and general sessions for Clinton county was held at Plattsburgh, on the 28th of October, 1788. Judge Charles Platt[1] presided. Peter Sailly, Theodorus Platt, William McAuley, Pliny Moore and Robert Cochran were the associate justices; Benjamin Mooers was sheriff; Melancton L. Woolsey,[2] clerk; John

---

[1] CHARLES PLATT was a native of Long Island and a brother of Zephaniah Platt. He removed to Plattsburgh soon after the organization of the town, was elected its first supervisor, and for several years was town clerk. He was first judge of the Clinton common pleas until the year 1804, and in 1808 was appointed to the office of county clerk, which he held until 1822.

[2] MELANCTON L. WOOLSEY was the youngest son of Melancton T.

Frontfreyde, coroner; and Robert Paul, Jonathan Stephenson, Lewis Lizotte and Jonathan Lynde, constables. One attorney only was in attendance, who appeared in behalf of the people; the prisoners were defended by the clerk. The first circuit and oyer and terminer for the northern part of the state, was held by Judge Benson, at the court house in Plattsburgh, on the 18th of August, 1796. The next year Judge Lansing held a circuit court at the block house in Willsborough, where the court also convened in 1798.

In 1789 George Clinton and Robert Yates were opposing candidates for governor. The canvass was so warmly contested that the supporters of Governor Clinton secured his reëlection by the small majority of four hundred and twenty nine votes. The entire vote of Clinton county at this election was forty-five, which was thus divided between the two candidates.

	Clinton.	Yates.
Crown Point,	10	
Willsborough,	15	3
Plattsburgh,	17[1]	

Woolsey of Long Island, and in early life had served as an officer in the army and as aid to Governor Clinton. He removed to Plattsburgh in 1785, was soon after appointed clerk of Clinton county, and was, for several years, collector of customs for the Champlain district.

[1] The poll list of this election was not preserved, but it can be conjectured who cast these seventeen votes, when it is known that the following *seventeen* persons were elected to town offices in Plattsburgh, at that election. Charles Platt, Kinner Newcomb, Theodorus Platt, Melancton L. Woolsey, Abraham Beeman, John Stephenson, John Cochran, Jr., Nathan Averill, Cyrenus Newcomb, Edward Everett, Peter Sailly, John B. Hardwick, Jonas Allen, Moses Soper, Titus Andrews, Benjamin Mooers and Lucius Reynolds.

In 1793 the vote of the county was increased to one hundred and thirty-four. George Clinton was elected governor over Stephen Van Rensselaer in 1801, by a majority of three thousand nine hundred and sixty-five. At this time Essex had been set off from Clinton, and several new towns had been organized in both counties. This year the vote was as follows:

Clinton County.

	Clinton.	Van Rensselaer.
Champlain,	42	45
Lisbon,	21	71
Plattsburgh,	107	21
Chateaugay,	11	52
Peru,	90	24
	271	213

Essex County.

	Clinton.	Van Rensselaer.
Willsborough,	50	82
Crown Point,	10	6
Elizabethtown,	69	9
Jay,	46	13
	175	110

The vote of both counties in 1803 was 749, which was increased to 929 in 1804. Two years later the number of votes polled in both counties was 1,247.

The increase of population on both sides of the lake, from 1790 to 1800, was nearly two hundred per cent. During this decade considerable progress was made in agriculture; particularly on the Vermont side, where the attention of the great body of the inhabitants was directed to the cultivation of the soil, the raising of sheep and the production of flax. The manufacture of pot and pearl ash was also carried on to a considerable extent. Some attention had likewise been given to the manufacture of iron. As early as 1792 four

forges were erected in Addison county and two in Chittenden, and prior to the year 1800 several other forges had
been erected at other points, upon both sides of the lake.
These forges were principally supplied from a bed near
Crown Point, which is yet celebrated for the quality and
quantity of its ore.[1] The country abounded with maple
trees from which large quantities of sugar were annually
made. Many of the maples were of very large size, and it
was not unusual for the farmers to make from twelve to fifteen pounds of sugar, in the course of the season, from a single tree.[2]

The first settlers were generally hunters and derived considerable profit from the sale of peltry, as the country then
abounded with moose, deer, bears, beavers, foxes, wolves,
rabbits, martins, &c. The lake was also celebrated for the
abundance, variety and delicate flavor of its fish. Salmon,
muskellunge, bass, shad, pike, pickerel and perch were
caught in great abundance in all parts of the lake, and in
the mouths of the principal streams. The lower part of the
lake near Wind-mill Point, and the Big Chazy River at the
foot of the first rapids, were especially celebrated for their
salmon fisheries. Champlain, in the account of his expedition in 1609, describes a large fish found in the lake which
the Indians called *chaousarou*, and which grew to the length
of eight or ten feet. He saw one five feet long, " as thick
as a thigh, with a head as big as two fists, with jaws two feet

---

[1] When Kalm was at Crown Point, in 1749, he noticed black sand
upon the shores of the lake, but he says it was not then known
whether there were iron mines in the neighborhood or not. Iron
ore was first found within the present limits of Clinton county, in
1800, when the Winter bed was discovered by Mr. George Shaffer.
The Arnold bed was first opened in 1809.

[2] Williams's *History of Vermont.*

and a half long and a double set of very sharp and dangerous teeth." "The form of the body," says Champlain, " resembles that of the pike, and and is armed with scales that a thrust of a poniard cannot pierce; and is of a silver grey color. The point of the head is like that of a hog."[1] This fish made war upon all others in the lake, who fled in terror at its approach. It was probably the *esox longirostris* or the *esox osseus* of Mitchell. The species, of smaller size, still exists in the lake, and is occasionally caught near Isle la Motte.[2]

A large quantity of pine and oak timber was annually cut on the borders of the lake, which was rafted through the Richelieu and St. Lawrence to Quebec, from whence it was shipped to England. The timber trade had furnished employment for the early settlers before the revolution. After the war it greatly increased, and for many years formed an important traffic for the inhabitants residing on the west side of the lake.

The commerce of the lake was principally limited to a small export and import trade with Canada. Vermont imported rum, wines, brandy, gin, coarse linens and woolens, tea, coffee, chocolate, and many articles necessary for building. Her exports were grain of all kinds, bar iron, wrought nails, pot and pearl ashes, beef, pork, lumber, peltry, maple sugar and some flax.[3] The exports on the New York side were lumber, pot and pearl ashes, peltry and iron.[4]

---

[1] *Voyages de la Nouv. France*, 1609.

[2] See De Kay's description of the gar fish and of the Buffalo bony pike, in the *Natural History of New York*.

[3] Williams's *History of Vermont*.

[4] "The manufactures here are of little importance, exclusive on iron works. There are five works on the New York side of the lake where iron is manufactured at once from very rich ore. Such iron sells from $100 to $120 per ton. There is also an anchor shop on a pretty large scale, and a furnace is erecting and nearly completed

Large quantities of grain and provisions were brought
from Vermont and Canada, to supply the inhabitants of
Clinton and Essex counties, who, from the first, had been
allured from the pursuits of agriculture, by the attractions
of the lumber trade.

Large tracts of land, lying in Clinton county, were set
apart in 1784 and 1786 for Canadian and Nova Scotia refugees, and for such of the inhabitants of the state as had
served in the United States army and were entitled to land
bounties under the act of 1782. These tracts were surveyed
and subdivided, and many of the lots were occupied under
the state grants. The greater portion, however, were for-
feited for want of actual occupation, and the lands were
afterwards patented by the state to other persons. Among
those acquiring title under these patents was William Bailey,[1]
who purchased an extensive tract in the present town of

---

in this vicinity (Plattsbugh). We have none but household
manufactures of cloth. There are a number of carding mills, and
nail cutting by water machinery is done to a considerable extent ;
all of which affords a very good profit. It does not come within
the spirit of your circular to speak of the great number of saw-
mills, nor of the manufacturing of ashes which here, as in every
other northern country newly settled, is an object of profit and
importance." *Peter Sailly Esq.*, collector of the district of Champlain, to the secretary of the treasury, September 7th, 1809.

[1] WILLIAM BAILEY was a son of Colonel John Bailey, of Dutchess
county. At the age of eighteen he was drafted into the Dutchess
county militia, and was sent to join the army at West Point. He
first visited Lake Champlain in 1786, and aided in the survey of
the lands belonging to Zephaniah Platt and his associates. He
was one of the associate justices of the Clinton common pleas in
1779, and was appointed first judge of the county in 1806. In
1800 he was appointed first major in Lt. Col. Benjamin Mooers's
regiment of militia, and was elected a member of the assembly in
1802, and again in 1806. He removed to Plattsburgh in 1811 where
he resided until his death, in the year 1840.

Chateaugay. He moved there in the year 1800, and cleared and cultivated a large farm near the four corners. At an early day he built a forge on the Chateaugay River, near the falls, which he intended to supply with ore from a bed at the south end of the upper Chateaugay Lake. This bed when first opened presented every indication of containing a large supply of ore, but it soon became exhausted and the forge was abandoned.

Before Mr. Bailey settled in Chateaugay[1] he was employed by the state to survey the lands set apart for the Canadian and Nova Scotia refugees. At this time the British occupied Point au Fer as a military post, and the commanding officer there refused to allow the surveying party to approach or to continue their survey to the point. The claim of the British commandant seems to have included all the territory north of the Big Chazy River, for after Judge Pliny Moore settled in Champlain in 1785, he was visited, on the first of each month, by a corporal and file of men, sent from Point au Fer to notify him that his claim of title from the state of New York would not be recognized. No attention was paid to these repeated warnings, which continued until the British gave up possession of Point au Fer, about the year 1788.

I have already had occasion to refer to the conflicting claims set up by various parties and at different times, to the title and sovereignty of the country bordering on Lake Champlain. The last of these claims had been adjusted in

---

[1] The town of Chateaugay (originally a part of Clinton county) was first settled in the year 1796 by Benjamin Roberts and Nathan Beman, who were soon followed by John Allen, Gates Hoit, Lewis Ransom, David Mallory and several others. Mallory was employed by Captain Nathaniel Platt, of Plattsburgh, to build a grist mill on Marble River, one mile and a half north of the present village of Chateaugay. Until this mill was completed (1798) the inhabitants procured their flour from Plattsburgh — a journey which usually required one week's time.

the year preceding the admission of Vermont into the Union. In the year 1792 the Caughnawaga and St. Regis Indians, calling themselves the Seven Nations of Canada, sent a deputation to the government of the state of New York, claiming a tract of land covering a large portion of the northern part of the state. A commission, consisting of Egbert Benson, Richard Varick and James Watson, was appointed to treat with the Indian chiefs upon the subject, and in the summer of 1796 an arrangement was effected, by virtue of which the Seven Nations relinquished their claim, with the exception of the St. Regis reservation, for a small sum in hand paid, and a yet smaller perpetual annuity.

As soon as the Seven Nations had completed their negotiations with the state of New York they advanced a similar claim against Vermont, for lands lying on the east side of Lake Champlain.

The subject was carefully examined by the legislature of Vermont, but no decision was had until the next year, when the governor of the state was requested to inform the claimants that the legislature was of the opinion that their claim, if it ever existed, had long since been done away and become extinct, in consequence of the treaty of peace between the king of Great Britain and the French king, in 1763, and the treaty of peace between the king of Great Britain and the United States, in the year 1783; and that the Indians had now no real claim either in justice or equity. This decision was communicated to the Indians, and the subject was dropped without any further negotiations by either party.

The Caughnawagas resided on the south bank of the St. Lawrence, near the island of Montreal, in Canada. The St. Regis Indians lived above and upon the same bank of that river. The latter still occupy the lands reserved to them by their agreement with the state, in 1796. These Indians were quiet and peaceable, and endeavored not only to preserve order within their own territory, but to prevent the violation of the laws of New York. An instance of their respect for order and good government occurred in 1804, under the following circumstances.

Jocco Lafrance, a St. Regis Indian, in the winter or spring of that year, killed a man near Chateaugay and escaped to the Indian village. He was immediately arrested by the chiefs and delivered up for trial. The evidence on the trial not being sufficient to convict Jocco of murder, he was acquitted of that charge, but was banished from the county. The chiefs were satisfied that Jocco was really guilty, and on his return banished him from their village also. They likewise addressed the following letter to Judge Bailey, who was then one of the magistrates of Chateaugay :

"This may certify to whom it may concern, that we, the chiefs and warriors of the village of St. Regis, are determined to hold among ourselves a strict regulation of justice, and that whereas, Jocco Lafrance has committed crimes not within our jurisdiction, but he belonging to our village, immediately apprehended said Jocco and delivered him up to justice where said crime was committed, to receive just punishment under their laws, according to the crime he had committed, which we esteem murder to be the most heinous crime in felony. Said Jocco has now, after his trial, returned to us again by banishment. For which now, said chiefs, having a full sense that the said Jocco has committed the heinous crime of murder, have passed a resolve that the said Jocco must immediately leave the territories under our jurisdiction, and also, if any person shall or may see said Jocco, it is our sincere wish that they may disappear him away from us, and never to have him seen among us while time shall be on earth.

St. Regis, October 17, 1804.

By order of the chiefs.

WILLIAM GRAY."

23

CHAPTER X.

Although Great Britain acknowledged the independence of the United States by the treaty of 1783, she could not forget that they had once formed the largest and most important of her colonial possessions. A feeling of dissatisfaction pervaded the British nation, and led to many acts of oppression towards the infant confederacy. Vessels sailing upon the high seas under the American flag were boarded by her ships of war; American seamen were impressed; trade with neutral nations was forbidden, and the territory of the United States invaded.

In June, 1807, the British ship of war Leopard fired into and boarded the United States frigate Chesapeake, while the latter vessel was yet within sight of the American coast. Ten days after this attack, Mr. Jefferson issued a proclamation interdicting all intercourse with the British armed vessels then within the waters of the United States. This proclamation was followed, on the 22d of December of the same year, by an act of congress declaring an unlimited embargo on every port in the Union.

During the year 1808 negotiations were conducted between the two countries in a temper that promised a pacific termination of the dispute, but no definite arrangement was concluded. The United States, in the mean time, was making preparations for defense. A large number of gun-boats were constructed for the protection of the sea coast, and in January, 1809, the president was directed to equip four new vessels of war. About the same time, Lieutenant Melancton T. Woolsey was sent north to build two gun-boats on Lake Champlain, and a brig of sixteen guns on Lake Ontario.[1]

When the news of the attack upon the Chesapeake first reached the people, there was a general cry of indignation throughout the country. Politics, however, ran high at the time, and this natural and national sentiment was soon consumed, in many quarters, by the fire of party strife. As the dispute with Great Britain progressed, the opposition of the anti-administration party developed itself more and more against the policy and measures of the government, until at length the authorities in Canada were induced to believe that a portion of the states were anxious to secede from the Union.[2] To encourage this feeling of discontent, Sir John Craig, governor of Canada, sent the notorious John Henry as an emissary among the Federalists of the New England states, with directions to ascertain how far, in case of their separation from the Union, they "would look to England for assistance, or be disposed to enter into connection with Great Britain."

Mr. Henry reached Burlington on the 12th of February, 1809, and at first was much pleased with the evidences of dis-

---

[1] The gun-boats on Lake Champlain were at first placed under the command of Lieutenant Haswell, U. S. Navy.

[2] This opposition was the most violent in the Eastern states, the inhabitants of which were more commercial, and had suffered more from the effects of the embargo than those of any other section of the Union.

content among the people. "On the subject of the embargo
laws," he writes Governor Craig, "there seems but one
opinion ; namely : that they are unnecessary, oppressive
and unconstitutional. It must also be observed that the execution of them is so invidious as to attract towards the officers of government, the enmity of the people, which is of
course transferred to the government itself; so that in case
the state of Massachusetts should take any bold step towards
resisting the execution of these laws, it is highly probable
that it may calculate upon the hearty coöperation of the
people of Vermont." A few days later Mr. Henry expresses
some doubts as to the correctness of his first opinions. "The
Federal party," he again writes Governor Craig, "declares
that in the event of war, the state of Vermont will treat sepa-
rately for itself with Great Britain, and support to the
utmost the stipulations in which it may enter, without any
regard to the policy of the general government. The Democrats on the other hand assert that, in such a case as that
contemplated, the people would be nearly divided into equal
numbers; one of which would support the government, if
it could be done without involving the people in a civil war ;
but at all events would risk every thing, in preference to a
coalition with Great Britain."

Henry's investigations were not satisfactory, and before
he left for Boston he evidently became convinced that
in the event of a dispute among the states, the citizens of
Vermont could not be relied upon to join the seceders, or to
unite in a strong opposition to the war. He had at first been
led astray by the loud clamor of politicians, and by the com-
plaints of those who had suffered most from the operation
of the embargo. These laws had severely injured the commerce of the lake, and had broken up the direct communication with the Canada markets, upon which the inhabitants of
the lake counties depended for a sale of their products, and
for a supply of foreign commodities.

The country was filled with smugglers, who frequently came in collision with the revenue officers. In some of these encounters blood had been shed and lives lost. The first serious affray occurred on the Winooski River, in 1808, between a party of government officers and a smuggling vessel called the Black Snake, in which two of the government officers were killed. Attempts were frequently made to seize the collectors and revenue officers stationed on both sides of the lake. These attempts always failed, but, on one occasion, two of the assailants were severely, although not mortally wounded. The feeling of opposition to the embargo was strong at the time of Henry's visit, in 1809, and induced him to attach greater importance to the representations of a few persons, as to the sentiments of the inhabitants of Western Vermont, than was warranted by the real inclinations of the people themselves. It is well known that when war was declared, the Vermontese were not only ready to repel an invasion of that state, but that many of them volunteered to cross the lake, and oppose the advance of the British into the state of New York.

The difficulties between the United States and Great Britain continued to increase, in number and importance, until the year 1812. On the 1st of June of that year, Mr. Madison sent a message to congress, in which he reviewed the various grounds of complaint against Great Britain, and set forth, at length, the unsatisfactory manner in which that power had received and treated the frequent remonstrances made on the part of the United States. This message was referred to the committee on foreign affairs, who, a few days afterwards, made a report in which they fully concurred in the sentiments expressed in the president's message.

In this report the committee declare that more than seven years had elapsed, since the commencement of a system of hostile aggressions, by the British government, on the rights and interests of the United States. That the United States had done every thing in their power to preserve the relations of friendship with Great Britain, and had given proof of this disposition at the moment when they were made the victims of an opposite policy. The committee then referred to the attack made by Great Britain upon the commerce between the United States and the colonies of France and Spain — a commerce which they declared was just in itself, sanctioned by the example of Great Britain in regard to the trade with her own colonies; sanctioned by a solemn act between the two governments in the last war, and by the practice of the British government in the then existing European war.

They refer, at length, to the different attacks made by Great Britain upon the rights and sovereignty of the United States; the interference with her neutral trade; the pretended blockade of the whole coast of Europe, from the Elbe to Brest, inclusive; the order of council of January, 1807, by which neutral powers were prohibited from trading from one port to another of France, or of her allies, or to any country with which Great Britain might not freely trade; the order of council of November of the same year; the claim of right to search vessels sailing under the American flag; impressment of American citizens into the British naval service, and the attempt to dismember the Union, by a secret mission to foment discontent and excite insurrection against the constituted authorities and laws of the nation.

Having clearly and plainly stated the facts upon which these charges were based, and reviewed the whole course of of Great Britain against the United States since 1804, the committee recommended an immediate appeal to arms, and introduced a bill declaring war between the United States and Great Britain. This bill passed the senate by a vote of nineteen to thirteen, and the house of representatives by a vote of seventy-nine to forty-nine, and was promulgated by the proclamation of President Madison, on the 17th day of June, 1812.

Active measures were immediately taken by many of the states to second the action of the general government. The state of New York approved warmly of the course of the administration and prepared to prosecute the war with vigor. Vermont was at the time under the control of the Democrats, and both the governor and legislature pledged themselves to support the country in the approaching contest. A law was immediately passed by the legislature of the latter state, prohibiting all intercourse with Canada without a permit from the governor, and measures were taken for calling out the militia whenever their services might be required.

The effective force in Canada, at the time of the declaration of the war, was about ten thousand men. These troops were principally concentrated around Quebec, but the greater part were soon afterwards removed to Upper Canada, which was threatened on the west by an army under General Hull. In the summer of 1812 General Bloomfield was ordered to the Champlain frontier, with several regiments. By the 1st of September he had about eight thousand men, including regulars, volunteers and militia, under his command. This force was stationed at Plattsburgh, with small advance parties thrown forward as far as Chazy and Champlain. The troops remained in quarters until the 16th of November, when they moved north, under the immediate command of Major General Dearborn, and on the 18th encamped about half a mile south of the Canada line. The army collected at this point numbered three thousand regulars and two thousand militia.

The entire British force on the northern frontier did not exceed three thousand men, and of these not more than one thousand were within striking distance of the American army. When Dearborn had concentrated his troops near the lines he prepared to cross into Canada. As he approached

Odletown, Major Salaberry, who commanded in that quarter, sent forward two companies of voltigeurs and three hundred Indians to support the two companies of embodied militia, who formed the British outposts on the La Colle. Major Salaberry followed, the next day, with the remainder of the voltigeurs and four companies of chasseurs.

Before day-break on the morning of the 20th, a detachment of Dearborn's army forded the La Colle and surrounded the guard-house which was occupied by the Canadian militia and a few Indians, who rushed out, broke through the American lines and escaped unhurt. In the mean time a second party of the Americans had advanced, and commenced a sharp fire upon those in possession of the ground, mistaking them for the British picket. This fire continued for nearly half an hour, when being undeceived, the two parties united and hastily retreated, leaving behind them five killed and as many wounded.[1] The troops immediately afterward returned to Champlain. The designs of the American general were so completely obscured that no one discovered the particular advantages intended to be gained by this singular and inefficient movement. It was a prelude to many similar military operations on the Champlain frontier during the war.

On the 23d of September the army returned to Plattsburgh, where the 6th, 15th and 16th regiments went into winter quarters. The militia were disbanded; the 9th, 11th, 21st and 25th regiments were sent to Burlington, and the light artillery and dragoons returned to Greenbush. Brigadier General Chandler commanded the troops left at Burlington, and Colonel Pike those stationed at Plattsburgh.

---

[1] Christie's *History of the War in Canada.* General Armstrong, then United States secretary of war, says this account does not differ materially from those given by the American officers.

On the 23d of October a gallant affair took place at St. Regis, where Major Young surprised a party of British, and took forty prisoners. But the campaign of 1812 did not add to the lustre of the American arms. On the Champlain frontier nothing was achieved beyond the little affair at St. Regis. The operations on the Ontario frontier were confined to a few skirmishes, the defense of Fort Niagara, and an unsuccessful and most disastrous assault upon Queenstown; while the incompetent and timid Hull surrendered Detroit and the north-western army, without a battle, or any effort to maintain the honor of the country.

In course of the winter preparations were made for the invasion of Upper Canada. The two brigades stationed on Lake Champlain moved for the Ontario frontier in February, leaving a small detachment at Burlington to protect the magazines and provisions collected there. The west side of the lake was left wholly unprotected, and remained so until the month of September following.

During the year 1811 a very active trade had been carried on between the United States and Canada. The value of exports for that year from the district of Champlain, which included the New York side of the lake only, exceeded half a million of dollars, of which four hundred and fifty thousand dollars was on property of American growth and manufacture. Among the articles exported were 1,513 barrels of beef, 2,678 barrels of pork, 70,269 pounds of butter, 53,049 pounds of cheese, and more than 2,000 head of cattle. The value of masts, spars, timber and sawed lumber exported exceeded two hundred thousand dollars. The number of clearances from the district, between the 10th of April and the 10th of December, was one hundred and ninety. Of these forty-two were rafts and the remainder sail vessels, bateaux and row-boats. A steam-boat, called the Vermont, made one trip each week to St. Johns.[1]

---

[1] The Vermont was the first steam-boat which navigated Lake

The commencement of hostilities between the United States and Great Britain broke up this trade with Canada, and again put in motion a numerous band of old and experienced smugglers who resided along the frontier, from Lake Memphremagog to the River St. Lawrence. The collectors used every precaution to put a stop to the illegal practices of these people, but on more than one occasion the ingenuity of the smugglers was an over match for the vigilance of the officers. Small row-boats would elude the revenue cutters in the darkness of the night, and pack horses, loaded with rich and valuable goods, would frequently escape through the thick woods which bounded the settlements on either side of the lake.

Among the many contrivances of the smugglers to escape detection was the following. John Banker, Jr., a resident in the city of New York, who had obtained from the collector of that port a commission authorizing him to fit out a privateer on Lake Champlain, equipped a small sail-boat of less than one ton burthen, which he called the Privateer Lark, and which was provided with an armament of three muskets. In this boat the Captain cruised around the lake, threatening vengeance to the enemies of his country. Indeed he carried his ardor so far on one occasion as to fire into the Essex ferry-boat, while it was crossing the lake, fifty miles south of the Canada line. After a profitless cruise in the

Champlain. She was built at Burlington by Winans and Lough in 1808, commenced running in 1809, and continued in service for five years. The following vessels were cleared at the Champlain custom house in 1811: schooner Liberty, Captain T. Babcock; sloops, Eagle, S. Boardman; Euretta, John Boynton; Jupiter, Justin Smith; Hunter, N. Hinckley; Independence, Z. Manning; Juno, A. Ferris; Champlain, E. Hurlbut; Essex, A. Rock; Rising Sun, Elijah Boynton; Mars, T. Clarke; Enterprise, E. Bellamy; Lady Washington, R. Jones; and Richard, Gideon King.

vicinity of Burlington, the gallant captain would run down
to Rouse's Point, and boldly lay at anchor upon the borders
of Canada, until some hostile barge loaded with goods should
incautiously run within range of his muskets. The approach
of the barge was the signal for attack, and doubtless many
a bloody battle would have been fought upon the quiet waters
of Rouse's Point Bay, had not the enemy surrendered at the
first appearance of the captain's guns.

The property thus forcibly captured by an armed privateer
was now beyond the reach of the revenue officers. Captain
Banker's next step was to appoint some trusty confederate
as prize master, in whose possession he placed the captured
property, with written instructions to deposit it in the government store houses at New York. When the prize master
reached New York, he delivered the goods to the owners for
whom they had been smuggled, upon receiving the stipulated
price of transportation. As soon as the government officers
ascertained that the goods did not reach the public store
houses, they seized the Lark, and thus put an end to pri-
vateering on Lake Champlain.

Prior to the commencement of the war, the whole naval
force on Lake Champlain consisted of two gun-boats, which
lay at Basin Harbor, on the Vermont side of the lake. In
the course of the summer of 1812. two small sloops were
fitted up and armed, to which were joined four scows,
carrying one long eighteen pounder each. These vessels
constituted the whole naval force of the Americans. The
British, at that time, had no vessels on the lake, nor any in
the Richelieu larger than gun-boats.

Late in the fall of 1812 Lieutenant Thomas Macdonough
was ordered north to take charge of the naval operations on
the lake, which until then had been confided to Lieutenant
Sidney Smith.[1]

---

[1] Mr. Smith was 5th lieutenant on board of the Chesapeake at

Macdonough brought out his vessels in the spring of 1813 as soon as the lake was free from ice. The American flotilla at this time consisted of the sloop President, fitted up during the winter, which was commanded by Macdonough in person ; the sloop Growler, Lieutenant Smith, and the sloop Eagle, Mr. Loomis. About the first of June Macdonough received information of an attack, by several British gun-boats, upon some small craft at the lower end of the lake. In consequence of this intelligence he ordered Lieutenant Smith to move towards Rouse's Point, with the Growler and Eagle, in order to attack the gun-boats, should they again make their appearance. Lieutenant Smith left Plattsburgh harbor with his vessels, on the morning of the 2d of June, and about dark cast anchor within a mile of the lines. The next morning, about day break, he got under way, and proceeded down the Richelieu as far as Ash Island (Isle aux Tetes), where he discovered and gave chase to three British gun-boats. The wind was blowing fresh from the south at the time, and soon brought the sloops, the Growler leading, within sight of the works at Isle aux Noix. The sloops now tacked and began to beat back towards the open lake, having the wind against them, with a slight adverse current in the river.

As soon as the British were aware of the advantages these circumstances gave them, three of their row-galleys came out from under the works at Isle aux Noix, and opened a brisk fire upon the sloops. As the galleys carried long

-----

the time of the Leopard's attack upon that vessel, in June, 1807, and on the return of the Chesapeake to Hampton Roads joined the other officers of that frigate in a letter to the secretary of the navy, preferring charges against Commodore Barron, and requesting a court of inquiry upon his conduct. He afterwards served on board the U. S. ship Wasp, and in March, 1810, was ordered to Lake Champlain, where he remained in command, until the arrival of Lieutenant Macdonough, in the fall of 1812. He married a daughter of Judge Bailey, of Plattsburgh, and died a commander, in 1827.

twenty-fours, while the largest guns on the sloops were eighteens, the former were able to select their own distance nor could the latter come to close quarters without running within range of the fire of the batteries on the island. To render the situation of the sloops still more critical, the British now lined the woods on each side of the river, and opened upon them with musketry. This fire was returned with constant discharges of grape and canister, and, in this manner, the contest was continued for several hours with great gallantry on both sides. About four hours after the commencement of the action a shot from one of the galleys struck the Eagle under her starboard quarter and passed out on the other side, ripping off a plank under water. The sloop went down almost immediately, but fortunately in shoal water, and her crew were taken off by boats sent from the shore; soon after this accident the Growler had her fore stay and main boom shot away, when she became unmanageable and ran ashore.

In this engagement the Growler had one killed and eight wounded, and the Eagle eleven wounded, including the pilot, Mr. Graves. The whole number of men on board both vessels, when they went into action, was one hundred and twelve, including Captain Herrick and thirty-three volunteers from his company. The officers and men were taken prisoners and sent to Canada. The two sloops, having been refitted, were transferred to the British service, their names being changed to the Finch and Chub, and were subsequently recaptured by Macdonough in September, 1814. The loss to the British, in this engagement, was never correctly ascertained. It must have been very severe, however, as their forces advanced to the bank of the river, where, destitute of shelter, they received broadside after broadside of canister and grape. A sergeant of the 11th regiment, who had volunteered on board one of the sloops, and who was paroled on account of his wounds, reported that he counted thirty of the enemy dead upon one small spot.[1]

The capture of the Growler and Eagle gave to the British the superiority on the lake. In July Macdonough increased his naval force, which by the loss of the Growler and Eagle had been reduced to one sloop, by the addition of six gunboats, and by the 20th of August had fitted out and armed three small sloops, mounting together 28 guns. This increased the American force on the lake to about fifty guns. In the official returns in the admiralty office, it is stated that the British had at Isle aux Noix or St. Johns, on the 24th of July, two sloops of eleven guns and forty men each, and three gun-boats of twenty men each. Other accounts state their naval force, in August, at three sloops, four gunboats and three row-galleys, mounting in all about forty-two guns. The efficacy of this arm was however less than the number of guns would seem to indicate, for the sloops, on both sides, were originally built and used in the transport service, and were not adapted to war purposes.

Before the American flotilla had been increased by the addition of the three sloops, a party of British, under Colonel Murray, made a descent upon Plattsburgh, and destroyed or took away a large amount of public and private property. Although this was in fact nothing but a predatory incursion, it was treated by the English at the time, as a most glorious achievement, and has been so considered by their historians up to the present day. Mr. Alison, in his history of Europe, a work replete with errors in relation to the military operations on this frontier during the war of 1812, refers to the expedition, and says that "the English flotilla, with nine hundred men on board, stretched across the lake, took

---

[1] The current belief, in the neighborhood of the action, was that the British loss exceeded two hundred, but this was probably an exaggeration.

Plattsburgh, which was evacuated by twelve hundred Americans, without firing a shot, burned part of the naval stores and brought away the rest, and also destroyed the American naval establishments at Champlain and Burlington."

A greater number of errors could not well be collected in so few words. Alison has overrated the number of Americans at Plattsburgh, diminished the actual strength of the British, and misstated every circumstance connected with the transaction. The force under Colonel Murray was embarked on two war sloops, three gun-boats and forty-seven long-boats, and numbered over fourteen hundred men, including infantry, sailors and marines. With this force Murray crossed the lines on the 30th of July, passed Champlain, where the Americans had not then, nor ever had, a naval establishment, and on the afternoon of Saturday, the 31st, arrived at Plattsburgh, where he landed without opposition, and began a work of destruction which continued until ten o'clock of the next day, when he reëmbarked and stood out of the bay. At the time the British landed there were no regular troops on the west side of the lake. Major General Hampton, it is true, was at Burlington on the opposite side, twenty miles distant, with between three and four thousand men under his command, but from some unaccountable cause he made no attempt to cross the lake or to protect the village of Plattsburgh, although he had twenty-four hours notice of the intended attack.[1] While the British were

---

[1] "I could not persuade myself that the American force stationed at Burlington, of 4,000 effective men, within twenty miles of this place, could be suffered to remain idle spectators of the destruction of the public property and of this village by comparatively a very small British force. Messengers were repeatedly sent to General Hampton with a request that one regiment might be sent here, but to no effect. It is a fact, that from the Canada line to the south end of Lake Champlain, on the west side, there is not a military post nor a soldier to be seen."—*Peter Sailly Esq., to Secretary of Treasury, August* 4, 1813.

at Plattsburgh, about three hundred militia were hastily collected, but they did not approach the village until the enemy had retired.

When Colonel Murray first entered the village he assured the civil authorities that private property should be respected, and that citizens, not in arms, should remain unmolested. These promises were, however, most shamefully violated, for the British, not satisfied with destroying the block-house, arsenal, armory and hospital in the village, and the military cantonment near Fredenburgh Falls, two miles above, wantonly burned three private store houses, took possession of about two thousand dollars worth of hardware belonging to merchants of the city of Boston, and plundered several private dwellings, destroying furniture and such articles as they could not use or carry away. The value of the private property plundered exceeded eight thousand dollars. Inventories of this property were prepared and published at the time, and include long lists of furniture, books, clothing, cooking utensils, groceries and dry goods. Soldiers would break into private dwellings and bear off back loads of property to the boats in the presence of British officers, who, when remonstrated with by the plundered citizens, replied that they could not prevent it, as the men did not belong to their company.[1] The value of the public property destroyed was estimated at twenty-five thousand dollars.

Colonel Murray, having accomplished the work of destruction, retired in great haste, leaving behind him a

---

[1] It appears by the inventories of plundered property, published at the time, that Judge De Lord lost $1,079.18; Peter Sailly Esq., $887.77; besides two store houses burned and valued at $900; Judge Palmer, $386.50; Doctor Miller, $1,200; Bostwick Buck, $150; Jacob Ferris, $700; several smaller amounts were lost by other citizens. A store house belonging to major Platt was also burned at the time.

picket guard of twenty-one men, who were made prisoners and sent to Burlington. The long-boats and two of the gun-boats then proceeded to Swanton, Vt., where the men burned some old barracks, and plundered several citizens of the place. On their way they landed at Cumberland Head and Point au Roche, and pillaged the houses and farms of Henry W. Brand, Judge Treadwell and Jeremiah Stowe. They also burned a store at Chazy Landing belonging to Judge Saxe. The two sloops and the other gun-boat, after leaving Plattsburgh, stood for the south and sailed ten or twelve miles above Burlington, when they returned towards Canada. As the vessels passed Burlington they fired a few shots at the place, but bore away as soon as the batteries on shore began to play upon them. While on the lake the British took or destroyed eight or ten long-boats engaged in the transportation business, and captured a Durham boat loaded with flour.

While Colonel Murray was at Plattsburgh he dropped a letter from his hat, which was afterwards picked up, and found to contain information as to the best mode of attack on Plattsburgh, together with a map of the encampment and miltary works at Burlington. A few days afterwards the person who wrote the letter was arrested on a charge of high treason and sent to Albany for safe keeping.

25

CHAPTER XI.

In July, 1813, Major General James Wilkinson assumed the command of the northern department. About the same time, the American secretary of war, Mr. Armstrong, repaired to Sackett's Harbor to supervise the military operations on the Ontario frontier. The plan of the secretary contemplated a descent upon Kingston, and a subsequent movement down the St. Lawrence. A large force was also collected at Burlington, on Lake Champlain, which was placed under the immediate command of Major General Hampton.

About the 1st of September Hampton was directed to move towards the British posts on the Richelieu, in order to create a diversion in favor of the western army, and to coöperate, if necessary, with Wilkinson in an attack upon Montreal. The American troops, numbering about four thousand men, were immediately concentrated at Cumberland Head, where they were joined by a body of New York militia, who had been called into service by Governor Tompkins. On the 19th the infantry and light troops moved from Cumberland Head in boats, flanked on the right by Macdonough's flotilla, and at twelve o'clock at night reached Chazy Landing. The next morning they entered the Big Chazy River, and disembarked at the foot of the rapids, near the village of Champlain, where they were joined by a squadron of horse and two companies of artillery. The same day the army moved north as far as Odletown, in Canada. Hampton remained one day in Canada, when learning that the springs and streams, in the direction of the St. Lawrence, had been dried up by an unusual drought, he determined to change his route, and to approach Montreal by the way of Chateaugay.

On the 21st the army returned to Champlain, and on the evening of the 24th reached Chateaugay Four Corners, where they remained inactive for twenty-six days. On the 16th of October Mr. Armstrong was at Sackett's Harbor, debating whether he should attack Kingston, or make an immediate descent upon Montreal. Hampton was ordered to advance to the mouth of the Chateaugay River, or to some other convenient point on the St. Lawrence, from which an easy and direct communication could be opened between the two armies. In pursuance of this order, he entered Canada on the 21st, and the next day encamped on the Chateaugay, at a point about twenty miles below the Four Corners. There he remained until the 20th, when he planned an expedition against a small body of British troops who were stationed about six miles below. The expedition failed, and Hampton returned to the Four Corners, with a loss of thirty-five men in killed and wounded. A few days afterwards he broke up his camp and returned to Plattsburgh, where the army was ordered into winter quarters.

While the army lay at Chateaugay, Colonel Isaac Clark,[1] who commanded a detachment of troops stationed at Champlain village, was ordered "to commence a petty war near Lake Champlain." "What I am aiming at," writes Hamp-

---

[1] Colonel Clark served in the revolutionary war. He was a lieutenant in Captain Ebenezer Allen's company, and took part in the surprise of Mount Defiance, in September, 1777.

ton, " is tranquility on the road, by kicking up a dust on the lines."[2] A better officer than Clark, to accomplish this object, could not have been selected. He had served with Herrick's rangers in the revolution, and was well skilled in border warfare.

On the evening of the 11th of October Clark crossed the lake with one hundred and ten men, a part of whom belonged to the rifle corps, and early the next morning reached the village of Missisco Bay, where a small party of British were stationed, under command of Major Powell. Clark placed himself at the head of the rifles, and advanced at double quick time until he met the main body of the enemy, who had been hastily drawn up near the guard house. Directing his men to halt, he approached the British and ordered them to lay down their arms. Major Powell advanced and attempted to speak, but Clark sternly ordered him to remain silent and march " to the rear of the American line." The boldness of the order, and the confident tone in which it was given, induced the major to believe that the rifles were supported by a large force, and he instantly obeyed. Clark ordered his men to advance against the main body, who, under command of their captain, was preparing to charge. A volley from the riflemen struck down the captain and several men, when the rest threw down their arms and surrendered themselves as prisoners of war. Captain Finch was now sent forward to watch a force of two hundred British, who were advancing under Colonel Lock. Finch proceeded with such promptness and secrecy, as to surprise an advance guard of cavalry, except one man who escaped and gave information of the approach of the Americans, when Colonel Lock immediately retreated with the rest of his command. The loss of the British in these attacks was nine killed and

---

[2] Letter to secretary of war, October 4th, 1813.

fourteen wounded. One hundred and one prisoners were taken by Clark and sent to Burlington.

During the autumn of this year a slight skirmishing war was carried on between the American and British picket guards, which kept the frontier in a state of excitement and alarm, without, however, doing much injury to either party. Upon one occasion, about the 1st of October, a small party of New York militia crossed the lines and attacked a picket guard stationed at Odletown, within the district under command of Major Perreault of the Canadian detached volunteers The audacity of this act excited the ire of the Canadian officer, who, in retaliation, discharged a gasconade at the whole town of Champlain.

"Citizens of Champlain!" exclaimed the indignant major, "I am happy that humanity should still have so much power over me as to inform you that, should any of the militia of Champlain be found hovering this side of the line, I will let loose upon your village and inhabitants the Canadian and Indian force under my command. You are probably aware that it has been with the greatest difficulty I have till now withheld them. But your cowardly attack at midnight, of a small picket of our's, has torn asunder the veil which hid you from them — *so beware!*" This message was enclosed in a note to Judge Moore, with a request that he would acquaint the people with "the tenor of the humane advertisement." Judge Moore preformed his duty, but the militia were obdurate.

As soon as the army had retired into winter quarters Hampton repaired to Washington, leaving General Izard in command at Plattsburgh, and General Parker at Burlington. Izard was soon afterwards ordered to join Wilkinson, who, on Hampton's return to Plattsburgh, had gone into winter quarters at French Mills. On the departure of Izard's brigade, the frontier on the western side of the lake was again left unprotected. About the middle of December, a strong detachment of British troops under command of Captain Barker of the frontier light infantry, crossed the lines into Vermont and destroyed some public store houses and barracks which had been erected at Derby. This attack, and the threatening movements of the British forces stationed along the Richelieu, induced the magistrates of Plattsburgh to address a letter to General Wilkinson, who was then at French Mills, in which they represented the exposed condition of the public property, and their apprehension that another invasion might soon be expected, unless a strong force was stationed on the west side of the lake. As soon as Wilkinson received this letter he ordered a company of dragoons to Plattsburgh from Burlington, and a detachment of infantry from Chateaugay Four Corners. The infantry reached Plattsburgh on 8th of January, having made a forced march of forty miles that day. Other detachments of troops soon afterwards arrived, and on the 10th Wilkinson repaired to Plattsburgh in person. The camp at French Mills was broken up, and all the magazines and provisions forwarded to Lake Champlain.

The operations on the lake, during the autumn of 1813, were of little importance. The British flotilla remained in the Richelieu, while the American vessels rode quietly at anchor on the lake. About the 1st of December Macdonough moved to King's Bay and anchored under Point au Fer. A few days after his arrival at that place, Captain Pring entered the lake with six armed galleys, landed at Rouse's Point, and burned a small shed there, which had been used as a public store house. As soon as Macdonough received information of the approach of the British galleys, he weighed anchor, and it being calm at the time, attempted to work out of the bay with sweeps. At the same time he sent Lieutenant Cassin forward with four row-galleys, with orders to bring the enemy into action, and thus detain them until the sloops could get up. The British, however, refused to engage, and Lieutenant Cassin returned after an unavailing pursuit of three miles.[1] Sir George Provost gives a different and erroneous account of this trifling affair. In a letter to Earl Bathurst, under date of December 12th, he says: " A division of gun-boats, with a detachment of troops, which I had ordered, on the 1st of the month, to advance into Lake Champlain, for the purpose of molesting General Hampton's division, succeeded in burning an extensive building lately erected at Plattsburgh, as a depot magazine; some bateaux, together with the ammunition, provisions and stores found in it, were either brought away or destroyed. The severity of the weather obliged Captain Pring, of the royal navy, under whose command I had placed the expedition, to return to Isle aux Noix on the 5th." Sir George was evidently misinformed as to the facts, by the officer in command of the expedition.

The "extensive building lately erected at Plattsburgh as a depot magazine," was a small shed near the lake shore at Champlain Landing, which *had formerly been* in public use, and the smoke from which gave the first information to Macdonough of the enemy's approach. A few days after this affair the ice blocked up the narrow channel below Rouse's Point, when Macdonough withdrew his vessels and laid them up for the winter in Otter Creek.

In November of this year a dispute arose between Governor Chittenden of Vermont, and some of the citizens of that state, involving the right of the militia, in certain cases, to pass without the territorial limits of their own state. The governor, in his annual message, had taken strong

---

[1] Macdonough to secretary of navy, December 5th, 1813.

grounds against the war, which he considered "doubtful as to its necessity, expediency or justice." He also declared that the militia were exclusively assigned for the service and protection of the respective states, except in the cases provided for by the national constitution. That it was never intended that they should, "by any kind of magic," be at once transformed into a regular army for the purpose of foreign conquest, and he regretted that a construction should have been given to the constitution, "so peculiarly burdensome and oppressive to that important class of our fellow citizens."

In opposition to these friendly suggestions, a portion of the militia, under Lieutenant Colonel Luther Dixon, crossed the lake and placed themselves under the orders of General Hampton. This movement called forth a proclamation from the governor, in which he ordered the militia to return and hold themselves in readiness to act under the orders of Brigadier General Davis, who had been appointed to the command of their brigade. "The military strength and resources of the state," says Governor Chittenden, "must be reserved for its own defense and protection, *exclusively*, except in cases provided for by the constitution of the United States, and then under orders derived *only* from the commander-in-chief."

The proclamation was distributed among the volunteers, who were men stationed at Plattsburgh, and created great excitement with both the officers and men. The agent, by whom it had been circulated, was arrested and held to bail, in a large amount, for his appearance before the United States district court. The officers also published a reply to the proclamation, in which, in very plain terms, they informed the governor that they should not obey his orders, but should remain in service until regularly discharged. In this reply they say : "If it is true, as your excellency states, that we are out of the jurisdiction or control of the executive of Vermont, we would ask from whence your excellency derives the right, or presumes to exercise the power of ordering us to return from the service in which we are engaged? If we are legally ordered into the service of the United States, your excellency must be sensible that you have no authority to order us out of that service. If we are illegally ordered into the service, our continuance in it is either voluntary or compulsory. If voluntary, it gives no one a right to remonstrate or complain; if compulsory, we can appeal to the laws of our country for redress against those who illegally restrain us of our liberty. In either case we cannot perceive the right your excellency has to interfere in the business."

This was pretty sharp firing and effectually silenced the governor's batteries. The brigade remained at Plattsburgh until it became known that the contemplated invasion of Canada had been abandoned for the winter, when the volunteers returned to Vermont, and probably put themselves " under the command of Brigadier General Davis."

The campaign of 1813 was directed towards the important military posts on Lake Ontario and the St. Lawrence River. It commenced with bright prospects of success, but failed through the imbecility of the officers who had been called to the head of the army. The people were deeply disappointed at the result. They had placed great confidence in their commanding generals, whose numerous dispatches were written in a lofty style, and were filled with predictions of most brilliant victories. " I am destined to and determined on the attack of Montreal, if not prevented by some act of God," cries Wilkinson, on the 6th of November, from the head of an army of 8,000 men.[1] " The Rubicon is now passed, and all that remains is to push forward to the capitol,"

---

[1] Letter to General Hampton.

is the bold declaration of Hampton.[1] Vain and empty
boasting! Two weeks later the one was quietly settled at
Plattsburgh, and the other was building winter quarters at
French Mills and Chateaugay.

The campaign of 1813 is closed. General Wilkinson
attributed its failure to the refusal of Hampton to join him
at St. Regis, on the St. Lawrence. He declared that by a
junction of the two armies he could have secured Montreal within eight or ten days. "It is a fact," he writes the
secretary of war, "for which I am authorized to pledge myself,
on the most confidential authority, that on the 4th of the
present month (November), the British garrison of Montreal
consisted solely of four hundred marines and two hundred
sailors, which had been sent up from Quebec. What a golden,
glorious opportunity has been lost by the caprice of Major
General Hampton."[2]

General Hampton, on the contrary, censured Wilkinson
for desiring a junction of the two armies, with the scanty
supply of provisions within reach of St. Regis. He contended that to have moved forward, with the 4,000 troops
under his command, would have seriously weakened, if it
did not destroy both armies. That his true course was to
throw himself upon his main depots at Plattsburgh, and from
that point to open a communication direct to Caughnawaga;
which would relieve the western army, and at the same time
retain all the benefits to be expected from a junction at St.
Regis.[3]

---

[1] Letter to secretary of war, Nov. 12.

[2] A glorious opportunity indeed, for two large armies to capture
six hundred men!

[3] About one month prior to this time Hampton attempted this
very route, and backed out before he had penetrated four miles
into Canada. Referring to the dispatches of the two northern
commanders, Mr. Niles, in his register, exclaims: "The *cacœthes*

In December General Hampton was withdrawn from the frontier, but General Wilkinson retained his command until after the unsuccessful attack upon a grist-mill in La Colle, when he too was ordered to head quarters. The assault on the La Colle mill was made on the 30th of March, 1814. About the first of that month Major Forsyth had been sent to the lines, near Champlain, with 300 riflemen and 60 dragoons to protect the frontier, and to break up an illicit intercourse which had been carried on with the enemy during the winter. Detachments had also been sent to the Vermont frontier, under command of General Macomb and Colonel Clark, for a similar purpose. About the same time General Wilkinson examined the country around Rouse's Point, with a view to the erection of batteries there, which should command the outlet of the lake and blockade the British flotilla within the Richelieu.

These movements alarmed the British, who hastened to strengthen their military posts in the vicinity of Rouse's Point. Major Hancock, of the 13th, occupied La Colle with six hundred men, and the forts at St. Johns and Isle aux Noix were garrisoned by about two thousand men, under command of Lieutenant Colonel Williams of the same regiment. When Wilkinson learned that the British force near the lines had been increased, he ordered the troops stationed at Plattsburgh to be advanced to Champlain, where he also directed Macomb and Clark to concentrate their respective commands. On the 29th of March four thousand men were collected at Champlain, of whom 100 were cavalry and 304 artillerists. The latter had with them eleven pieces of cannon of small calibre. Wilkinson now planned an attack against Major Hancock, who occupied a grist-mill on

---

scribendi again rages with singular violence in the army, with symptoms fatal to gallons of ink and hundreds of goose quills!"

the banks of the La Colle river, about five miles north of
the lines.

On the morning of the 30th the American army marched
out of Champlain, upon the Odletown road. The advance
guard was composed of the rifles under Major Forsyth, and
the 30th and 31st and part of the 11th infantry, under Colonel Clark ; in all about 600 men. They were followed by
two corps of infantry, under Brigadier Generals Bissell and
Smith. A reserve of 800 men, under General Macomb,
brought up the rear. The roads at this time were obstructed
by fallen trees and by heavy drifts of snow, and were nearly
impassable for artillery. The guides, too, were ignorant of
the country, and led the army off from the main road into
a very narrow and crooked winter path, leading from Odletown to La Colle. On the way to La Colle, Bissell's corps
was attacked by, and after a short skirmish repulsed a party
of Canadian militia, who had been stationed as a picket on
the main road at Odletown.

The La Colle mill, against which the Americans were
now advancing, was a strong stone building. The walls had
been braced on the inside with heavy timbers, the windows
closed up, and port holes made in every direction, for the
fire of musketry. A small clearing, of from one to two
hundred yards in width on each side of the river, surrounded
the mill. The woods adjacent were of small growth but
very thick. The river, at the mill, was frozen over, but
below it was open to its mouth. The Richelieu was also
open from the mouth of the La Colle to Isle aux Noix.

The American troops did not reach the ground until between one and two o'clock in the afternoon, when a portion
of Bissell's brigade took a position to the south of the building and commenced the attack, which for the first half hour
was confined to a fire of musketry. Major McPherson then
brought up a twelve pounder, which he planted about two

hundred and fifty yards to the south of the mill. With this
gun a brisk but ineffectual fire was directed against the
rear of the building, and afterwards against the side wall.

When it was ascertained that the gun was too light to
break down the walls, orders were given to bring up an
eighteen pounder, but its carriage had broken down, three
miles back, and could not be repaired in time to be of service during the day. The cannonade upon the mill was
returned by a brisk discharge of musketry, which was kept
up during the whole attack, but did little damage, as the
American troops were posted out of range of the fire. In
the course of the afternoon an unsuccessful assault was made
upon a detachment of Americans who guarded the north
banks of the La Colle, by two companies of the 13th Regiment, sent from Isle aux Noix to reinforce the garrison in the
mill. While these companies were engaged a sortie was
made against the centre of the American line. The attack
was executed with great gallantry but did not succeed,
although the artillery were driven from the gun, which would
have been captured had not a portion of General Bissell's
brigade been sent to its rescue. A short time afterwards
another attack was made upon the gun by a grenadier company of the Canadian fencibles and a company of voltigeurs,
who had followed the movement of the troops from the
Odletown road. This attack was also unsuccessful. The two
companies, however, succeeded in gaining a block house
which stood below the mill. The loss of the Americans in
these attacks was 104 killed and wounded, while that of the
British was reported by them at ten killed and forty-six
wounded. Among the wounded on the side of the Americans were Captain McPherson and Lieutenant Larabee of
the artillery, Lieutenants Green and Parker of the infantry
and Lieutenant Kerr of the rifles. Lieutenant Parker was
struck by a random shot. He survived his wounds for several

days, and expressed a most sincere regret that he had not fallen in close action : " Hard is my lot," he exclaimed, " that I should have received this wound at such a distance from the enemy, and where I was wholly inactive." Captain McPherson, on the contrary, was wounded while fighting at the head of his men, and, at the time, was not expected to recover. As they were bearing him from the field, several officers offered their personal services to carry him to Plattsburgh. The gallant captain paused a few moments, and then, thanking them for the interest and regard they had manifested, added " I shall be sufficiently honored when you bear me to my grave." The same spirit of firmness was shown by the other officers, and by the wounded and bleeding privates. Lieut. Larabee, when some persons were pitying his misfortune, as he was passing to the rear of the field, exclaimed, " Have you never seen a man die ?" A private, on receiving similar sympathy, cried, " Never mind it, I'll give them another fight !" Another private, when struck down, cried out, " Give it to them, my boys, never flinch !"

At the commencement of the assault a few cannon shots and several rockets were fired from a sloop and from some gun-boats lying in the river below, but the fire was not continued, as it was soon ascertained that the American troops were perfectly protected by the intervening ground.[1] About sundown Wilkinson called in the detachments which had been sent to the north side of the river, and shortly afterwards retired with the whole army to Odletown. The next day he returned to Champlain. From this place General Macomb was sent to Burlington, while the main army fell

---

[1] Late in the day, Lieutenant Creswick, of the royal navy, succeeded in landing two field pieces and getting them to the block house, but they were not fired during the engagement.

back upon Chazy and Plattsburgh, to protect the military
stores at the latter place.[1]

On the 9th of May, Captain Pring, of the British navy,
ascended the Richelieu in the brig Linnet, accompanied by
five sloops and thirteen row-galleys, and the next day came
to anchor under Providence Island,[2] where he remained until
the evening of the 13th. Macdonough was at this time at
Vergennes, on Otter Creek, busily engaged in fitting out
the American fleet which lay at that place. As soon as he
was informed that the British flotilla had entered the lake,
he ordered Lieutenant Cassin, with a small party of sailors,
to reinforce Captain Thornton, who had been sent from
Burlington with a detachment of light artillery to man a
battery which had been erected at the mouth of Otter Creek.
A brigade of the Vermont militia was also ordered out, and
was advantageously posted to oppose the enemy, in case he
should attempt to land.

At day-break on the morning of the 14th, eight of the
British galleys and a bomb-sloop anchored off the mouth of
Otter Creek and commenced a warm fire upon the battery,
which was promptly returned. A brisk cannonade was
kept up by both parties for one hour and a half, when the
attack was abandoned.

After this repulse the galleys entered the Bouquet River,
and ascended that stream for the purpose of seizing some
government flour, which had been deposited in the grist-
mill at the falls. On their return, the boats were fired into

---

[1] This account of the affair at La Colle is derived from the testi-
mony of Bissel, Macomb, Clark, Totten, McPherson and others
before the court martial, on the trial of General Wilkinson, in
January, 1815, and from the official report of Adj. General Baynes
of the British army.

[2] This is one of the small islands lying near the south end of
Grand Island, opposite Valcour.

by a company of militia who had hastily collected on the south bank of the river near its mouth. This fire killed or wounded nearly all the men in the rear galley. The boat afterwards drifted into the lake, and was towed off by small boats sent to its assistance. The galleys then joined the brig and the three sloops, which, during the attack on the battery, had remained at anchor near the Four Brothers. On the 16th Captain Pring returned to Isle aux Noix. A few days afterwards Macdonough brought his fleet out of Otter Creek, and on the 29th cast anchor in Cumberland Bay, off Plattsburgh.

During the summer the British and Americans were actively engaged in strengthening their positions along the Champlain frontier. Large reinforcements joined the army at Plattsburgh, while the garrisons at Chambly, St. Johns and Isle aux Noix were increased by detachments of troops drawn from Montreal and Quebec. Major General Izard, who had succeeded to the command on the withdrawal of Wilkinson, was directed to erect a heavy battery at Rouse's Point, to guard the entrance from the Richelieu into the lake. Considering the occupation of that point hazardous, from its proximity to the enemy's posts at La Colle and Isle aux Noix, he objected to erecting works there, and instead, caused a battery of four eighteen pounders and a large redoubt to be constructed on Cumberland Head.[1]

On the 11th of June, a light brigade under command of General Smith, Forsyth's regiment of riflemen, and two companies of artillery were encamped near the mouth of Dead Creek, about two miles north of the village of Plattsburgh. These troops advanced as far as Chazy on the

---

[1] The works on Cumberland Head were commenced in opposition to the views of Colonel Totten, who considered they would not impede or materially injure a passing fleet. They proved useless and were abandoned on the first approach of the British.

17th, and on the 27th occupied the village of Champlain. Smith's brigade was 1,400 strong. At the latter date, Colonel Pierce, of the 13th regiment, was at Chazy with 800 men, and about 1,200 men occupied the works on Cumberland Head, at Dead Creek and in the village of Plattsburgh. Macdonough's fleet lay at anchor in King's Bay. The British then held La Colle with a force of 3,600 men. They also had strong garrisons at Isle aux Noix and St. Johns. Muron's regiment, 1,000 strong, was at L'Acadie, two brigades of artillery and 300 cavalry at Chambly, and 2,000 regulars at Montreal. Their fleet lay at Isle aux Tetes.

On the 24th of June, Lieutenant Colonel Forsyth, with 70 of his riflemen, penetrated into Canada as far as Odletown, where he was attacked by a detachment of two hundred British light troops. Forsyth returned to Champlain, with the loss of one killed and five wounded. A few days afterwards he was ordered again to enter Canada, for the purpose of drawing the British across the lines into an ambuscade. He advanced a few men on the main road leading to Odletown, who soon met a party of the enemy, when they retreated, closely pursued by about one hundred and fifty Canadians and Indians, under command of Captain Mahew, until they reached a point about half a mile south of the lines, where the main body of the rifles lay concealed. As the enemy approached the ambuscade, Colonel Forsyth stepped upon a log to watch their movements. He had scarcely taken this exposed position when he was shot down by an Indian, the ball passing through his breast. The rifles immediately uncovered and fired upon the enemy, who retreated in great haste, leaving seventeen of their number dead upon the field[1].

---

[1] Forsyth was the best partisan officer in the army. His men declared that they would avenge his death, and a few days after-

A few days afterwards, Captain Nelson, of the 10th infantry, crossed into Canada with a small detachment, surprised a British picket in Odletown, took some of them prisoners and put the rest to flight. Skirmishes were very frequent along the borders during the months of July and August, although seldom attended with any considerable loss to either side.

On the 31st of July, Macomb's brigade, consisting of the 6th, 13th, 15th, 16th and 29th regiments, set out in boats from Cumberland Head, for Chazy landing. The same day, Bissell's brigade, of the 5th, 14th, 30th, 31st, 33d, 34th and 45th regiments, started for Chazy by land. This movement placed three brigades, in all 4,500 strong, at and in rear of the village of Champlain. The invalids and 200 effectives of Macomb's brigade were left behind, to finish the works at Cumberland Head, and a working party of about 400 strong of Bissell's brigade was left at Plattsburgh under Colonel Fenwick, to complete three redoubts which had been commenced near that village.

In the month of August Sir George Provost repaired to the Isle aux Noix, where he had concentrated a large body of men, including several veteran regiments who had lately distinguished themselves on the banks of the Adour and the Garronne. Every thing now indicated that a battle was soon to be fought on the Champlain frontier, which would decide the fate of the campaign, and the control of the whole country bordering on the lake. It was at this moment that the government determined to remove the troops from Lake Champlain, and to abandon the large amount of military

---

wards crossed the lines and shot Captain Mahew, who commanded the Canadians and Indians at the time of Forsyth's death. Mahew was taken to the residence of Judge Moore in Champlain, where he lingered about a week and died.

stores and provisions collected at Plattsburgh, the lives and property of its citizens, and the great military key of the northern and eastern states to the protection of a few raw, worn out, sick or disabled men. This strange movement evinced a reckless indifference on the part of the government as to the result of the war in this quarter.[1]

General Izard strongly protested against the removal of the troops, and repeatedly represented to the war department the fatal results that might be expected from such a movement. As late as the 20th of August, he writes the secretary of war as follows: " I must not be responsible for the consequences of abandoning my present strong position. I will obey orders and execute them as well as I know how. Major General Brisbane commands at Odletown ; he is said to have between five and six thousand men with him. Those at Chambly are stated to be about four thousand." On the 23d he again writes that he has decided to move west, by way of Lake George and Schenectady, with 4,000 men, leaving the sick and convalescents, and about 1,200 men, to garrison Plattsburgh and Cumberland Head, under command of Brigadier General Macomb.

---

[1] It has been asserted in certain quarters, that the authorities at Washington never intended a real invasion of Canada, for fear that the reduction of Montreal and the other important points upon the St. Lawrence might ultimately lead to annexation, and to a consequent increase of political power, north of Mason and Dixon's line. While old and superannuated generals commanded on this frontier, they were allowed, *ad libitum*, to lead their armies to and fro along the outskirts of Canada, but the moment a fighting man, with the regular snap of war in him, was found to be in command, the army was broken up and its best fragments sent to aid in some distant operations, where the most triumphant success could not endanger the cities of Montreal and Quebec, which were justly considered as the keys of the British provinces.

Receiving no counter orders, Izard, on the 29th of August, left Champlain and Chazy with the 4th, 5th, 10th, 12th, 13th, 14th, 15th, 16th and 45th infantry, the light artillery armed as infantry and the dragoons, and slowly and reluctantly moved towards the west. On the 3d of September his corps reached Lake George, where they remained two days, anxiously expecting orders to return to Plattsburgh. No such orders arrived, and Izard again put his column in motion. On the 7th he reached Schenectady, from which place he urged on more rapidly.

As soon as Izard left General Macomb concentrated his whole force at Plattsburgh, where he commenced immediate preparations to resist an attack. From the returns of the 28th of August it appears that on that day he had the following troops within the limits of his command :

Detachments of the regiments and corps that marched,	77
Capt. Leonard's company of light artillery,.............	100
Capt. McGlassin's company, 15th regt.,...................	50
The 6th, 29th, 30th, 31st, 33d and 34th regiments, reported from the aggregate present on the 31st July,...	1,771
Capt. Sproul's detachment of 13th regiment,.............	200
Sick and invalids of the regiments and corps that left,	803
Aggregate,..	3,001

There were two veteran companies of artillery under Captain Alexander Brooks, which were omitted in the return. Two hundred and fifty infantry were also on board the fleet doing duty as marines. This brought the whole force to about 3,400 men, of whom over 1,400 were invalids or non-combatants.[1] With this force Macomb prepared to resist the advance of fourteen thousand veteran British soldiers.

---

[1] General Macomb, in his detailed report of the battle of Plattsburgh, says: "Except the four companies of the 6th regiment, I had not an organized battalion among those remaining; the garrison was composed of convalescents and the recruits of the new regiments —all in the greatest confusion, as well as the ordinance and stores; and the works in no state of defense."

CHAPTER XII.

General Izard abandoned the camp at Champlain on the 29th of August, and the next day Major General Brisbane advanced his division from Odletown to that place. On the 3d of September fourteen thousand British troops were collected at Champlain. This force was composed of four troops of the 19th light dragoons, 300 men; two companies royal artillery, 400 men; one brigade of rocketeers, twenty-five men; one brigade royal sappers and miners, seventy-five men; the first brigade of infantry, consisting of the first battallion of the 27th regiment, the 58th and 5th, and the 3d or buffs, in all 3,700 men, under command of Major General Robinson; the second brigade, formed by the 88th and 39th, and the third battallions of the 27th and 76th, in all 3,600 men, under Major General Powers; the third brigade, composed of the second battallion of the 8th or king's, and the 18th, 49th and 6th, 3,100 men, under Major General Brisbane. There was also a light brigade 2,800 strong, composed of Muron's Swiss regiment, the Canadian chasseurs, the voltiguers and the frontier light infantry. The whole was under Sir George Provost, governor general of Canada; Lieutenant General De Rottenburgh being second in command.

On the 4th the main body reached Chazy village, and the next night encamped near Sampson's, about eight miles from the village of Plattsburgh. At the same time Captain Pring, with a number of gun-boats, moved up the lake as far as Isle la Motte, and erected a battery of three long 18 pounders on the west side of that island, to cover the landing of the supplies for the troops.

Brigadier General Macomb was now at Plattsburgh actively engaged in preparations to resist the expected attack. On the 3d of September he issued a general order detailing his plan of defense. "The troops (says this order) will line the parapet in two ranks, leaving intervals for the artillery. sufficient number of infantry to line all the faces (in single A reserve of one fifth of the whole force in infantry will be detailed and paraded, fronting the several angles, which it will be their particular duty to sustain. To each bastion are to be assigned, by the several commanders of forts, a rank) of each tier. Should the enemy gain the ditch, the front rank of the part assailed will mount the parapet and repel him with its fire and bayonet. If the men of this rank are determined, no human force can dispossess them of that position."

The American works were built upon an elevated plain, lying between the banks of the river Saranac and Lake Champlain. The river descends from the west until it approaches within about one hundred and sixty rods of the lake, and then turns towards the north and runs about one mile in a northeasterly direction to the lake. The land, between the river and lake, at this point, is nearly in the shape of a right angled triangle, the perpendicular being formed by the lake shore. About eighty rods above the mouth of the river, and near the centre of the village, is the lower bridge, and about one mile higher up, following the course of the stream, was another bridge, on the road leading south to Salmon River, called the upper bridge. One mile and a half above the upper bridge is a ford of the

river.[1] The stream can also be forded at the bridges, and
at a point about midway between them. The south bank
of the river, above the village, is from fifty to sixty feet
high, and steep. About sixty rods above the lower
bridge is a deep ravine, running back from the river and
extending nearly to the lake shore. The principal work,
called Fort Moreau, stood opposite the bend of the river,
and about half way between it and the lake. It was three
fourths of a mile south of the lower bridge. A redoubt,
called Fort Brown, stood on the bank of the river, directly
opposite the bend, and about fifty rods west of Fort Moreau.
There was another redoubt to the east of Fort Moreau, near
the bank of the lake, called Fort Scott. On the point, near
the mouth of the river, was a block house and battery. Another block house stood on the south side of the ravine, about
half way between the river and the lake. The defense of
Fort Moreau was entrusted to Colonel Melancton Smith,
who had for its garrison the 29th and 6th regiments. Lieutenant Colonel Storrs was stationed in Fort Brown, with
detachments of the 30th and 31st, and Major Vinson in
Fort Scott, with the 33d and 34th. The block house near the
ravine, was entrusted to Captain Smith of the rifles, and
had for its defense a part of his company and of the convalescents of one of the absent regiments. The block house
on the point was garrisoned by a detachment of artillery,
under Lieutenant Fowler. The light artillery were ordered
to take such position as would best annoy the enemy. When
not employed they were to take post in the ravine with the
light troops.

As soon as the British had advanced to Chazy village,
Captain Sproul was ordered by General Macomb, with two
hundred men of the 13th, and two field pieces, to take

---

[1] This ford is near the spot where General Pike encamped in
1812. The buildings were burned by Colonel Murray in 1813.

28

PLATTSBURGH AND VICINITY, Sept., 1814.

position near the Dead Creek bridge, and to abattis the road beyond, while Lieutenant Colonel Appling was stationed in advance with one hundred and ten riflemen, and a troop of New York state cavalry, under Captain Safford and Lieutenant M. M. Standish, to watch the movements of the enemy. Macomb also made arrangements with Major General Mooers for calling out the New York militia, and addressed a letter to Governor Chittenden, of Vermont, requesting aid from that state. On the 4th seven hundred of the Clinton and Essex militia had collected at Plattsburgh. They were advanced the next day about five miles on the north road, and lay during the night in the vicinity of the present stone church in Beekmantown. The militia were directed to watch the enemy, skirmish with him as he advanced, break up the bridges and obstruct the road with fallen trees.

On the 5th, as we have already stated, the British occupied a position near Sampson's, on the lake road. The troops were there divided into two columns, and moved towards the village of Plattsburgh on the morning of the 6th, before day-light, the right column crossing over to the Beekmantown road and the left following the lake road leading to the Dead Creek bridge. The right column was composed of Major General Powers's brigade, supported by four companies of light infantry and a demi-brigade under Major General Robinson. The left was led by Major General Brisbane's brigade. Information of this contemplated movement having reached General Macomb on the evening of the 5th, he ordered Major Wool, with a detachment of two hundred and fifty men, to advance on the Beekmantown road to the support of the militia. Captain Leonard, of the light artillery, was also directed to be on the ground before day-light, with two field pieces.

The right column of the British advanced more rapidly than the left, and at an early hour met Major Wool's detachment and the militia, who had taken a position near the residence of Ira Howe, in Beekmantown. Wool's party opened a brisk fire of musketry upon the head of the British column as it approached, severely wounding Lieutenant West of the the 3d Buffs, and about twenty privates. Near this place, Goodspeed and Jay, two men of Captain Atwood's company of militia, were wounded and taken prisoners. Wool, with his men, now fell back as far as Culver's Hill, four and a half miles from the village, where he awaited the approach of the British. He was supported by a few of the militia, but the greater portion retreated precipitately after the first fire near Howe's. The resistance at Culver's Hill was intrepid but momentary, for the British troops pressed firmly forward, occupying the whole road, and only returning the fire by their flanks and leading platoons; the latter were once driven to the base of the hill, after having reached its summit. At this point, Lieutenant Colonel Willington, of the 3d Buffs, fell as he was ascending the hill at the head of his regiment. Ensign Chapman, of the same regiment, was also killed there, and Captain Westropp, of the 58th, severely wounded. Several of the Americans were killed, including Patridge, of the Essex militia.

Learning that a large body of the British were advancing on a parallel road, leading from Beekmantown Corners, to gain his rear, Wool fell back as far as Halsey's Corners, about one and a half miles from the village bridge. He was there joined, about eight o'clock in the morning, by Captain Leonard with two pieces of light artillery. Leonard placed his guns in battery at an angle in the road, masked by Wool's infantry and a small body of militia, and as the British approached opened a most galling fire upon the head of the column, the balls cutting a narrow and bloody lane through the moving mass. Three times were the guns discharged, but even this terrible fire did not check the progress of the column, for the men, throwing aside their knapsacks, pressed forward, the bugles sounding the charge, and forced Leonard hastily to withdraw towards the village. At this place a number of the British were killed or wounded. Among the latter was Lieutenant Kingsbury, of the 3d Buffs, who was taken into the adjoining farm house of Isaac C. Platt Esq., where he soon afterwards died.

Finding that the enemy's right column was steadily approaching the village, General Macomb ordered in the detachments at Dead Creek, at the same time directing Lieutenant Colonel Appling to fall on the British flank. The rapid advance of the column on the Beekmantown road had reversed Appling's position, and he had barely time to save his retreat, coming in a few rods ahead as the British debouched from the woods a little north of the village. There he poured in a destructive fire from his riflemen at rest, and continued to annoy the enemy until he formed a junction with Wool, who was slowly retiring towards the lower bridge. The field pieces were taken across the bridge and formed a battery for its protection, and to cover the retreat of Wool's, Appling's and Sproul's men. These detachments retired alternately, keeping up a brisk fire until they got under cover of the works.

The left column of the British army did not arrive near the village until after Sproul's and Appling's detachments had been withdrawn, their march having been retarded by the obstructions placed in the road, and by the removal of the bridge at Dead Creek. As this column passed along the beach of the lake it was much annoyed by a brisk fire from several galleys, which Macdonough had ordered to the head of the bay. After this fire had continued for about two hours the wind began to blow so heavy from the south as to endanger the safety of the galleys. Mr. Duncan, a midshipman of the Saratoga, was therefore sent in a gig to order them to return. As that officer approached he received a severe wound from the enemy's fire, which for a few minutes was concentrated upon his boat.[1] About this time one of the galleys drifted under the guns of the British and sustained some loss, but was eventually brought off.

As soon as the American troops had crossed the river, the planks were removed from the lower bridge, and were piled up at its east end to form a breast-work for the infantry. A similar breast-work was made by the militia, at the upper bridge. The British light troops made several attempts in the course of the day, to cross at the village, but were repulsed by the guards at the bridge, and by the sharp fire of a company of volunteers who had taken possession of a stone grist mill near by.[1] An attempt was also made to cross at the upper bridge, which was gallantly resisted by the militia. The loss this day, on both sides, was greater than the whole loss during the rest of the siege, forty-five of the Americans, and more than two hundred British having been killed or wounded.[2]

---

[1] On the 26th of May, 1826, congress passed a resolution of thanks to Midshipman Silas Duncan for his gallant conduct on this occasion.

[1] This company was called Aiken's volunteers and was composed of the following young men, none of whom were old enough to be liable to perform military duty; Martin J. Aiken, Azariah C. Flagg, Ira A. Wood, Gustavus A. Bird, James Trowbridge, Hazen Mooers, Henry K. Averill, St. John B. L. Skinner, Frederick P. Allen, Hiram Walworth, Ethan Everest, Amos Soper, James Patten, Bartemus Brooks, Smith Bateman, Melancton W. Travis and Flavius Williams. They had been out on the Beckmantown road in the morning, where they behaved with great gallantry. In May, 1826, congress authorized the president to cause to be delivered to each, "One rifle promised to them by General Macomb, while commanding the Champlain department, for their gallantry and patriotic services as a volunteer corps during the siege of Plattsburgh in September, 1814."

[2] General Macomb, in his general order of the 7th, estimates the British loss at from two to three hundred. The Burlington *Sentinel* of the 9th states it to have about three hundred.

The configuration of the land on the north side of the river differs somewhat from that on the south side. The bank at the mouth of the river is abrupt and about thirty feet high. This bank, with a depression above the lower bridge, opposite the mill pond, follows the margin of the stream, until within about eighty rods of Fort Brown, when the hill recedes from the river and is less abrupt. The flat and hill opposite Fort Brown were covered with small trees and bushes. About one mile back from the river is an elevated ridge running to the north. At Allen's farm house, which stood upon this ridge at the distance of about one and one fourth miles from the American forts, Sir George Provost established his head quarters. The army were encamped upon the ridge, and on the high ground north of the village.

From the 7th to the 10th Provost was busily engaged in bringing up his battering trains and supplies, and in preparing his approaches. He erected a battery on the bank of the lake north of the mouth of the river; and another near the edge of the steep bank above the mill pond; another near the burial ground, and one, supplied with rocket works, on the hill opposite Fort Brown. Besides these, there were three smaller batteries erected at other points, within range of the American forts.

While Provost was thus engaged the American troops were diligently at work, day and night, in strengthening their defenses. The barracks and hospitals in the vicinity of the forts were burned, and the sick removed to Crab Island, about two miles distant, where they were protected from the weather by tents. A small battery was erected on that island, mounting two six pounders, which was manned by convalescents. The Americans also, during this time, fired hot shot into and burned some fifteen or sixteen build-

ings, on the north side of the river, which had afforded protection to the British light troops.[1]

From the 7th to the 10th the pickets and militia were
engaged in frequent skirmishes with the enemy at the two
bridges, and at the different fords along the river. On the
morning of the 7th, a party of British, under Captain Noa-
die, attempted to cross the river at a ford about five miles
west of the village. They were, however, met by a company
of Colonel Miller's regiment of militia, under command of
Captain Vaughan, and were repulsed with a loss of two
killed and several wounded. The same day, Lieutenant
Runk, of the 6th, was mortally wounded, as he was passing
in the street, near the present dwelling of A. C. Moore Esq.

On the night of the 9th, while the British were engaged in
erecting their rocket battery near Fort Brown, Captain Mc-
Glassin, of the 15th infantry, obtained permission from General Macomb to take a party of fifty men and attack a
detachment of British troops at work upon the battery. The
night was dark and stormy and favored such an enterprise.
Ordering his men to take the flints from their muskets, Mc-
Glassin crossed the river, and passing through a small clump
of dwarf oaks, reached, unobserved, the foot of the hill upon
which the enemy were at work. There he divided his
force into two parties, one of which was sent, by a circuit-
ous route, to the rear of the battery. As soon as this party
had reached its position, McGlassin, in a loud voice, ordered
his men to charge " on the front and rear, " when they

---

[1] The Burlington *Sentinel* says that up to the evening of the 8th
the following buildings had been burned : Jonathan Griffin's house
and store ; Roswell Wait's house and store ; Mr. Savage's house ;
B. Buck's house ; Mr. Powers's store ; Widow Beaumont's house
and store ; Charles Backus's house and store ; Joseph Thomas's two
stores, and Mr. Goldsmith's house. The court house and jail were
also burned.

rushed forward with all the noise it was possible for them to make, and entered the work at both sides on the run. The working party were taken by surprise, and supposing themselves attacked by overwhelming numbers, retreated precipitately towards the main camp. McGlassin spiked the guns and led his party back to the American fort without losing a man. The whole affair was boldly conceived and most gallantly executed. It was long before the British officers would believe that fifty men could make so much noise, or so badly frighten over three hundred of their veteran troops.

When the British army reached Plattsburgh their gun-boats had advanced as far as the Isle la Motte, where they remained under command of Captain Pring. On the 8th Captain Downie reached that place with the rest of the fleet, and on the morning of the 11th the whole weighed anchor and stood south to attack the Americans, who lay in the bay off Plattsburgh.

As the British vessels rounded Cumberland Head, about eight o'clock in the morning, they found Macdonough at anchor a little south of the mouth of the Saranac River, and abreast, but out of gun shot of the forts. His vessels lay in a line running north from Crab Island, and nearly parallel with the west shore. The brig Eagle, Captain Henly, lay at the head of the line, inside the point of the Head. This vessel mounted twenty guns and had on board one hundred and fifty men. Next to her and on the south lay Macdonough's flag ship, the Saratoga, mounting twenty-six guns, with two hundred and twelve men. Next south was the schooner Ticonderoga, of seventeen guns, Lieutenant Cassin, with one hundred and ten men, and next to her, and at the southern extremity of the line, lay the sloop Preble, Lieutenant Charles Budd. This vessel carried seven guns and was manned by thirty men. She lay so near the shoal extending

29

north-east from Crab Island, as to prevent the enemy from
turning that end of the line. To the rear of the line were
ten gun-boats, six of which mounted one long twenty-four
pounder and one eighteen pound columbiad each ; the other
four carried one twelve pounder. The gun-boats had, on
an average, thirty-five men each. Two of the gun-boats lay
a little north and in rear of the Eagle, to sustain the head
of the line ; the others were placed opposite the intervals
between the different vessels, and about forty rods to their
rear. The gun-boats were kept in position by their sweeps.

The British fleet was composed of the frigate Confiance,
carrying thirty-seven guns,[1] with over three hundred men,
commanded by Captain Downie ; the brig Linnet, Captain
Pring, of sixteen guns and one hundred and twenty men ;
the sloop Chub, Lieutenant McGhee, and the sloop Finch,
Lieutenant Hicks, each carrying eleven guns and about forty-
five men. To these vessels were added twelve gun-boats of
about forty-five men each. Eight of them carried two guns,
and four, one gun each. Thus the force of the Americans
consisted of one ship, one brig, one schooner, one sloop and
ten gun-boats, manned by eight hundred and eighty-two men,
and carrying in all eighty-six guns. The British had one
frigate, one brig, two sloops and twelve gun-boats, manned
by over one thousand men, and carrying in all ninety-five guns.
The metal of the vessels on both sides was unusually heavy.
The Saratoga mounted eight long twenty-fours, six forty-
twos, and twelve thirty-twos, while the Confiance had the
gun-deck of a heavy frigate, with thirty long twenty-fours
upon it. She also had a spacious top gallant forecastle, and
a poop that came no further forward than the mizen mast.
On the first were a long twenty-four on a circle, and four heavy

---

[1] There were thirty-nine guns on board the Confiance, but two
of them were not mounted.— *Cooper.*

carronades; two heavy carronades were mounted on the poop.[1]

When the British fleet appeared in sight the Finch led and kept in a course toward Crab Island, while the other vessels hove to opposite the point of Cumberland Head, to allow the gun-boats to come up, and to receive final instructions as to the plan of attack. The vessels then filled and headed in towards the American fleet, passing inside of the point of Cumberland Head; the Chub laying her course a little to windward of the Eagle, in order to support the Linnet, which stood directly towards that vessel. Captain Downie had determined to lay the Confiance athwart the Saratoga, but the wind baffling, he was obliged to anchor at about two cables length from that ship.[2] The Finch, which had run about half way to Crab Island, tacked and took her station, with the gun-boats, opposite the Ticonderoga and Preble.

---

[1] Cooper's *Naval History.* Mr. Alison (*History of England,* vol. IV) says:

"The relative strength of the squadron on this, as in every other naval action during the war where the British were defeated, was decidedly in favor of the Americans"— a statement unwarranted by the facts, and unnecessary to sustain the high reputation of the British navy. The following are the number and size of the guns used on both fleets.

AMERICAN.	BRITISH.
14 long 24 pounders.	31 long 24 pounders.
6 42 pound carronades.	7 18 "
29 32 " "	16 12 "
12 long 18 pounders.	5 6 "
12 " 12 "	12 32 pound carronades.
7 " 9 "	6 24 " "
6 18 pound Columbiads.	17 18 " "
—	1 18 " Columbiad.
86 guns.	—
	95 guns.

[2] Captain Pring's account of the battle, Sept. 12th, 1814.

As the British vessels approached they received the fire
of the American fleet; the brig Eagle firing first, and
being soon followed by the Saratoga and the sloop and
schooner.[1] The Linnet poured her broadside into the
Saratoga as she passed that ship to take her position
opposite the Eagle. Captain Downie brought his vessel
into action in the most gallant manner, and did not fire
a gun until he was perfectly secured, although his vessel suffered severely from the fire of the Americans. As soon,
however, as the Confiance had been brought into position she
discharged all her larboard guns at nearly the same instant.
The effect of this broadside, thrown from long twenty-four
pounders, double shotted, in smooth water, was terrible.
The Saratoga trembled to her very keel; about forty of
her crew were disabled, including her first lieutenant,
Mr. Gamble, who was killed while sighting the bow gun.

Soon after the commencement of the engagement, the
Chub, while manœuvering near the head of the American
line, received a broadside from the Eagle which so crippled
her that she drifted down between the opposing vessels and
struck. She was taken possession of by Mr. Charles Platt,
one of the Saratoga's midshipmen, and was towed in shore
and anchored. The Chub had suffered severely, nearly
half of her men having been killed or wounded. About

---

[1] The first gun fired on board the Saratoga was a long twenty-
four, which Macdonough himself sighted. The shot is said to
have struck the Confiance near the outer hawse hole, and to have
passed the length of her deck, killing and wounding several men,
and carrying away the wheel. In clearing the decks of the
Saratoga, some hen coops were thrown overboard and the poultry
permitted to run at large. Startled by the report of the opening
gun of the Eagle, a young cock flew upon a gun slide, clapped
his wings and crowed. The men gave three cheers and considered
the little incidence as a happy omen. — Cooper's *Naval History*, and
Niles's Weekly Register.

an hour later the Finch was driven from her position by the Ticonderoga, and being badly injured, drifted upon the shoal near Crab Island, where she grounded. After being fired into from the small battery on the island, she struck and was taken possession of by the invalids who manned the battery.[1]

After the loss of the Finch the British gun-boats made several efforts to close, and succeeded in compelling the sloop Preble to cut her cables and to anchor in shore of the line, where she was of no more service during the engagement. The gun-boats, emboldened by this success, now directed their efforts towards the Ticonderoga, against which they made several very gallant assaults, bringing the boats, upon two or three occasions, within a few feet of the schooner's side. They were, however, as often beaten back, and the schooner, during the remainder of the day, completely covered that extremity of the line.

While these changes were taking place at the lower end of the line a change was also made at the other extremity. The Eagle, having lost her springs and finding herself

---

[1] Mr. Alison (*History of England*, vol. IV), referring to this event, says ; " The Finch, a British *brig*, grounded out of shot and *did not engage*; " and again, " The Finch struck on a reef of rocks and could not get into action." Had Mr. Alison examined Captain Pring's official account of the engagement he would have found in it the following statement: "Lieutenant Hicks, of the Finch, had the mortification to strike on a reef of rocks, to the eastward of Crab Island, about the middle of the engagement, which prevented his rendering that assistance to the squadron that might, from an officer of such ability, have been expected." It is very convenient for the English historian to convert a small sloop of eleven guns and forty men into a *brig*, and to keep that large vessel out of the action altogether ; but as I have before said such statements are unnecessary to preserve the well earned reputation of the British navy for bravery or gallantry in action.

exposed to the fire of both the Linnet and Confiance, dropped down and anchored between the Saratoga and Ticonderoga, and a little in shore of both. From this position she opened afresh on the Confiance and the British gun-boats, with her larboard guns. This change relieved the brig, but left the Saratoga exposed to the whole fire of the Linnet, which sprung her broadsides in such a manner as to rake the ship on her bows.

The fire from the Saratoga and Confiance now began materially to lessen, as gun after gun on both vessels became disabled, until at last the Saratoga had not a single available gun, and the Confiance was but little better off. It therefore became necessary that both vessels should wind, to continue the action with any success. This the Saratoga did after considerable delay, but the Confiance was less fortunate, as the only effect of her efforts was to force the vessel ahead. As soon as the Saratoga came around she poured a fresh broadside from her larboard guns into the Confiance, which stood the fire for a few minutes and then struck. The ship then brought her guns to bear on the Linnet, which surrendered in about fifteen minutes afterwards. At this time the British gun-boats lay half a mile in the rear, where they had been driven by the sharp fire of the Ticonderoga and Eagle. These boats lowered their colors as soon as they found the larger vessels had submitted, but not being pursued, for the American gun-boats were sent to aid the Confiance and Linnet which were reported to be in a sinking condition, they escaped together with a store sloop which lay near the point of Cumberland Head during the battle.

The engagement continued for two hours and a half, and was the most severely fought naval battle of the war. The Saratoga had twenty-eight men killed and twenty-nine wounded; the Eagle thirteen killed and twenty wounded; the Ticonderoga six killed and six wounded, and the Preble

MACDONOUGH'S VICTORY ON LAKE CHAMPLAIN,

September 11th, 1814.

—

Position of the Vessels after the Battle.

two killed. The loss on the gun-boats was three killed and three wounded. Total killed and wounded, one hundred and ten, being equal to every eighth man in the fleet. Besides, the Saratoga had been hulled fifty-five times and was twice on fire; the Eagle was hulled thirty-nine times. The carnage and destruction had been as great on the other side. The Confiance had forty-one men killed and eighty-three wounded; the Linnet reported her casualties at ten killed and fourteen wounded, but the killed and wounded probably exceeded fifty; the Chub was reported at six killed and ten wounded, and the Finch at two wounded. No account is given of the loss on the gun-boats, but, from their close and severe contest with the Ticonderoga, it must have been large. The total of killed and wounded on the British side was equal to at least one fifth of the whole number of men in their fleet. The Confiance had been hulled one hundred and five times. So severe had been the contest, that at the close of the action there was not a mast in either fleet fit for use.[1]

Among those killed on the side of the British were Captain Downie, who fell soon after the action commenced, Captain Alexander Anderson, of the marines, Midshipman William Gunn, of the Confiance, and Lieutenant William Paul and Boatswain Charles Jackson, of the Linnet. Among the wounded were Midshipman Lee, of the Confiance, Midshipman John Sinclair, of the Linnet, and Lieutenant James McGhee, of the Chub. The American officers killed were Peter Gamble, 1st Lieutenant of the Saratoga, John Stans-

---

[1] "I could only look at the enemy's galleys going off, in a shattered condition ; for there was not a mast in either squadron that could stand to make sail on; the lower rigging being nearly all shot away, hung down as though it had been just placed over the mast heads." — *Macdonough's Report of the battle.* "Our masts, yards and sails were so shattered, that one looked like so many bunches of matches, and the other like a bundle of rags."—*Letter of Midshipman Lee, of the Confiance.*

bury, 1st Lieutenant of the Ticonderoga, Midshipman James
M. Baldwin and Sailing Master Rogers Carter. Referring
to the death of three of these officers, Mr. Cooper, in his
History of the Navy, says: — "Lieutenant Gamble was on
his knees, sighting the bow-gun, when a shot entered the
port, split the quoin, drove a portion of it against his breast
and laid him dead on the quarter deck without breaking his
skin. Fifteen minutes later one of the American shots struck
the muzzle of a twenty-four on the Confiance, dismounted it,
sending it bodily inboard against the groin of Captain Downie, killing him also without breaking the skin. Lieutenant
Stansbury suddenly disappeared from the bulwarks forward,
while superintending some duty with the springs of the Ticonderoga. Two days after the action his body rose to the
surface of the water, and it was found that it had been cut
in two by a round shot."

It is said that scarcely an individual escaped on board of
either the Confiance or Saratoga without some injury.
Macdonough was twice knocked down; once by the spanker-
boom, which was cut in two by a shot and fell upon his
back, as he was bending his body to sight a gun; and again
by the head of a gunner, which was driven against him, and
knocked him into the scuppers. Mr. Brum, the sailing master of the Saratoga, had his clothes torn off by a splinter,
while winding the ship. Mr. Vallette, acting Lieutenant,
had a shot-box, on which he was standing, knocked from
under his feet, and he too was once knocked down by the
head of a seaman. It appears to have been agreed on both
sides to call no man wounded who could keep out of the
hospital.[1] Midshipman Lee, of the Confiance, who was
wounded in the action, thus describes the condition of that
vessel. "The havoc on both sides is dreadful. I don't think

---

[1] Cooper's *Naval History.*

there are more than five of our men, out of three hundred, but what are killed or wounded. Never was a shower of hail so thick, as the shot whistling about our ears. Were you to see my jacket, waist-coat and trowsers, you would be astonished how I escaped as I did, for they are literally torn all to rags with shot and splinters; the upper part of my hat was also shot away. There is one of our marines who was in the Trafalgar action with Lord Nelson, who says it was a mere *flea-bite* in comparison with this."[1]

As soon as the British fleet were observed approaching Cumberland Head, on the morning of the 11th, Sir George Provost ordered General Power's brigade, and a part of General Robinson's brigade, consisting of four companies of light infantry, and the 3d battalions of the 27th and 76th, to force the fords of the Saranac, and to assault the American works. The advance was made, and the batteries were opened, the moment the action on the lake commenced.

The British attempted to cross the river at three points; at the village bridge, where they were repulsed by the artillery and guards under Captains Brooks, Richards and Smith; at the upper bridge, where they were foiled by the pickets and riflemen, under Captain Grovenor and Lieutenants Hamilton and Smith, supported by a detachment of militia; and at the ford near Pike's cantonment, where they were resisted by the New York militia, under Major General Mooers and Brigadier General Wright. At this latter point several companies succeeded in crossing, dri-

---

[1] Letter to his brother, published in *Niles's Register*, vol. VIII. The result of the engagement depended, from the first, upon the Saratoga and Confiance. When Macdonough anchored his vessel he not only attached springs to the cables, but also laid a kedge broad off on each bow of the Saratoga, and brought the hawsers in upon the two quarters. To this timely precaution he was indebted for the victory, for without the larboard hawser he could not have brought his fresh broadside into action.

ving the militia before them towards Salmon River. The British advanced, firing by platoons, but with such carelessness of aim as to do but little injury.[1] At Salmon River the militia were joined by a large detachment of the Vermont volunteers, and were soon afterwards reinforced by Lieutenant Sumpter, with a party of artillery and a field-piece. Here they rallied and were drawn up to meet the attack of the British troops, who were rapidly approaching. Just at this moment an officer[2] rode up to the ranks, proclaiming the welcome intelligence that the British fleet had surrendered. With three hearty cheers the militia immediately pressed forward against the enemy, who, having been at the same moment recalled, were now rapidly retiring toward the ford. In their retreat a company of the 76th lost their way among the thick pines, where they were surrounded and attacked by several companies of militia and Vermont volunteers. Three Lieutenants and twenty-seven men were made prisoners, and Captain Purchase and the rest of the company killed.[3] The rest of the British detachment regained the north bank of the Sarauac without much loss.[4]

---

[1] I have conversed with several who boast of their *activity* during this retreat, and who felt a personal interest in the subject at the time, and they all state that the balls, at each volley, struck the pine trees at least fifteen feet from the ground.

[2] Chancellor Walworth, then aid-de-camp to Major General Mooers.

[3] It is said Captain Purchase was shot down while waving a handkerchief over his head as a notice that he had surrendered.

[4] Sir George Provost, in his account of the battle, says: "Scarcely had his majesty's troops forced a passage across the Saranac *and ascended the heights on which stand the American works*," &c. — This would imply that the British had gained ground near the forts, but such was not the case. They crossed nearly two miles above the forts, and followed the militia *from*, instead of *towards* the American works.

Although no further attempt was made to cross the river, the British batteries continued their fire upon the American works until sun-down. This fire was returned by the guns of Fort Brown, which were managed during the day with great skill, by Captain Alexander Brooks and the corps of veteran artillery under his command.

Sir George Provost had now under his command over thirteen thousand troops, more than half of whom had served with distinction under Wellington, while the American force did not exceed fifteen hundred regulars fit for duty, two thousand five hundred Vermont volunteers, under Major General Strong, six hundred of whom had just arrived, and General Wright's brigade of Clinton and Essex militia, seven hundred strong, under command of Major General Mooers. With his superior force Provost could have forced the passage of the Saranac, and have crushed Macomb by the mere weight of numbers. But the victory would have been attended with great sacrifice of life, and would have led to no permanent advantage to the British. Macdonough was in command of the lake; reinforcements of regulars were hastening to the support of Macomb; the militia were rising *en masse* in every quarter, and within two weeks Provost would have been surrounded, his supplies from Canada cut off, and an only alternative left to force his way back with the loss of half his army, or to have surrendered. In a dispatch to Earl Bathurst, after referring to the loss of the fleet, he says: "This unlooked for event depriving me of the coöperation of the fleet, without which the further prosecution of the service was become impracticable, I did not hesitate to arrest the course of the troops advancing to the attack, because the most complete success would have been unavailing; and the possession of the enemy's works offered no advantage to compensate for the loss we must have sustained in acquiring possession of them.

This was a just and merited compliment to the skill and bravery of the American regulars and militia. The former were few in number, but resolute and unflinching. Among the latter the greatest enthusiasm now prevailed. They had become accustomed to the "smell of powder," and animated by the recollection of Macdonough's victory, were ready to oppose any force that might attempt the passage of the Saranac. It is due to the patriotism of the citizens of Vermont to mention the fact, that as soon as Governor Chittenden received information from General Macomb of the invasion by the enemy, he issued a spirited address, calling on the Vermont militia to rally to the aid of their countrymen on the opposite side of the lake. This address was most nobly responded to, for when the requisition of the president for a reinforcement of two thousand militia reached the governor, he replied that the order had not only been anticipated, but far exceeded, by the voluntary enrollment of his fellow citizens. The same enthusiasm pervaded the militia on the New York side. When Major General Mooers's orders were received for the militia of Warren and Washington counties to assemble and march to the frontier, there appeared under arms two hundred and fifty men *more* than had ever mustered at an inspection or review.

Acting upon the considerations stated in his dispatch to Earl Bathurst, Sir George Provost prepared for an instant and hasty retreat. As soon as the sun went down he dismantled his batteries, and, at 9 o'clock at night, sent off his heavy baggage and artillery, which were quickly followed by the main army; the rear guard, consisting of a light brigade, started a little before day-break, leaving behind them vast quantities of provisions, tents, camp equipage, ammunition, &c. The sick and wounded were also left behind, consigned to the generosity and humane care of General Macomb. So silent and rapid was the retreat, that the main army had passed through Beckmantown before its absence was known in the American camp. The light troops, volunteers and militia were immediately sent in pursuit. They followed the retiring column as far as Chazy, and took a few prisoners. The roads were muddy, and very heavy at the time, which not only prevented further pursuit, but delayed Provost's retreat. The last of the British army did not leave Champlain until the 24th.

General Macomb, in his returns, states the number of killed, wounded and missing of the regular force under his command, during the skirmishes and bombardment, at one hundred and twenty-three. The only commissioned officer killed was Lieutenant George W. Runk, of the 6th regiment, who was severely wounded on the 7th and died the next day. The loss among the volunteers and militia was small. That of the British has never been correctly ascertained. Their accounts fix the casualties of the expedition at under two hundred killed and wounded, and four hundred lost by desertion. This, however, is far below the true number. At the time, the American officers believed the total loss of the British, from the time they first crossed the lines until they again entered Canada, in killed, wounded and prisoners, and by desertion, was over two thousand men. Seventy-five prisoners were taken.[1]

---

[1] The following list of British officers killed or wounded during the invasion, was published in the *London Gazette* of the 19th and 20th November, 1814.

Killed. — Captain (Brevet Lieut. Col.) James Willington and Ensign John Chapman, of the 3d Buffs. Captain John Purchase, 76th regiment, foot.

Wounded. — Captain T. Crosse, A. D. C. (slightly); Lieut. R. Kingsbury, severely (since dead); Lieut. John West (severely); Lieutenants Benson and Holmes (slightly); all of the 3d Buffs. Captain L. Westropp (severely,); Lieut. C. Brohier and Adjutant Lewis (slightly); of the 58th regiment, foot.

On the 12th the Vermont volunteers returned home, and on the 13th the New York militia were disbanded by General Macomb, and orders issued countermanding the march of thousands who were flocking to the frontier.

On the morning of the 13th of September the remains of the lamented GAMBLE, STANSBURY, BALDWIN, CARTER and BARRON were placed in separate boats, which, manned by crews from their respective vessels, proceeded to the Confinance, where they were joined by the British officers, with the bodies of DOWNIE, ANDERSON, PAUL, GUNN and JACKSON. At the shore of the lake the procession was joined by a large concourse of the military and citizens of Plattsburgh, who accompanied the bodies to the village burial ground. Near the centre of the grave-yard, beneath the shade of two pines, now rest the ashes of those gallant officers. The sailors and marines who fell in the engagement were buried on Crab Island, side by side in one common grave.

With the battle of Plattsburgh closed all active operations upon the Champlain frontier. For several months, however, the inhabitants were kept in a state of alarm, as it was rumored that the British authorities contemplated another campaign. Major General Mooers, of New York, and Major General Strong, of Vermont, ordered their respective divisions of militia to hold themselves in readiness for active service. General Macomb remained at Plattsburgh with a small force, and caused two redoubts to be thrown up a short distance to the south of Fort Moreau, which he named Fort Tompkins and Fort Gaines.

The treaty of Ghent was signed on the 24th of December, 1814, and, on the 17th of February following, was ratified by the United States senate. With the publication of this treaty all fears of further hostilies ceased.

APPENDIX.

AN ACCOUNT of the Celebration of the Anniversary of the Battle of Plattsburgh, by the Citizens of Plattsburgh and the Clinton County Military Association, September 11th, 1843.

At a meeting of the Clinton county Military association, held on the 21st of August, 1843, it was, on motion of Major A. A. Prescott,

Resolved, That this association do celebrate, in some appropriate manner, the anniversary of the Battle of Plattsburgh on the eleventh of September next.

Resolved, That a committee of three be appointed to confer with the trustees of the village, and make arrangements for the celebration.

Maj. Gen. Skinner, Brig. Gen. Halsey and Col. Moore were appointed said committee.

The following named gentlemen were duly appointed a committee on the part of the citizens to confer with the committee of the Military association in making the necessary arrangements for the proper celebration of the day:

William F. Haile, Moss K. Platt, D. B. McNeil, C. S. Mooers, R. A. Gilman, G. M. Beckwith, G. W. Palmer, S. Couch, Benj. Ketchum, R. A. Weed, J. Bailey, Peter S. Palmer, T. Deforris, William H. Morgan, J. W. Tuttle.

31

At a meeting of the joint committee of arrangements, Col. D. B. McNeil (who was acting assistant adjutant general of the militia forces at Plattsburgh, in Sept., 1814) was designated to act as president of the day, and the following resolutions were adopted :

Resolved, That the citizens of Plattsburgh, in connection with such other persons as may unite with them, will, on the 11th of September, instantly proceed to the erection of plain marble monuments to mark the several spots where rest the mortal remains of the American and British officers who fell at the memorable battle of Plattsburgh.

Resolved, That R. A. Gilman, George Moore and Roby G. Stone be a committee to procure the monuments and make the necessary arrangements to carry out the foregoing resolution.

Resolved, That Brig. Gen. Wool, and Lt. Col. B. Riley, of the U. S. Army, be requested to unite with the citizens and military of this place, in the proposed celebration, and the erection of the monuments above mentioned.

Resolved, That Gen. Skinner, Gen. Halsey, and Col. R. G. Stone be the committee of invitation.

Resolutions were also passed inviting the United States Officers and troops stationed at this post, the surviving officers and soldiers of the regular army, the Clinton and Essex militia, and the Vermont volunteers who participated in the events of that time, to unite with us in the proposed celebration.

In accordance with the above arrangements, the anniversary of the battle of Plattsburgh was celebrated in an appropriate manner by the Clinton county Military association and the citizens of Plattsburgh and its vicinity generally, on Monday last. General Wool and suite, and several other gentlemen who were in the battle of the 11th, were present by special invitation.

The procession was formed at Fouquet's Hotel at 10 o'clock, under the direction of Gen. C. Halsey, chief marshal, assisted by Messrs. C. S. Mooers, G. W. Palmer and R. G. Stone, escorted by the United States troops at this post, under the command of Capt. C. A. Waite, and moved to the park, in front of the court house, where an able and patriotic address was delivered by Col. A. C. Moore, to a large and attentive audience of ladies and gentlemen.

After the address the procession was again formed and moved to the burying ground, where a square was formed by the U. S. troops and the Military association, around the unmarked graves of those who fell in the battle of Plattsburgh.

After a prayer by the Rev. Mr. Witherspoon, and an address by Gen. Skinner, the president of the day (Col. McNiel) said :

"Fellow citizens: The president of the day has designated our distinguished guest, Brigadier General Wool, of the United States army, who commanded the detachment of American regular troops opposed to that division of the British army which advanced upon Plattsburgh by the Beekmantown Road, on the 6th of September, 1814, to erect a monument at the head of the grave of Col. Willington, of the 3d regiment of British Buffs, who gallantly fell at the head of his regiment at Culver's Hill, on the Beekmantown Road, in the memorable battle of the 6th of September, 1814.

"The division of the British army in which the brave and lamented Willington fell, was not less than 4,000 strong ; and when we take into view the fact that General Wool (then a major), with a light corps of but 250 regular troops all told, contested every inch of ground with this formidable force in their descent upon Plattsburgh, the selection of General Wool to perform the melancholy duty assigned to him cannot fail to give deep interest to the solemn occasion which brought us together upon this hallowed spot. Nothing can be more appropriate than that the monument about to be erected should be raised by the hand of an officer who bore an honorable and conspicuous part in the events of the memorable day on which the gallant Willington fell. It is a pleasing spectacle to see the living brave doing honor to the memory of the illustrious dead."

Gen. Wool proceeded to discharge the duty assigned him, and said :

" Fellow citizens and soldiers : The duty assigned me by the president of the day, in behalf of the citizens of Plattsburgh and the Military association of the county of Clinton, is no less gratifying to me than it is honorable and magnanimous to its authors, and will furnish an example worthy of imitation for all time to come. It is not less a holy and pious offering to the illustrious dead, than the offspring of noble and generous hearts to a fallen foe, and will furnish themes of praise to the end of time. It will be a healing balm to the wounded hearts of relatives and friends whilst it will not fail to call forth from every Briton who passes this consecrated spot, tears of gratitude as well as tears of sympathy.

" With these brief remarks, I now erect, in behalf of the citizens of Plattsburgh and the Military association of Clinton county, this monument to the memory of Colonel Willington, who fell the 6th of September, 1814, at Culver's Hill, leading to the charge the advance of the British army marching on Plattsburgh."

The President of the day said :

" Fellow citizens : Our esteemed fellow citizen, Judge Haile, late a captain in the United States army, will now proceed to place monuments at the respective graves of Captain Purchase, late of the British army, Lieut. Runk, late of the 6th regiment United States infantry, and Ensign John Chapman, late of the 3d Buffs."

The president of the day, in designating Judge Haile to perform the duty assigned to him, did so from a full knowledge of the fact, that no officer of his rank ever left the army of the United States with a higher and more enviable reputation as a fearless and fighting officer, than did Captain Haile.

Judge Haile proceeded to the duty assigned him with suitable remarks.

The President of the day then said :

" Fellow citizens : To Colonels Miller and Manley, and Maj. Gen. Skinner, all of whom bore a distinguished part in the battles of Beckmantown and Plattsburgh, is assigned the honor of erecting monuments to the memory of Lieutenant Peter Gamble, United States navy, John Stansbury, United States navy, and Midshipman James M. Baldwin, United States navy."

The gentlemen above mentioned proceeded to discharge the duty assigned them, accompanied by appropriate remarks.

The President said :

" To our esteemed fellow citizen, Platt R. Halsted Esq., late a Lieutenant in the United States army, I assign the honor of placing monuments at the graves of Captain Alexander Anderson, of the British marines; Lieutenant William Paul, midshipman ; William Gunn and Boatswain Charles Jackson, of the British navy, and Joseph Barron, pilot on board Commodore Macdonough's ship — all of whom fell in the naval engagement in Cumberland Bay, off Plattsburgh, on the 11th of September, 1814.

" Joseph Barron, pilot, was personally known to Lieut. Halsted and myself, and was a man held in high estimation for his intelligence and patriotism by all who had the pleasure of his acquaintance."

Lieut. Halsted, in the discharge of the duty assigned him, erected the monuments at the head of the graves of the three lieutenants of the British navy, and proceeded to the grave of Joseph Barron, and as near as we could catch his remarks, spoke as follows :

"I take a melancholy pleasure in erecting this monument at the head of the grave of Joseph Barron, Commodore Macdonough's confidential pilot. I knew him well — he was about my own age — we were school boys together — a warmer hearted or a braver man never trod the deck of a ship."

Lieut. Springer, late of the United States army, was designated by the president of the day, to erect the monument at the head of the grave of Sailing Master Rogers Carter, United States navy, and proceeded to discharge that duty.

A benediction was then pronounced by Rev. Mr. Witherspoon, and the procession returned to Fouquet's Hotel, where the committee of arrangements, the invited guests and the Military association partook of an excellent dinner, got up in Fouquet's best style.

Among the sentiments offered on this occasion was the following by General Skinner :

Brig. General Wool, United States army — the hero of Beekmantown as well as Queenstown.

"His laurels are green, though his locks are gray."

General Wool, with much feeling, responded to this sentiment as follows :

"Mr. President: I rise with a heart overflowing with gratitude to respond to the sentiment just given by my friend at the other end of the table. I find it impossible, however, filled as I am with emotion, to make a speech, or give utterance to my feelings in a manner worthy of the occasion. Were it otherwise, I could say but little that

has not already been said. I might speak of the campaigns
of 1812 and '13, which closed with the most gloomy
forebodings. I might also speak of the campaigns of 1814,
when the mantle of darkness was cast off, and a blaze of
light shone forth along the frontier from Fort Erie to
Plattsburgh, and finally closed, with a brilliancy seldom
equalled, on the plains of New Orleans. But these periods
have already been noticed and described in the most
eloquent and stirring language. Therefore, little remains
for me to add, could I give utterance to my feelings, but to
express my warmest thanks for the kind partiality with
which you have been pleased to allude to my services. I
would, however, remark that although at one period of the
war darkness and despondency appeared to pervade our
beloved country, there was one bright spot exempt from the
general gloom. It was here in this place, Plattsburgh, that
the patriotic inhabitants never wavered nor quailed before
the legions of Great Britain. They stood by their country
in the darkest hour, and never failed to cheer and comfort
the war worn soldier, and to receive him with open arms,
whether he returned victorious, or was driven back by the
force of circumstances. Who that was at Plattsburgh in
1812, ' 13 and ' 14, does not remember with delight Mooers,
Smith, Sailly, Delord, Bailey, Palmer and Ransom, all
patriotic citizens and devoted friends of their country in
war as well as in peace, but who now rest in the mansions
of eternal bliss. With these few remarks, Mr. President, I
would offer this sentiment —

"The citizens of Plattsburgh and the Military association
of Clinton county — This day attests their magnanimity
and greatness of soul, by the homage paid to the illustrious
dead who fell fighting the battles of their country."

POSITION OF THE GRAVES,

WEST.

Lieut. G. W. RUNK, 6th Regt. U. S. Army, 8th Sept. 1814.	Colonel WILLINGTON, 3d Regt. Buffs, B. Army, 6th Sept. 1814.	Ensign J. CHAPMAN, 3d Buffs, B. Army, 6th Sept. 1814.	Lieut. R. KINGSBURY, 3d Buffs, B. Army. 6th Sept., 1814.
Lieut. PETER GAMBLE, U. S. N. 11th Sept. 1814.	Lieut. John Stansbury U. S. N. 11th Sept. 1814.	Sailing Master ROGERS CARTER, U. S. N. 11th Sept. 1814.	Midshipman J. M. BALDWIN, U. S. N. 11th Sept. 1814.

SOUTH.   **NORTH.**

Pilot JOSEPH BARRON Ship Saratoga, 11th Sept. 1814.	(PINE TREE.) SACRED to the memory of GEORGE DOWNIE, Esq., A Post Captain in the Royal Brit. Navy, who gloriously fell on board His B. M. S. the Confiance, while leading the vessels under his command to the attack of the American Flotilla, at anchor in Cumberland Bay, off Plattsburgh, on the 11th September, 1814, — To mark the spot where the remains of a gallant officer and sincere friend were honorably interred, this stone has been erected by his affectionate Sister-in-Law, MARY DOWNIE. (PINE TREE.)	Boatswain CHAS. JACKSON, B. Navy, 11th Sept. 1814.

CAPT. PURCHASE 76th Regt. B. Army. 11th Sept. 1814.	ALX. ANDERSON, Capt. Marines, B. Navy. 11th Sept. 1814.	Acting Lieut. WILLIAM PAUL, B. Navy. 11th Sept. 1814.	Midshipman WILLIAM GUNN, B. Navy. 11th Sept. 1814.

EAST.

Anecdotes of the Battle of Plattsburgh.

The following anecdotes are copied from *Niles's Weekly Register*, vol. VIII.

The wounded of both fleets and our army, the same evening, were landed at our cantonment on the island. The enemy was not neglected; prompt assistance was indiscriminately rendered. Those who had but one hour previous been deadly foes, now lodged by each other's side, like brothers and friends, giving and receiving the tenderest words of consolation.

It is as true that Macdonough is religous, as that he is a brave man. He made a most appropriate prayer over the dead, previous to their interment. The following anecdote will interest you. At the moment the British were bearing down, an officer asked permission of the commodore to issue an extra ration of grog to the men. "No," was the reply, "my men shall go cool into action, excited by no stimulus except their native valor."

On the 11th September, after the British column, which crossed the Saranac, had broken, and the men were making the best of their way back, Hazen Mooers and Mr. Brooks and Stafford pursued a party of the enemy's light troops, double their number, for nearly two miles, keeping up a constant fire upon them, which they returned occasionally. At length the British party hesitated about the course they were pursuing, and our men told them they were lost and called upon them to surrender, which they consented to after obtaining a pledge from the militiamen that they should be well treated. Scarcely had the captors made their disposition for bringing in their prize, when two other British soldiers came back and commenced a fire on them, reproaching their

32

comrades for having, five of them completely equipped, surrendered to three militia riflemen. With five prisoners in custody, who might attempt to retake themselves, encumbered with the equipment of their captives, and no aid within reach, our riflemen were eager only to get off with the prisoners; but the soldiers were so obstinate in the pursuit, finding no resistance, that Mr. Stafford concealed himself and waited their near approach, when he gave one of the soldiers a deadly shot, and the other relinquished the pursuit. The prisoners, a corporal and four men, were brought in to General Mooers.

On the same day, a few of our militia, conducted by Captain Aiken, of Essex county, overtook a party who had Major Skinner, whom they had made prisoner—the party attempted to ford the river. When about half way across, the men who held the major were shot down by his side—one of them held so fast to his sleeve as to tear off the cuff of his coat, and the current took them down the stream. Maj. Skinner, however, extricated himself and swam ashore. The residue of the party threw down their arms, and cried out, "For God's sake spare our lives." The firing ceased: Captain Aiken brought in several prisoners, and Major Skinner, whom he rescued from their hands. Major S. was previously robbed of his equipage and about one hundred dollars in money, which he did not recover.

During the siege, Abel Chamberlin and Eli Lewis crossed the Saranac, and made an officer prisoner. He was in a house about twenty rods from a British picket—they took him out of the back door, put one of their coats upon him, and piloted him through the woods to the upper bridge, and from thence to Salmon River, a distance of about twelve or fourteen miles.

On the morning of the 9th September, two citizens of the town found a soldier of the British army asleep in his tent, and made him prisoner. In coming into town they were joined by another citizen — none of them had arms: About a quarter of a mile west of the village they met three British soldiers, armed, going on to join the army. When within a few paces of each other, the citizens sprang upon the soldiers, disarmed and brought them in prisoners. In the affray, Mr. Samuel Norcross, a respectable, industrious citizen, was shot through the thigh, and expired in about two hours. Shelden Durkee and Ephraim Rand were the two other citizens.

The following narrative of the death of Norcross is copied from an address delivered at Plattsburgh, September 11th, 1843, by A. C. Moore Esq.

It was on the morning of the 12th, that Shelden Durkee, Ephraim Rand and Samuel Norcross, entirely unarmed, met three British soldiers on the retreat, and simultaneously sprang upon them and seized their guns. A most desperate personal recontre ensued — a struggle for life. Rand and his antagonist, equally matched in point of strength, strained every sinew for the mastery, which neither could obtain; Norcross sunk before the superior power of his adversary, who threw him on the ground and poured the blazing contents of his musket into his body, then turned from the dying Norcross and rushed upon the struggling Rand. At this critical moment, Durkee, who with a convulsive effort had wrenched his gun from the third soldier and stretched him upon the ground, prostrated the antagonist of Rand with its butt, and pointing its loaded muzzle at the other soldier compelled him to surrender. Then leaving Rand to bind up the wounds of poor expiring Norcross, the victorious Durkee marched his three prisoners into camp.

Loss of the American Fleet on Lake Champlain, October, 1776.

The following is General Arnold's official account of the loss of his fleet on the 13th of October, 1776. The sunken wrecks of the vessels are yet to be seen in Adam's Bay, in Panton, nearly opposite Barber's Point.

Ticonderoga, October 15, 1776.

Dear General: I make no doubt before this you have received a copy of my letter to General Gates of the 12th instant, dated at Schuyler's Island, advising of an action between our fleet and the enemy the preceding day, in which we lost a schooner and a gondola. We remained no longer at Schuyler's Island than to stop our leaks, and mend the sails of the Washington. At two o'clock P. M., the 12th, weighed anchor with a fresh breeze to the southward. The enemy's fleet at the same time got under way; our gondola made very little way ahead. In the evening the wind moderated, and we made such progress that at 6 o'clock next morning we were about off Willsborough, twenty-eight miles from Crown Point. The enemy's fleet were very little way above Schuyler's Island; the wind breezed up to the southward, so that we gained very little by beating or rowing, at the same time the enemy took a fresh breeze from the north cast, and by the time we had reached Split Rock were alongside of us. The Washington and Congress were in the rear; the rest of our fleet were ahead except two gondolas sunk at Schuyler's Island. The Washington galley was in such a shattered condition, and had so many men killed and wounded, she struck to the enemy after receiving a few broadsides. We were then attacked in the Congress galley by a ship mounting twelve eighteen pounders, a schooner of fourteen sixes, and one of twelve sixes, two under our stern, and one on our broadside, within musket shot. They kept up an incessant fire on us for about five glasses, with round and grape shot, which we returned as briskly. The sails, rigging and hull of the Congress were shattered and torn in pieces, the first lieutenant and three men killed, when to prevent her falling into the enemy's hands, who had seven sail around me, I ran her ashore in a small creek ten miles from Crown Point, on the east side, when, after saving our small arms, I set her on fire with four gondolas, with whose crews I reached Crown Point through the woods that evening, and very luckily escaped the savages, who waylaid the road in two hours after we passed. At four o'clock yesterday morning I reached this place, exceedingly fatigued and unwell, having been without sleep or refreshment for near three days.

Of our whole fleet we have saved only two galleys, two small schooners, one gondola, and one sloop. General Waterbury, with one hundred and ten prisoners, were returned by Carleton last night. On board of the Congress we had twenty odd men killed and wounded. Our whole loss amounts to eighty odd.

The enemy's fleet were last night three miles below Crown Point; their army is doubtless at their heels. We are busily employed in completing our lines and redoubts, which I am sorry to say are not so forward as I could wish. We have very few heavy cannon, but are mounting every piece we have. It is the opinion of General Gates and St. Clair that eight or ten thousand militia should be immediately sent to our assistance, if they can be spared from below. I am of opinion the enemy will attack us with their fleet and army at the same time. The former is very formidable, a list of which I am favored with by General Waterbury, and have enclosed. The season is so far advanced, our people are daily growing more healthy.

We have about nine thousand effectives, and if properly supported, make no doubt of stopping the career of the enemy. All your letters to me of late have miscarried. I am extremely sorry to hear by General Gates you are unwell. I have sent you by General Waterbury a small box containing all my publick and private papers, and accounts, with a considerable sum of hard and paper money, which beg the favor of your taking care of.

I am, dear General, your most affectionate, humble servant,
                                                    B. ARNOLD.
To Hon. Major General Schuyler.

N. B. Two of the enemy's gondolas sunk by our fleet the first day, and one blown up with sixty men.

Captain Thomas Pringle to Mr. Stephens, Secretary of the Admiralty.

On board the Maria, off Crown Point, October 15, 1776.

It is with the greatest pleasure that I embrace this opportunity of congratulating their lordships upon the victory completed the 13th of this month, by his majesty's fleet under my command, upon Lake Champlain.

Upon the 11th I came up with the rebel fleet commanded by Benedict Arnold; they were at anchor under the Island Valcour, and formed a strong line, extending from the island to the west side of the continent. The wind was so unfavorable, that, for a considerable time, nothing could be brought into action with them but the gun-boats. The Carleton schooner, commanded by Mr. Dacres, who brings their lordships this, by much perseverance, at last got to their assistance; but as none of the other vessels of the fleet could then get up, I did not think it by any means advisable to continue so partial and unequal a combat; consequently with the approbation of his excellency general Carleton, who did me the honor of being on board the Maria, I called off the Carleton and gun-boats, and brought the whole fleet to anchor in a line as near as possible to the rebels, that their retreat might be cut off, which purpose was, however, frustrated by the extreme obscurity of the night; and in the morning the rebels had got a considerable distance from us up the lake.

Upon the 13th I again saw eleven sail of their fleet making off to Crown Point, who, after a chase of seven hours, I came up with in the Maria, having the Carleton and Inflexible a small distance astern; the rest of the fleet almost out of sight. The action began at twelve o'clock, and lasted two hours, at which time Arnold, in the Congress galley and five gondolas, ran on shore, and were directly abandoned and blown up by the enemy, a circumstance they were greatly favored in by the wind being off shore, and the narrowness of the lake. The Washington galley struck during the action, and the rest made their escape to Ticonderoga.

The killed and wounded in his majesty's fleet, including the artillery in the gun-boats, do not amount to forty; but from every information I have yet got, the loss of the enemy must indeed be very considerable.

THE END.

INDEX.

33

34

www.ingramcontent.com/pod-product-compliance
Lightning Source LLC
Chambersburg PA
CBHW030630030726
47497CB00006B/1723